To: Alan

From: Grandpa & Grandma Allbright
1981

THE CHILD'S WORLD

Consultant editor Brian Dicks

LDREN'S ATLAS

CELESTIAL ARTS
A DAWNE – LEIGH BOOK

A QED BOOK

Celestial Arts
231 Adrian Road
Millbrae, CA 94030

A Dawne-Leigh book

First published 1981
© QED Publishing Limited and Intercontinental Book Productions
Cartography © QED Publishing Limited

This book was designed and produced by
QED Publishing Ltd
32 Kingly Court
London W1

Art director Alastair Campbell
Production director Edward Kinsey
Editorial director Jeremy Harwood
Senior editor Kathy Rooney
Project editor Nicola Thompson
Art editor Heather Jackson
Designers Clive Hayball
Editorial Tim Healey, Keith Lye, Juila Kirk
Picture research Anne Lyons
Illustrators Marilyn Bruce, Chris Forsey, Gail Gibson,
Arka Graphics (maps), Elaine Keenan, Edwina Keene,
Abdul Aziz Khan, Elly King, Sally Kindberg (projects),
Susan Kinsey, Sally Launder, Gary Marsh, David Staples,
Perry Taylor, Martin Woodford

Filmset in Great Britain by Flowery Typesetting,
London
Colour origination in Hong Kong by Hong Kong
Graphic Arts Limited
Printed in Hong Kong by Leefung Asco Limited

ISBN 0-89742-052-7

Library of Congress Cataloging in Publication Data
Main entry under title:

The Children's World Atlas.

Includes index.
Summary: In addition to maps, presents facts and
photos of countries and introduces basic geography.
1. Atlases. [1. Atlases. 2. Geography]
I. Dicks, Brian.
G1021.C5 1981 912 81-65884
ISBN 0-89087-401-8 AACR2

FOREWORD

This book is designed to give the younger reader
a fuller understanding of our fascinating and
varied planet. The approach is strongly visual –
the maps, illustrations and photographs have
been carefully selected to show both the world's
exciting general features and the detailed
geographical characteristics of individual
countries, regions and continents.
The book is divided into two sections. The first
introduces the reader to maps, scales and
reference points, initially at the level of the
reader's own experience – their immediate
environment and area. Through successive
spreads, the context is broadened to include the
town, region, country and continent. In this way,
the reader becomes aware of ever larger areas
and scales of experience. Next, this section covers
the natural world – how it was formed, how it
moves, how immense forces of nature create
mountains, move continents and produce
earthquakes and volcanoes. The earth's land-
forms and scenery, weather and climate,
vegetation and mineral resources are all dealt with.
The second section examines the countries of the
world with the aid of maps and photographs.
Each map shows the main physical features,
economic and natural resources, as well as towns,
roads and rail communication. Picture symbols
ensure clear visual understanding. This type of
presentation enables the younger reader to learn
about his or her own country and, at the same
time, to compare and contrast it with other
countries in the world. For this purpose an
information panel provides such details as total
land area of the country, population, language,
currency and capital city.

Brian Dicks
Consultant editor

CONTENTS

YOUR WORLD

Your room

Where are you? Are you sitting in a room? How many windows does the room have? Where are they? Where is the door. How would you describe the room to someone else? Are you at school or at home?

One way of showing where things are in a room is to make a map of it. A map is a special kind of diagram of a place which shows exactly where things are. A map can be of a room or a house, but more often shows a town or a country.

A map of your classroom would show where the windows, door and furniture are. A map of your town would show, for example, where the streets and main buildings are. On a map of your country you would see larger features like rivers, mountains and towns. Maps can also include other information, such as where the political boundaries are or what a country produces. Such information is shown using signs which are called symbols. A map has a key which shows what the symbols and the different colors on it mean.

So that the map can show accurately where things are, it is drawn to scale. A scale is a system by which actual distances – for example one mile or one kilometer – are shown by much smaller distances – such as one inch or one centimeter. This means that many miles can be reduced to a size that will fit on a page, as well as still giving exact information about where places are. A collection of maps is called an atlas.

This picture and map both show the same classroom from above. It is easy to see what is in the picture, but the map would not make sense without the key. The key is very important as it explains what all the colors represent. For example, the chairs and desks would just be strange shapes on the map if the key was not there to explain what the different colors mean. Not everything in the picture is shown on the map. The people are not shown as they are not part of the room.

◀ If you want to be good at making maps you should try to remember everything you see in detail. For example, you often see your school but how well can you describe it from memory? Where are the doors and windows? What is the shape of the school? Is it made up of one building or many? Before you begin to draw a map you should note down as much information as possible.

▶ This is a simple map of the school illustrated here. The roof looks flat and none of the walls, windows or doors can be seen. This is because a map is like an aerial view. An aerial view means that something is only seen from directly above it. It is much easier to see what shape the building is from the map, which is like a diagram, rather than from the picture.

◀ Maps are usually of large places — continents, countries or towns. However, if you want to make a map you could start with a small area like your classroom. A plan is another name for a map of a house or room.

Key

 Floor
◯ Window
⬤ Door
⬤ Blackboard
◯ Wall
⬤ Chair
◯ Table
◯ Other furniture

Make a map of your classroom
1. Take a large piece of squared paper, a long tape measure, a ruler and some pencils. Measure your classroom with the tape measure and note down the measurements. Work out a scale for your map.

2. A scale is a way of showing a long distance by means of a shorter one. For example, one foot (25cms) could be shown as one square on your paper. Draw the scaled measurements of your classroom on to the paper lightly in pencil.

3. Next, measure where all the main objects in the room are. This should include, for example, the door, windows, desks and chairs. Draw the shapes in on the map to show their position in the room using the same scale as for the outline.

4. After drawing all the lines in pencil, go over the outline of the map in a colored pencil or felt-tip pen. Then fill in the shapes of the objects in different colors. Use the same color for all the chairs, another for all the desks and so on.

5. Next make the key at one side of the map. The key is an important part of the map, as it says what the colors or symbols on the map mean. Fill in one of the squares on the paper with the color used for the desks and write 'desk'

beside it. Repeat for the other colors. Underneath the key write the scale you have used. When you look at a map, always look at the key and scale too. They help you to understand what the map means.

Your neighborhood

Your home and your school are both part of a neighborhood. If you live in a town, your neighborhood will probably include streets, stores, houses, and perhaps parks, railroad lines, churches and factories. This kind of neighborhood is called urban. If you live in the country, your neighborhood may include farms, hills, rivers, small towns or villages. This kind of neighborhood is called rural. Roads, railroads and rivers may link rural and urban areas. What kind of neighborhood do you live in? Make a list of the main features of your neighborhood.

In the past most people lived in rural areas; but today most people live in urban areas. Large towns and cities have two main parts – the inner city where there are offices and large stores for example, and the outer city or suburbs where most people live. Inner cities tend to be crowded with people and traffic. Roads and bus or rail routes link the inner with the outer city. The city is usually the center of local government and administration which may cover both the urban and rural areas. Do you live in a city? If not, what is the nearest city to your home? What is its population?

Town and regional maps
If you want to see on a map where you live, you could look at two different kinds of map. Maps of towns show detailed information like the names of streets and where parks and buildings are. Regional maps show a whole region so that there is not room for as much detail. The regional map on the opposite page shows only general information. You can see where towns are in relation to each other but you cannot see street names or where the roads go through a town. Regional maps are useful if you want to see how near one town is to another. Town maps help visitors find their way around the town.

Your town

Key
● Building
● Municipal building
○ Church
● Train station
○ Street
● Commercial property
● Residential area
● School
○ Undeveloped land
● Football field
● Lake
● Municipal property
● Railroad
● Park
● Trees

▲ Contour lines
If you want to know how high the land is in a particular area, you should look on a large-scale map which has contour lines. These are imaginary lines which join up places which are at the same height on the earth's surface. From the aerial view of the river (left) it is not clear what height the land around it is. However, the map (right) and the section of land (center) have simple contours marked out on them.

Key

— Road
— River
— Railroad
◯ Farmland
● Town
● Woodland
◯ Sea

Your region

Make a contour landscape
1. Draw a large square on a contour map and trace all the contour lines in the square onto a piece of paper.

2. Take a piece of thick card – or use two pieces of thin card instead. Trace the lowest contour onto it and then cut it out carefully along the line.

3. Use one piece of card as a base for the landscape and stick the contour onto it with paper glue. Wipe away any excess glue.

4. Trace and cut out the other contour lines in order of height. Stick the layers on top of each other.

5. Paint each contour level a different color. To finish the landscape, mark the contour height on the layers.

6. The completed model will clearly show how much the land varies in height even over short distances.

Your country

Your neighborhood is part of your country. Your country may be large, like the United States and Australia, or small like Switzerland or Austria. A country is an area of land with its own people, government and laws.

Your country may join on to other countries. The dividing line between countries is called a boundary. Boundaries may follow natural features, such as the Pyrenees Mountains which separate Spain from France. Boundaries can also be straight lines which follow no natural features. For example, the boundary between the United States and Canada follows a line of latitude. Other countries, like Australia and Japan, are islands and have no land boundaries with other countries. What kind of boundaries does your country have? Does it border on any other countries?

All countries have a city called the capital. Often the government and main administration is here. The capital is usually also the center of the country's communications. What is the capital of your country?

Your country has many resources. These include soil for agriculture and farming and minerals such as coal, oil and iron, which industry uses. All the things which farmers grow or industry makes are called products. A country with many farms and little industry is called an agricultural country, and a country with many industries and few farms is an industrial country. Is your country agricultural or industrial? What are its main products?

Scales
A scale is a system by which large distances on the earth's surface can be represented on a map as a short distance. There are three main ways of giving a scale. One is to write it in words — one inch to one mile, for example. Another type of scale uses numbers either as a fraction or as a ratio. 1/100 or 1:100 could mean that one inch (or one centimeter) on the map represents 100 inches (or 100 centimeters) in reality. This is a useful type of scale as it works with any measurement. The third way of showing a scale is to mark out distances on a line and put it under the map.

▶ Relief map
Maps which show the features of a country such as mountains and rivers are called physical maps. There are two main types of physical map. A relief map is like a picture of the country taken from above. It shows the mountains and rivers as on a photograph. The tops of mountains sometimes appear white, to indicate snow. The United States is flatter in the east than it is in the west where the Rocky Mountains are. The lower range of mountains in the east is called the Appalachians.

▶ Contour map
The second main type of physical map is the contour map. Contours are lines drawn on maps along lines of height. On some contour maps, the lines themselves are shown. Others, as here, shade in the areas of the different contours. Contours are a good way of showing heights — they can vary between showing small differences in height (50 feet/20 meters) and large differences such as 1,000 feet/300 meters.

Key
- Up to 1,500 feet/500 meters
- Up to 3,000 feet/1,000 meters
- Up to 6,000 feet/2,000 meters
- Over 6,000 feet/2,000 meters

Your country

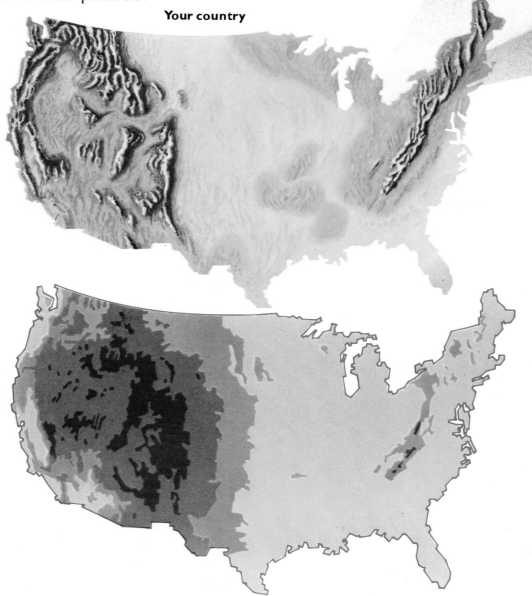

Your school

Your neighborhood

Your region

This series of pictures shows how your neighborhood relates to your region and country.

▼ Political map

Most countries are divided into different areas. Maps which show these areas are called political maps. In the United States there are 50 states, 48 are shown here with Alaska and Hawaii not shown. The country's government is in Washington DC, but each state has its own government which takes care of local affairs.

When someone writes you a letter from abroad, they start with the most detailed information and end with the most general. First they write your name, then your house or box number and street, then your town, then the abbreviated letters of your state with the zip code number. Last comes your country.

Jane Smith,
860 Valley Road,
ANYTOWN,
KY 20013,
U.S.A.

▶ Economic map

Maps which show how land is used are called economic maps. The map shows the main types of farming in your country.

Key

- Dairy
- Fruit and vegetables
- Farming
- Cattle
- Cotton
- Tobacco
- Grain

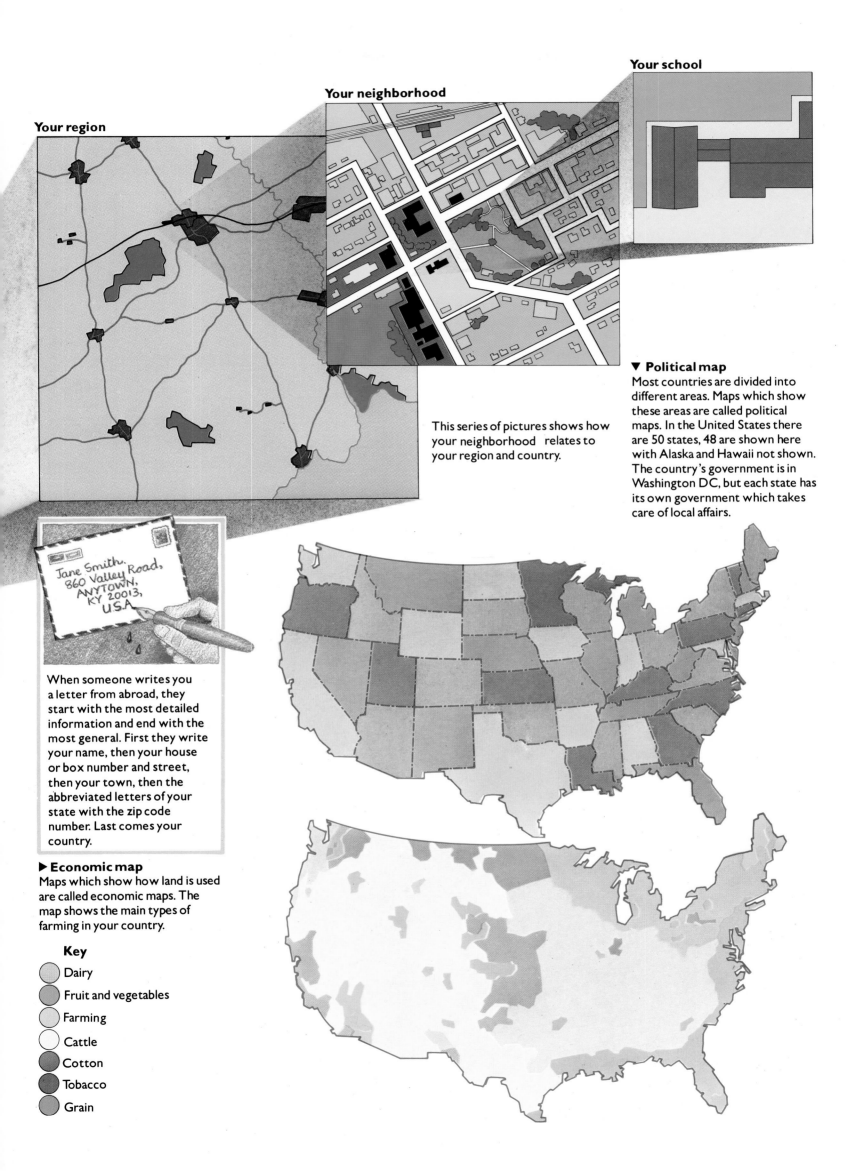

Your continent

Your country is part of a continent. The world has seven continents. Some, such as Europe and Asia, contain many countries. Others such as North America have fewer. How many countries does your continent have?

A continent is a large land area, one of the main sections of the earth's surface. The continents are Asia, Africa, North America, South America, Antarctica, Europe and Australasia. Most of the earth's land surface is in the northern hemisphere. However, only about one third of the earth's surface is land; the rest is covered by water. In the northern hemisphere about two fifths is land; in the southern hemisphere only about one fifth is land-covered.

Continents have many natural features which often cross country boundaries. These include many rivers and mountain ranges. What are the main features of your continent?

A continental island is an island off the coast of a continent which still is part of that continent. For example, Japan is a group of continental islands belonging to Asia. Newfoundland is a continental island which is part of North America. Does your continent have any continental islands?

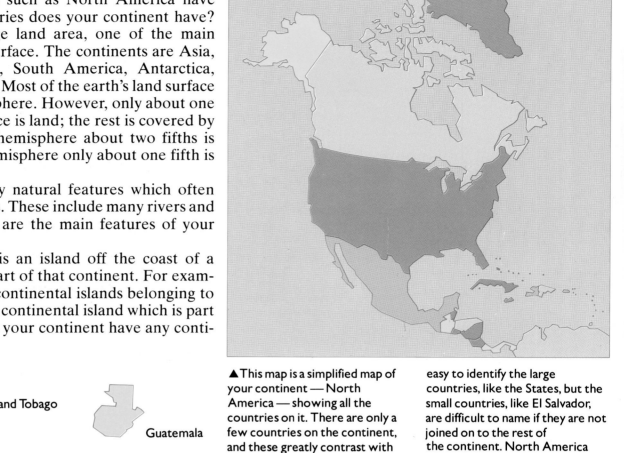

▲ This map is a simplified map of your continent — North America — showing all the countries on it. There are only a few countries on the continent, and these greatly contrast with each other. The United States and Canada, for example, are very large when they are compared with the much smaller countries which can be found in Central America south of Mexico.

Given below are the countries of North America as though they were separate islands. It is quite easy to identify the large countries, like the States, but the small countries, like El Salvador, are difficult to name if they are not joined on to the rest of the continent. North America has many islands which belong to it. The northern part of Canada particularly has a large number of islands. The land here is thinly populated compared to the mainland. Greenland, which is also in the northern part of the continent is another island. This, in fact, belongs to Denmark which is in Europe.

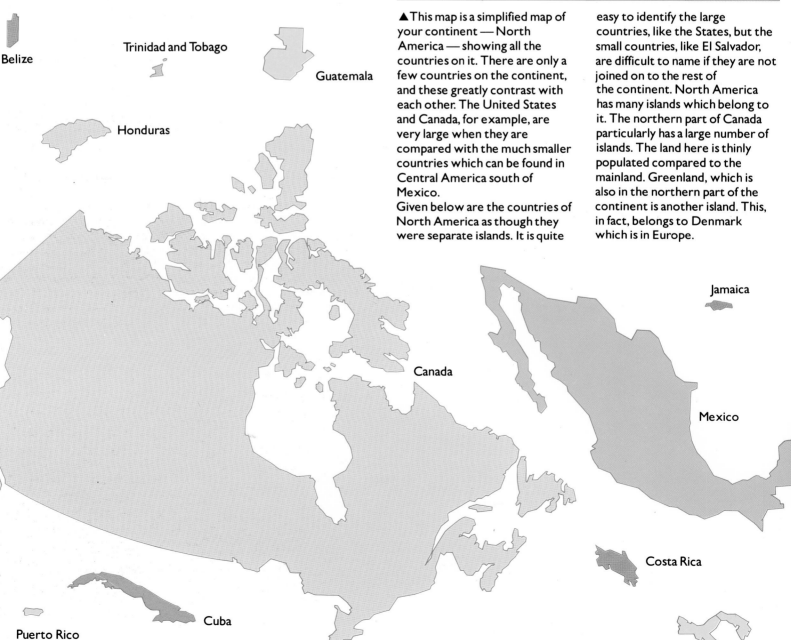

Belize

Trinidad and Tobago

Guatemala

Honduras

Canada

Jamaica

Mexico

Costa Rica

Puerto Rico

Cuba

Panama

▲The Lesser Antilles are a chain of small islands which are part of the West Indies. These islands belong to the North American continent. They cover about 2,500 miles (4,020 kms) from Florida in the United States to the coast of Venezuela in South America.

Make a jigsaw of North America

1. First you will need a map. You can use either the countries on this page or an atlas. Make sure that the map is large enough and the lines between the countries dark enough to see through a piece of tracing paper. Maps from large atlases are best. If it is a small book, it may be difficult to flatten out the page and keep the tracing paper straight.

2. Take a piece of tracing paper and place it over the map. The tracing paper should cover the entire map and not be too heavy or you will not be able to see through it. If the map you are tracing is one sheet of paper, you can secure the map and tracing paper with thumb tacks. If the map is in a book, small pieces of masking tape can be placed on the corners to hold the paper steady as you work.

3. You are now ready to begin tracing the outlines of the countries. The country borders will be the darkest lines. Be careful not to confuse them with other lines. With a dark pencil trace over all the lines which you need to make the map. When you have traced all the country borders, turn the tracing paper over. Now scribble on the back of each line so that it is completely covered.

4. Once the country borders are completed, lift the tracing paper off the map. Take a piece of white paper the same size as the tracing paper and, turn the tracing paper over again so that the scribbled pencil marks are touching the white paper. Secure both sheets with thumb tacks or pieces of masking tape. With a black pencil, draw over your outlines, pressing hard. Work slowly and carefully.

5. When you have finished tracing all the country borders (make sure you have traced all of them), lift off the tracing paper. You will have before you the continent of North America. With five or six colored pencils, carefully fill in the countries, making sure not to go over the borders. Try not to use the same color for countries next to one another, but you do not have to use a different color for each of the countries.

6. After you have colored in all the countries, take a pair of small, sharp scissors and very carefully cut out each country, following the black borders. Take a piece of colored paper (blue paper can represent the oceans and seas) and some paper glue, and stick down the countries as they are in the atlas. You can then write in the country names, cities, rivers and mountains with a black pen.

Alaska

Nicaragua

Dominican Republic

Greenland

El Salvador

Haiti

United States of America

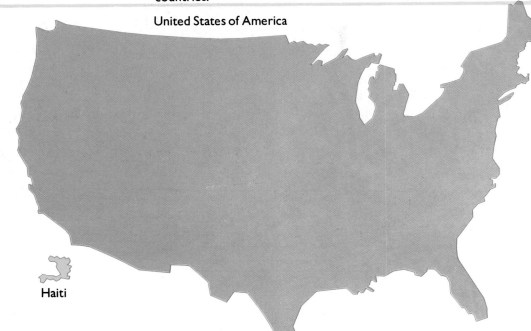

The world's continents

The largest of the world's seven continents is Asia. It covers an area of about 17,000,000 square miles (43,000,000 sq kms). Africa is the next largest continent, covering about 12,000,000 square miles (30,000,000 sq kms). North and South America are near to one another in size – North America is slightly larger having an area of 9,400,000 square miles (24,300,000 sq kms), while South America covers 6,800,000 square miles (17,800,000 sq kms). The second smallest continent is Antarctica (5,500,000 square miles/14,250,000 sq kms). Australasia is the smallest continent. Its land area is about 3,200,000 square miles (8,510,000 sq kms).

Several of the world's continents are like triangles in shape. These are North America, South America and Africa, all of which become narrower towards the south. Europe is also triangular with the base of the triangle in the Ural Mountains and the top or apex in Spain and Portugal.

The continents are separated from one another by oceans and seas. The Mediterranean Sea, for example, lies between Europe and Africa. The longest land boundary between continents is along the Ural Mountains which separate Europe from Asia.

▼ The large, revolving globes show the earth as it might appear from different angles in space. Look at the small pictures of the continents. Can you find them on the globes?

▲ Africa bulges broadly in the north and tapers away to a rounded curve in the south. A large island — Madagascar — is to the south-east.

▲ Antarctica is not as well known as other continents. It is almost completely covered with ice and snow.

◄ South America is roughly triangular. It tapers away to a sharp tip in the south. An island group — Tierra del Fuego — lies just off the southern tip of the continent.

▲ North America is another triangular continent. It includes huge islands — Greenland and neighboring territories — to the north.

▲ Europe has a very jagged coastline, with many peninsulas — fingers of land — stretching into the sea. Europe itself is sometimes thought of as a large peninsula joined on to the much larger continent of Asia.

▲ Most of Australasia's land mass is made up by the bulging horseshoe shape of Australia. The islands of New Zealand are to the south-east. Thousands of smaller islands lie to the east.

▲ Asia is the largest of the world's continents in both area and population. Its main peninsulas are the Indian subcontinent and the Malaysian Peninsula.

Mapping the world

The world is a sphere, like a ball, but it is slightly flattened at the North and South Poles and bulges a little at the Equator. So that countries and continents can be located accurately, a number of imaginary curved lines are drawn on a globe to divide the world into sections.

The lines are lines of latitude and longitude. The lines of latitude run around the globe parallel to the Equator. This is rather like someone cutting an apple or tomato into even slices starting at the top. The Equator is called 0° latitude and each half of the world – or hemisphere – is split into 90 slices, so the North Pole is 90° north and the South Pole 90° south.

In order to pinpoint exactly where a place is on the earth's surface another set of lines, running from north to south are needed. These are lines of longitude. These divide the world into segments like those of an orange, which are wider in the middle (the Equator) than at the top and bottom (North and South Poles).

A globe is a way of showing all the world's countries on a sphere. However, maps in books are flat. If you peel an orange, it is impossible to lay the peel out flat without cutting, stretching or tearing it. The same applies to making flat maps of the round earth. There are many ways of flattening the round shape of the earth to make maps of it. These are called map projections.

The problem with map projections is that they cannot show the earth accurately; this is only possible on a globe. For example, in Mercator's map projection the world is seen as a rectangle. It works by showing the lines of longitude as a parallel rather than meeting at the Poles. This means that places near the Poles, such as Greenland, seem much larger. Many map projections show eastern Russia on the right and Alaska on the left of the map. It is also possible to show Australia at the center.

◀ The world is round. Imagine that you are looking at it from space. You can easily recognize the shapes of the oceans and continents. However, mapping the world presents a problem to map-makers. They need to draw an accurate picture of its *round* surface on a *flat* piece of paper. Systems of projection have been invented to overcome the problem. They are not perfect, but they are important aids.

◀ One aid to map-making involves using imaginary lines called longitude and latitude. These provide a grid, making it easier to judge distances between places, and to find where one place is in relation to another.
Lines of latitude run around the earth from east to west. They are measured according to their angle from the very center of the earth. They are parallel to the Equator which is at 0° (0 degrees). This is the line that is most often close to the sun. The North and South Poles are at 90°. These are the points that are most often far from the sun. All the other places on earth can be mapped in degrees north or south of the Equator. They are all between 0° and 90°. Lines of longitude run from the North Pole to the South Pole. They are measured in degrees east or west of Greenwich in England.

Making your own globe
To make your own globe you will need some tracing paper; a pencil; paints, crayons or felt-tip pens; thin card; scissors and paper glue.

1. Place a sheet of tracing paper over the outline shown on the facing page. Now use a pencil to trace around the shape and tabs.

2. Turn the tracing paper over and scribble lightly over the outlines you have just drawn. Make sure that each line is covered.

3. Turn the tracing paper over again and place it on thin card. Draw over the outlines again. An image will appear on the card.

4. Now color in your map, and label the countries and the oceans. When you have finished, cut around the outline.

5. Glue the tabs one by one and stick each one under the neighboring piece of card. Wipe off any excess glue with a cloth.

6. Wait for the glue to dry. You can now hang your globe from the ceiling as a mobile, or make a stand for it with wire and a cork.

▶ Making a flat map of the world is rather like peeling an orange. If you take the peel off an orange in sections from top to bottom you can then lay it out flat even though the orange is a sphere. In the same way, map-makers may draw the shapes of the continents as if they had been peeled away from the outer crust of the earth. This is one system of projection.

Goode's equal-area projection

Mollweide's equal-area projection of the earth

▶ These maps are drawn according to three different systems of projection. The top system shows the earth's surface as if it had been cut up and laid flat like the peel of an orange. It shows the continents fairly accurately, but the oceans are all cut up. The middle system shows the earth's surface as if it were on a single curve rather than a complete sphere. Outer regions such as Australasia look narrower than they are.

The bottom map also distorts distances. Lines of longitude really meet at the poles. Here they are evenly spaced. Places near the poles — such as Greenland — look much wider than they really are. All three systems fail to show that the earth's surface is continuous. Alaska and Siberia look far apart. In fact, they are close together.

A simple cylindrical equal-space projection of the earth

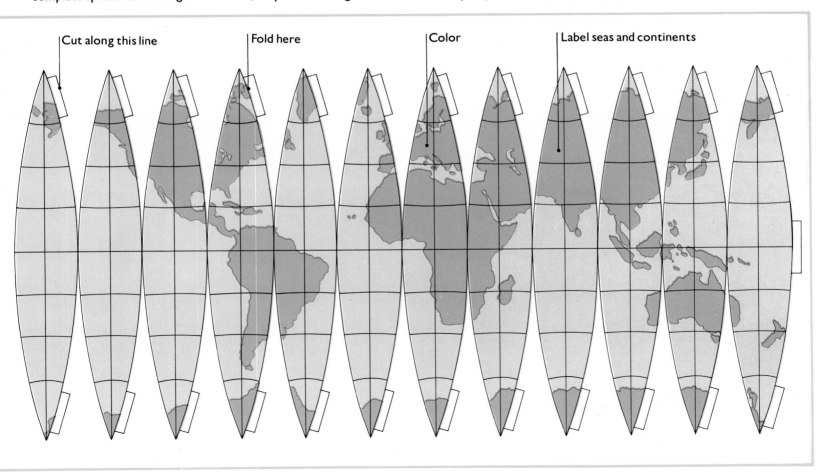

Cut along this line   Fold here   Color   Label seas and continents

The world

There are over 100 countries in the world. The Union of Soviet Socialist Republics (USSR), usually called the Soviet Union or Russia, is the largest in area. China has the largest population. Many countries are very small, for example the islands of the Pacific Ocean. Some groups of small countries have grouped themselves together into larger units. The United Arab Emirates in the Middle East is one such group, made up of seven small states on the Persian Gulf. Most countries have their own government. Countries which do not have an independent government are usually called colonies or dependencies. Most countries also have their own money (currency), capital town or city and language. Some countries have more than one language.

Facts and figures about the earth
Total surface area 197,000,000 sq miles/510,000,000 sq kms
Land surface 57,500,000 sq miles/149,000,000 sq kms
Land as percentage of surface 29%
Water surface area 139,500,000 sq miles/361,300,000 sq kms
Water as percentage of surface 71%
Circumference at Equator 24,830 miles/40,000 kms
Diameter at Equator 7,926 miles/12,760 kms
Highest land point (Mount Everest, Asia) 29,028 ft/8,848 m
Deepest ocean point (Marianus Trench, Pacific) 36,198 ft/11,033 m
Distance from sun 93,000,000 miles/150,000,000 kms
Total population 3,800,000,000

Highest mountains
Everest, Asia, 29,028ft/8,848m
Godwin-Austen(K2), Asia, 28,250ft/8,611m
Kangchenjunga, Asia, 28,168ft/8,588m
Makalu, Asia, 27,805ft/8,477m
Dhaulagiri, Asia, 26,810ft/8,174m
Nanga Parbat, Asia, 26,660ft/8,128m
Annapurna, Asia, 26,504ft/8,080m
Gasherbrum, Asia, 26,470ft/8,070m
Gosainthan, Asia, 26,291ft/8,016m

Longest rivers
Nile, Africa 4,132miles/6,912kms
Amazon, S America 3,900miles/6,240kms.
Mississippi, N America 3,860miles/6,176kms
Irtys, Asia 3,461miles/5,538kms
Yangtse, Asia 3,430miles/5,488kms
Hwang Ho, Asia 2,903miles/4,645kms
Zaire, Africa 2,900miles/4,640kms
Amur, Asia 2,802miles/4,483kms
Lena, Asia 2,653miles/4,249kms
Mackenzie, N America 2,635/4,216kms

Oceans and seas
Pacific Ocean 63,855,000sq miles/165,384,000 sq kms
Atlantic Ocean 31,744,000sq miles/82,217,000 sq kms
Indian Ocean 28,371,000sq miles /73,481,000 sq kms
Arctic Ocean 5,427,000sq miles/14,056,000 sq kms
Mediterranean Sea 967,000sq miles/2,506,000sq kms
South China Sea 895,000sq miles/2,318,000sq kms
Bering Sea 876,000sq miles/2,269,000sq kms
Caribbean Sea 750,000sq miles/1,813,000sq kms
Gulf of Mexico 596,000sq miles/1,544,000sq kms
Sea of Okhotsk 590,000sq miles/1,528,000sq kms

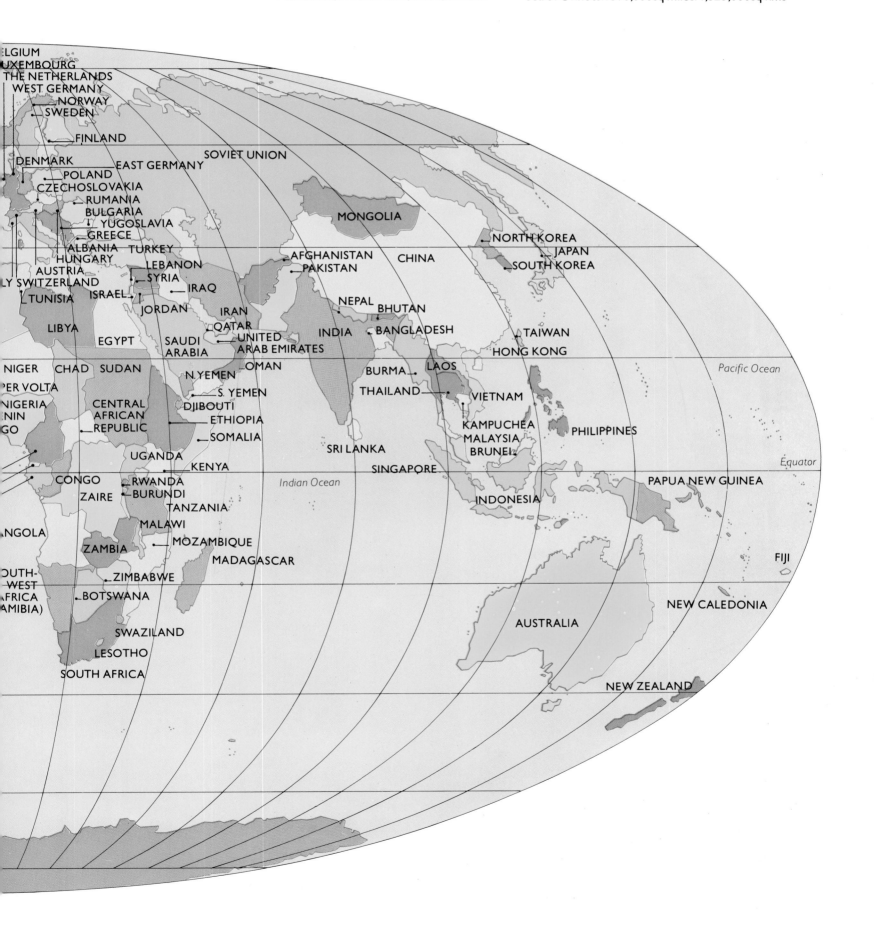

The structure of the earth

The earth is one of the nine planets in the solar system which revolve around the sun. The earth is solid and rocky and it is 93 million miles (150 million kms) from the sun.

Scientists believe that 4,500 million years ago the earth's surface was covered by molten rock. This is rock which is so hot that it melts. As the rock cooled and hardened, the heavier materials sank towards the center of the earth, while the lighter materials stayed near the surface. The rock released steam which condensed and became the seas and oceans. The cooling rocks also gave off gases. These formed a kind of atmosphere.

The earth is still cooling very slowly. It has three main layers – the core, the mantle and the crust. The crust is made up of several rigid but slowly moving plates on which the continents sit. Scientists believe that there was originally only one large land mass. Gradually this split up and the continents drifted to where they are today. The continents split up because at the edges of the plates new material came up from the earth's mantle and forced the plates apart. The main mountain ranges in the world are found where the plates are being pushed together.

◄ The earth revolves around the sun in a counter-clockwise direction. All the other planets except Venus move in the same way. The earth's path around the sun is known as its orbit. The earth does not orbit the sun in a perfect circle, but in an elongated one known as an ellipse. It takes a year for the orbit to be completed.

► The structure of the earth is rather like that of an apple. At the center is the core. Next comes a second layer, like the flesh of the apple. This is known as the earth's mantle. The skin of the earth is called the crust. It is very thin compared to the inner core and mantle. The thickest parts of the crust lie beneath very high mountain ranges. It is much thinner beneath the oceans.

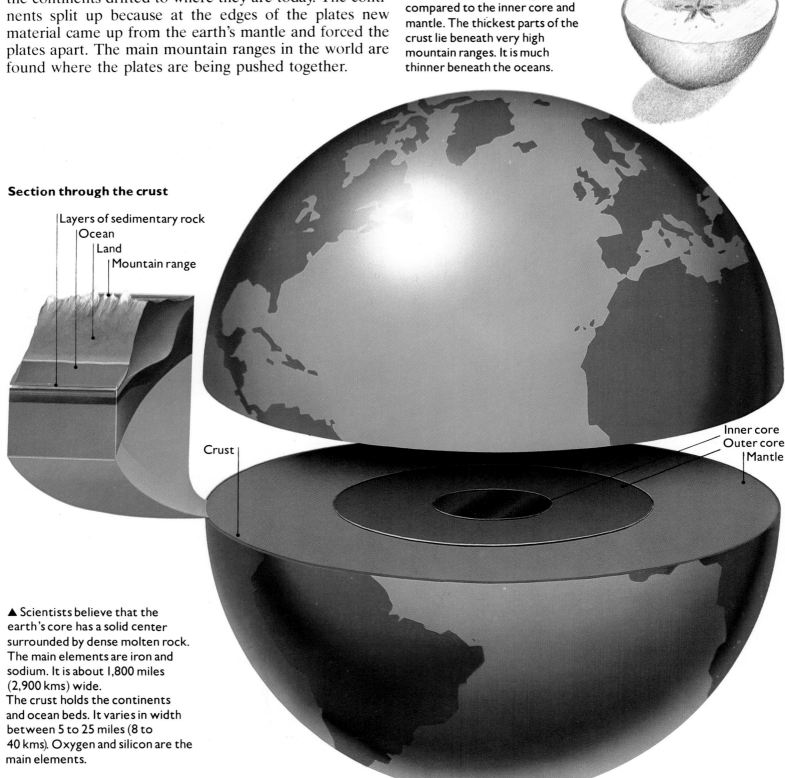

Section through the crust

Layers of sedimentary rock
Ocean
Land
Mountain range

Crust

Inner core
Outer core
Mantle

▲ Scientists believe that the earth's core has a solid center surrounded by dense molten rock. The main elements are iron and sodium. It is about 1,800 miles (2,900 kms) wide.
The crust holds the continents and ocean beds. It varies in width between 5 to 25 miles (8 to 40 kms). Oxygen and silicon are the main elements.

▲ Pangaea, the earth's original land mass, began to split up about 200 million years ago.

This created two basic continental regions, Laurasia and Gondwanaland.

The shapes of today's continents began to emerge about 100 million years ago.

The continents today are Asia, Africa, Australia, the Americas, Antarctica and Europe.

▲The earth's surface has grooves and ridges, like the skin of a wrinkled apple. All the little grooves on an apple's surface are like ridges on the earth, only much smaller. The earth may look as if it only has mountains on land, but in fact it has them under the sea too.

▶ If you drained the world's oceans, you could see its uneven surface more clearly. The earth's upper crust is composed of separate sections which are locked together. They are known as plates, and lie on a layer of hot, dense rock. The plates are constantly drifting, but so slowly that you do not notice their movement. Here you can see how the bulging west coast of Africa once fitted into the concave east coast of the Americas.

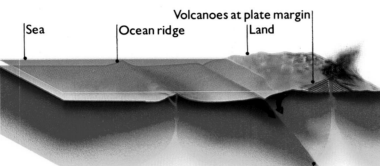

Sea | Ocean ridge | Volcanoes at plate margin | Land

Plate boundary

◀ The earth's crust is always on the move. Sometimes, land masses drift apart. This drifting causes cracks, known as faults, to appear. Sometimes, land masses push against each other, forcing rock layers upwards. These layers are then said to be folded. Many folds create mountain ranges.

   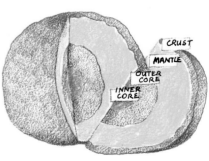

CRUST
MANTLE
OUTER CORE
INNER CORE

Make a model of the earth
1. To make a cross section of the earth, you will need four different colors of modeling clay, one for each layer. Roll a piece of clay into a ball about one inch (2.5cms) across. This represents the inner core of the earth. Now roll out a second, larger piece of clay for the second layer.

2. Place the inner core in the middle of the second sheet. This should be quite thick as it represents the outer core which is much thicker than the inner core. The outer core is also much cooler than the inner one. Try to choose colors for the layers that will show up well against each other.

3. Make sure the second sheet of modeling clay covers the inner core fully. Press the two lots of clay together with your fingers so that they stick together. Cut away any excess clay and smooth the surface so the joins do not show. Repeat this process with the third color.

4. The fourth color must be rolled out flat so that it is as thin as possible. This layer of clay is to be the earth's crust which is much thinner than the two cores or the mantle — the third layer. To see the cross section, cut through the clay with a knife or a piece of wire held taut.

Earthquakes and volcanoes

Earthquakes and volcanic eruptions often happen at the edges of the plates in the earth's crust. When one plate moves against another, a series of violent jerks and shudders occur. This is an earthquake.

Like the waves which spread out from the center when you throw a stone into a pond, the vibrations of an earthquake travel out from a center called the focus. The surface of the earth above the focus is the epicenter. If an earthquake is very strong it can start landslides and floods.

Volcanoes are openings in the earth's crust out of which molten rock (called lava), rocks, ashes, dust and gases come from inside the earth. The lava, rocks and ashes sometimes form a mountain shaped like a cone. Sometimes the lava comes up through long cracks and flows over large areas to make a flat area called a plateau. Many volcanoes do not erupt for long periods. These are called dormant volcanoes. In volcanic regions there are also many geysers. These are springs which produce steam and hot water.

Earthquakes and volcanic eruptions occur mainly in certain areas of the earth. These areas are often at the edges of the plates on the earth's crust. For example, the largest belt is called the 'Fiery Girdle' and goes around the shores of the Pacific Ocean. A second belt follows the ridge in the middle of the Atlantic. A third belt runs from the Mediterranean to the Himalayas.

◄ The earth seems solid. But below its surface lie seething masses of hot gases and molten rock. These are known as magma. This is very hot and exists at great pressure. Magma which has reached the surface is called lava.

◄ As the earth's plates drift, cracks may appear in the surface of the crust. Magma may force its way up at high pressure. As it reaches the surface, a volcano is born.

◄ Molten lava moves to the surface. It may rise slowly and seep out to form a lake of lava. It may also force its way up at great pressure and erupt in a series of explosions.

◄ As layers of lava and ash cool, they harden. In some volcanic areas, eruptions often occur in the same place. The layers of ash and lava build up over the years and form a mountainous cone.

► The shapes of volcanoes vary. Mauna Loa in Hawaii has a low cone. The lava seeps out from the pipe at the center.

▲ Guatemala in Central America has a range of volcanoes along its Pacific coast. Some of these, such as Tacaná and Agua, are still active.

▲ This shows the shape of Mount Pelée – a volcano on the island of Martinique in the West Indies. When this volcano erupted violently in 1902, magma forced its way out through vents in the side rather than out through the top.

► This diagram shows the structure of a volcano. Lava rises through the central pipe. After many eruptions, the pipe may get blocked. Vents appear at the sides. They sometimes form separate peaks as the lava hardens. Some lava never reaches the surface. It may form a slanting channel which hardens beneath the surface. This is called a dyke. Laccoliths are lava lakes which may harden underground in the same way. Volcanoes which are no longer active are called dormant.

Gases/Steam
Crater
Volcanic cone
Layers of ash and lava
Volcanic pipe
Subsidiary cone
Molten lava
Ash
Magma reservoir
Dyke

▼ As land masses shift, the rock tends to fold. A downfold is called a syncline. An upfold is an anticline. Underground reservoirs of gas and oil may collect between layers of rock in an anticline. Before people drill for oil, they study rock folds carefully.

▼ As the rock folds, layers of earth fall away from its peaks. The bare rock is exposed. Wind and weather erode the surface leaving pits and crags.

▲ As land moves and shifts it may bend and crack. These cracks in the earth's crust are faults. There are several different types of fault. A thrust fault happens when one section of land breaks away and slides over another next to it.

If a wedge of rock sinks between two neighboring masses it is called a graben or rift valley. These valleys form when two parallel faults occur. They have steep sides and flat floors.

If it is forced upwards between its

neighbors it is known as a horst. When a mass of rock slides sideways along a fault, the fault is called a strike slip.

These changes occur over millions of years. They cannot often be seen as clearly as on the diagram.

Direction of plate movement

Epicenter

▲ When two plates slide side by side along a fault, danger threatens. The grinding masses lock together and pressure builds up. It may be released in the sudden shudder of an earthquake.

▲ The origin of the earthquake lies underground at the focus. Shock waves travel out from the epicenter above this. The Richter Scale is used to measure the strength of the waves.

Make a fold mountain
This demonstrates how mountains are formed.
1. You need lots of modeling clay in at least four different colors. First roll each color into a ball so the clay is soft and easy to work with.

2. Each ball of clay represents a layer of rocks in the earth's crust. Take each ball and roll it out flat with a rolling pin. An empty bottle will do if you have not got one. Roll each ball so it is about $\frac{1}{2}$ inch (1.25cms) all over.

3. When you have flattened the clay, place the layers one on top of another like strata. Press them together quite firmly so they stick together but do not squash them too much. Tidy up the edge by trimming the clay with a knife.

4. Take hold of each end of the clay and gently push the two ends towards each other. This is like two plates in the earth's crust pushing together. With more pressure from your hands, a ridge like a mountain will form in the middle of the clay.

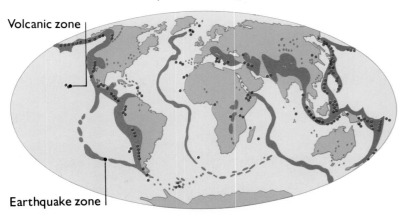

Volcanic zone

Earthquake zone

▲ The most violent areas of earthquakes and volcanic activity are the edges of the earth's

plates. Tokyo and San Francisco lie on them. Both have experienced disastrous earthquakes.

Rocks and minerals

Three kinds of rock make up the crust of the earth. These are called igneous rocks, sedimentary rocks and metamorphic rocks. Igneous rocks are formed when hot, molten material, which has come up from the earth's interior, hardens. There are two types of igneous rock – volcanic and intrusive. Volcanic rocks have cooled and hardened on the surface. Basalt is a common volcanic rock. The second type – intrusive rock – forms when molten rock does not reach the earth's surface and hardens underground. Granite is an important intrusive igneous rock.

Most of the earth's surface is now made up of sedimentary rocks. But at one time all rocks were igneous rocks. Gradually water, wind and ice wore away the rocks on the surface. Over a long period of time the materials which had been worn away – they are called sediments – collected in the oceans. This collection took many million years and is still going on. As the sediments pressed together they formed new kinds of rock.

Metamorphic rocks are the third type of rock in the earth's crust. 'Metamorphic' means that the rocks have been changed – by heat, pressure or by having their chemical structure altered. For example, heat can change limestone into marble and pressure changes shale to slate.

A rock is a collection of particles of various minerals. For example, the rock granite is composed of the minerals felspar, quartz and mica. There are over 2,000 different minerals, but most rocks consist of about 12 minerals. Gold, silver and uranium are metallic minerals.

◄ Igneous rocks form when magma hardens, either above or below ground. Intrusive igneous rocks such as granite often contain crystals. Granite contains quartz, felspar and sometimes mica. The crystals give granite its distinctive mottled appearance.

◄ Sedimentary rock is formed when tiny particles are pressed flat and harden. Rivers and seas have generally helped to form it. The particles may be of other rocks (sandstone is formed in this way). The sediment may be of vegetable matter – coal is formed from ancient leaves and branches.

◄ Metamorphic rock forms when a layer of sedimentary rock is exposed to heat, pressure, or chemical action. For example, the pressure built up by the earth's shifting land masses may turn sedimentary shale to slate. Heat from underground magma may turn limestone to marble.

▼ This diagram shows how different types of rock have been formed. The processes have often taken millions of years.
Oolitic limestone is a sedimentary rock formed by the action of deep water on tiny clusters of calcium carbonate.
A conglomerate is a mixture of sedimentary rocks. They may vary greatly in size.
Slate is a metamorphic rock. It forms when sedimentary shale is under pressure and heated by magma.
Basalt is an igneous rock. It forms fairly quickly as magma cools and hardens above the ground.
Granite is an intrusive igneous rock. It hardens slowly below the surface.

▲The Devil's Tower National Monument is a huge mass of igneous rock columns. It is 865 feet (284 meters) high.

▲Ice expanding in cracks made these limestone boulders break away from cliffs. They are in a desert in New Mexico.

▲Slate is a metamorphic rock which is quarried in many countries. It is often made into tiles and used for roofing.

Limestone   Conglomerate of sedimentary rock   Slate   Basalt   Granite

▶ Millions of years ago, the earth's ancient forests decayed. They were gradually covered with layers of sediment. The sediment turned to rock. The rotten vegetation was pressed flat. It gradually hardened and turned to coal. The layers of coal are called seams. To reach them, people have dug shafts underground. Miners hack at the coal face. Winding gear is needed to take them up and down. Pumps and fans keep fresh air circulating while they work. Machines are often used in mining today.

▶ Oil was formed when millions of tiny sea creatures and plants died and decomposed. Layers of rock gradually covered them. The decayed remains turned to liquid oil and natural gas. These substances seeped into soft, porous rocks and collected in gaps between soft and hard layers. An oil company's first task is to find these underground reservoirs by drilling in likely areas. Then they need pumping equipment to control the flow of oil to the surface. Pipelines then take the oil to refineries.

Mine buildings
Main shaft
Fault
Coal seam
Tilted strata
Oil rig
Coal face
Trapped oil
Folded strata

Fertilizer
Plastic
Medicine
Soap and detergents

▲ Coal and oil are known as fossil fuels, because both had their origins in living matter. They are not only used as fuel. People make plastics, insecticides, road surfaces, chemicals, fertilizers, soaps and antiseptics from them.

▶ Coal and oil are perhaps the most important natural sources of energy. Modern society depends heavily on them. This map shows the main centers of production. The stocks will not last forever. Today, people are urgently exploring alternative sources of energy. Nuclear power is one. Harnessing solar energy, wind and waves are others.

Coal
Oil

▲ Most rocks contain some metallic minerals. They are called ores, and can often be seen as a thin vein where the mineral has seeped into a crevice.
The metal is generally extracted in a heat process known as smelting. Oxygen is taken from the ore to purify the metal. Here, copper has been extracted from its ore in a furnace.

Satchel or bag
Newspaper for wrapping fossils in for protection
Water for cleaning rocks
Notebook and pencil
Old toothbrush for cleaning fossils and rocks
Small hammer
Magnifying glass

▲ These men are working at a diamond mine. This mineral is made of carbon. It is the hardest natural substance in the world and it can cut glass.

◀ Precious metals include gold and silver. Gold ore may be mined, or extracted from river beds in the form of gold dust or nuggets. Gold is a soft metal which is very easy to work.

How to find fossils
Fossils are the remains or imprints of prehistoric animals and plants. They are not easy to find but if you have got lots of time to spare they are fun to look for and collect.

Chalk cliffs and disused slate quarries are usually good places for finding fossils but you should always make sure it is safe for you to go there. You will find all the things in the picture very useful.

How the landscape is formed

The earth's scenery is formed by processes called weathering and erosion which begin as soon as the land forms. Weathering and erosion mean that the land is worn away by changes in temperature or by wind, water or ice.

In cold areas such as mountain tops, rainwater collects in the cracks in rocks. When it freezes the water expands and makes the rock split apart. In hot deserts, the surfaces of rocks expand during the day and contract at night when the temperature falls. This change gradually weakens the rock and makes the outer layers peel off. Tree roots and burrowing animals also make rocks split apart.

Water can alter the minerals in some rocks. For example, water dissolves chalk and limestone rocks to make features such as limestone caves.

A river is one of the main agents of erosion. As a river flows downhill, it gathers more and more material such as stones and sediment and deposits it in the lowland areas. This is how river deltas are formed. A glacier, which is a river of ice, is like a harsh file which scrapes away more of the earth's surface than a river. Much of the earth's surface was shaped by glaciers in the past, and the same process continues in cold mountain regions and around the poles.

The wind is another important shaper of the land. For example, in the deserts, the wind blows sand away and deposits it to make dunes. The sea can both wear land away and build it up. Bays, cliffs and caves result from the sea wearing away the land. Beaches and sand bars are examples of how the sea builds up land.

The sole and heel of an old boot are a simple example of erosion. When they have been walked on for a long time they become worn away.

▶ If you dry out an onion, the layers of skin will blister, crack and peel away. Some rocks are composed of layers of sediment. They react like the skin of an onion to changes in temperature. The layers expand and contract. They blister and crack. This is called mechanical weathering and it takes many years.

▶ Scree can be found in the Grand Canyon, Arizona, USA. Scree is the name given to lots of pieces of rock that have broken away from larger boulders. Weathering by wind and rain causes the scree to form.

◀ When rain falls on mountains it collects in pools and lakes. It also seeps into cracks in the rock itself. In cold weather, the water freezes and forms ice.

▼ Chemical erosion often occurs in limestone regions. The rock contains chemicals which react with other chemicals in water to produce a weak solution of carbonic acid. This dissolves limestone. It seeps into surface cracks and these are enlarged to form ridges and grooves called clints and grikes. The acid also makes vertical and horizontal shafts – joints and bedding planes. Caves with stalactites and stalagmites are found in limestone areas.

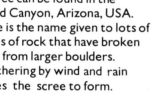

◀ Water expands as it freezes. The ice presses against the surface of the rock. Pressure builds up. New cracks appear in the rock and pieces begin to crumble away.

◀ The rock falls and tumbles down the mountainside. It often collects at the base in the form of scree. The mountain begins to look craggy. This is mechanical erosion.

Clints

Grikes

Swallow hole

Stalactite

Stalagmite

Gallery

Limestone boulders

Underground stream

Resurgence (where stream resurfaces)

▼ When a river flows down a mountainside it passes through three stages: youth, maturity and old age. In youth it flows swiftly down steep slopes. It carves out a deep V-shaped valley. In maturity it flows more slowly. It begins to swerve, and forms a broader valley. In old age it winds very slowly over flat land to the sea. It brings down much sediment which collects as mudflats.

Origin of river
Rock layers
Crags
River cliffs
Tributary stream
Meander

Youthful valley section

River valley in maturity

Flood plains
Islands
River in old age
Coastal marsh

Flood plain section

Lake dammed by ice
Moraine
Hanging valley
Crevasse
Meltwater lake
Hill of clay
Alluvial fan

▲ A glacier is a river of frozen water. It grinds slowly through the landscape in a broad U-shape. When the glacier melts, it leaves distinctive, U-shaped valleys.

▲ A glacier produces a very special sort of landscape. The glacier itself is pitted with deep cracks called crevasses. The ice walls sheer away the neighboring valleys. They become hanging valleys which often end in waterfalls. The glacier pushes mud and boulders ahead of it, and to each side. These deposits are called moraines. Ice melts and trickles down to form a meltwater lake. Then water often seeps out of the lake to produce an alluvial fan of streams. An alluvial fan is a fertile area of deposited mud and sand which is fan-shaped. Crops grow well in this soil.

▼ The wind is often the main eroding force in hot, dry countries. The dry atmosphere makes plants wither. Little is left to hold the earth together. It dries and turns to dust. The wind gathers up the dust and sweeps it around the landscape. It scours at the surrounding rocks. They begin to erode. The shifting, dusty soil makes it even harder for plants to flourish. However, in some places cacti and coarse grasses grow well.

▲ In desert lands, the wind collects sand. This cuts into the surrounding rocks. In some deserts, the swirling wind has carved startling rock towers out of the landscape.

▲ The Aletsch Glacier in the Swiss Alps is the largest glacier in these mountains. The landscape here has been shaped by the slow eroding movement of the ice.

▲ The sea acts as a powerful eroding force around the world's coastlines. The continual crashing of the waves breaks down the rocks. Sand and pebbles strike the cliffs with great force. Water forces its way into cracks. As it rushes out again it sucks out the fragments that have broken away. This process forms caves. Some rocks dissolve slowly in seawater. Chalk dissolves even in calm seas. The chalk is eroded at the base of a cliff. After a while, the rocks above fall down. The process forms steep, white cliffs like those of Flamborough Head in north-east England (above). The white cliffs of Dover are another good example of chalk cliffs. Chalk is easily dissolved, but it takes many years for other types of rock, such as granite, to be eroded.

The seasons

The earth orbits the sun which is at the center of the solar system. This process takes one year. At the same time, the earth spins on its axis once every 24 hours. The earth's spinning produces light and darkness – day and night.

The revolution of the earth around the sun and the angle at which the earth is tilted causes the seasons. These are spring, summer, fall and winter. When the North Pole is tilted towards the sun, the northern hemisphere has its summer and the southern hemisphere has its winter. It is summer in the southern hemisphere when the South Pole is tilted to the sun.

Time is measured by the earth's rotation and is linked to lines of longitude. It is always the same time at all the places which are along a line of longitude. For example, if it is noon in Greenwich, England, then it is also noon in France, Ghana and all the countries through which the 0° line of longitude passes. This line is called the Prime Meridian. Time throughout the world is calculated from this line.

There are 24 time zones in the world each with their own time. Travelers going east must put their watches on an hour for every time zone boundary they cross. Travelers going west must put their watches back.

The date changes near the 180th meridian. This lies almost completely in the Pacific Ocean and not many people cross it. It is known as the International Date Line.

▼The earth revolves around the sun once every 365¼ days. This makes a full year. To make things simpler for ourselves, we count 365 days in a normal year. Every fourth year we add a day. This is a leap year. There are 366 days in a leap year. While the earth revolves around the sun it is also spinning on its axis. So two things are going on at the same time: the earth revolving around the sun produces the year; and the earth spinning on its axis produces day and night. The sun looks as if it is moving, but it is still all the time.

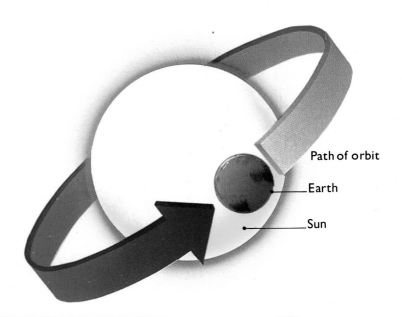

Path of orbit

Earth

Sun

▲The earth is like a great ball. It spins on its axis. The axis is like an imaginary rod passing through the middle of the ball. The angle of the axis always stays the same.

▲As the earth spins on its axis, only half of its surface is in sunlight at any one time. The rest is in darkness. The sunlight gives us our daytime. The darkness gives us our night. The darkness does not fall suddenly. The blurred areas between darkness and light are the twilight zones of dawn and dusk. Dawn begins when the first light shows and dusk begins when the sun starts to set.

▲ If you shine a flashlight on a ball you can see how the sun lights up the world. The light can only reach half of the surface at one time. The rest of the surface of the ball remains in shadow.

▲ Look at the ball from above. The point at which the rod emerges is called the pole of the axis. In our world, the North Pole is at one end of the axis. The South Pole is at the other end. Of course, the axis itself is invisible. The poles are regions of ice and snow where temperatures are very low so that few people live there and vegetation is scarce.

▲ The world does not stand upright on its axis. It is tilted. As the world spins on its axis, different regions are lit up by the sunlight. One by one, the countries of the world pass through the same cycle: dawn, daylight, dusk and night. The whole process takes 24 hours, or one full day. When countries on one side of the world have their day, it is night on the other side.

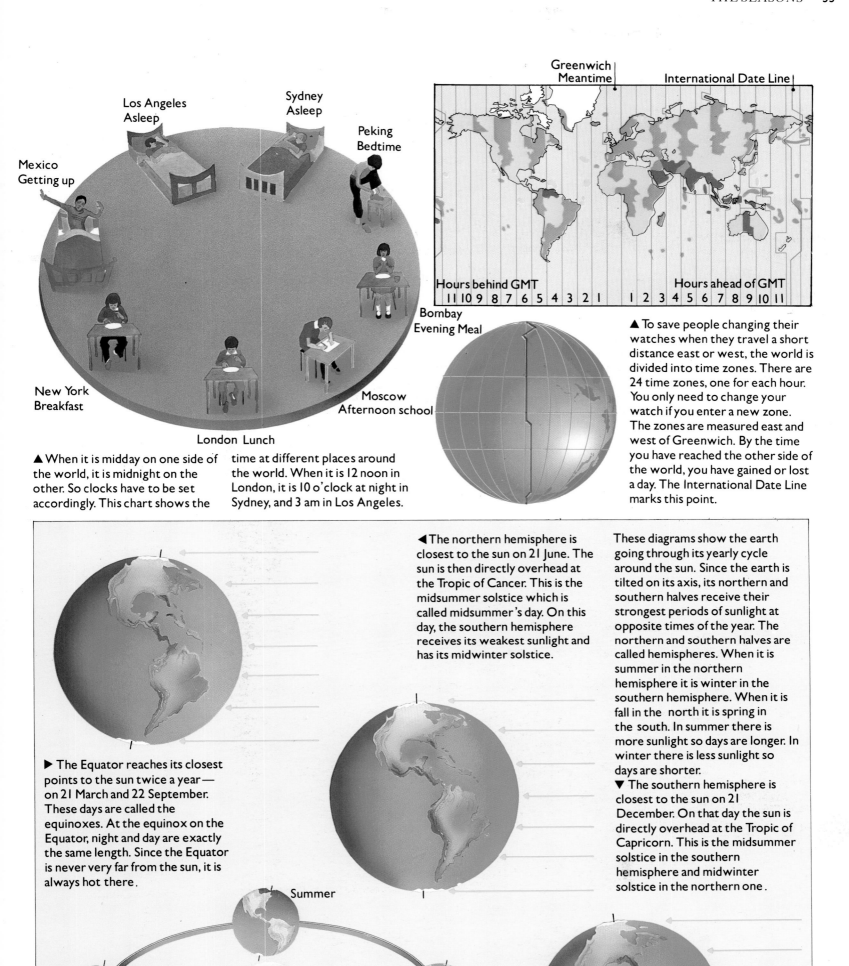

Los Angeles
Asleep

Sydney
Asleep

Peking
Bedtime

Mexico
Getting up

Bombay
Evening Meal

New York
Breakfast

Moscow
Afternoon school

London Lunch

Greenwich
Meantime

International Date Line

Hours behind GMT
11 10 9 8 7 6 5 4 3 2 1

Hours ahead of GMT
1 2 3 4 5 6 7 8 9 10 11

▲ When it is midday on one side of the world, it is midnight on the other. So clocks have to be set accordingly. This chart shows the time at different places around the world. When it is 12 noon in London, it is 10 o'clock at night in Sydney, and 3 am in Los Angeles.

▲ To save people changing their watches when they travel a short distance east or west, the world is divided into time zones. There are 24 time zones, one for each hour. You only need to change your watch if you enter a new zone. The zones are measured east and west of Greenwich. By the time you have reached the other side of the world, you have gained or lost a day. The International Date Line marks this point.

◄ The northern hemisphere is closest to the sun on 21 June. The sun is then directly overhead at the Tropic of Cancer. This is the midsummer solstice which is called midsummer's day. On this day, the southern hemisphere receives its weakest sunlight and has its midwinter solstice.

These diagrams show the earth going through its yearly cycle around the sun. Since the earth is tilted on its axis, its northern and southern halves receive their strongest periods of sunlight at opposite times of the year. The northern and southern halves are called hemispheres. When it is summer in the northern hemisphere it is winter in the southern hemisphere. When it is fall in the north it is spring in the south. In summer there is more sunlight so days are longer. In winter there is less sunlight so days are shorter.

▼ The southern hemisphere is closest to the sun on 21 December. On that day the sun is directly overhead at the Tropic of Capricorn. This is the midsummer solstice in the southern hemisphere and midwinter solstice in the northern one.

► The Equator reaches its closest points to the sun twice a year— on 21 March and 22 September. These days are called the equinoxes. At the equinox on the Equator, night and day are exactly the same length. Since the Equator is never very far from the sun, it is always hot there.

Summer

Fall

Spring

Winter

Weather and climate

The surface of the earth is wrapped in an envelope of gases which is called the atmosphere. The main gases are nitrogen and oxygen. The lowest layer of the atmosphere is the troposphere. The troposphere consists of many masses of air which are always moving. Air masses determine the world's weather. A front develops where two different types of air mass meet. For example, a cold front is where a mass of cold air moves into a warm air area. A warm front is where warm air pushes into a cold air area.

Weather means the day-to-day conditions of the troposphere – temperature, air pressure, wind, clouds and humidity. Humidity is the amount of water vapor which the air contains. Climate is like a yearly average or summary of weather conditions. The three main types of climate are tropical, temperate and polar. A tropical climate is very hot and is found around the Equator. Temperate climates are less hot and are found north and south of the tropics. Polar climates are the coldest and are found in the far north and south. The nearness of a place to the sea affects its climate. The sea stores warmth from the sun. This means that the climate of places near the sea have fairly even temperatures. Areas far away from the sea are hotter in summer and colder in winter. This type of climate is called continental. It has only a little rainfall in early summer.

Height above the sea – or altitude – also affects climate. For every 1,000 feet (300 meters) above sea level the temperature falls by about 7°F (3°C). This means that mountains like Mount Kilimanjaro in Africa have snow on their peaks even though they are very near the Equator.

◄ Seen from space, the earth looks like this. Some areas are covered by cloud, making dull weather. Others are free of clouds and the weather is sunny.
As the earth's air masses move, the weather changes. Clouds hide the sun from some areas, and the sky is clear in others. This process is going on all the time. Weather forecasting depends on studying cloud movements.

► Clouds form when air becomes saturated with water vapor. Tiny droplets of moisture condense. They hang in the air as clouds. You can see how clouds form when you breathe out on a cold winter's day. Your breath is warm and moist. It condenses as it reaches the cold air outside.

▲ Nome in Alaska is close to the Arctic Circle. Temperatures stay below freezing point for most of the year. They only reach 50° F/ 10°C in midsummer.

▲ Moscow is in a temperate zone. It is also in the middle of a great continent, so temperatures vary. It is bitterly cold in winter and very hot in summer.

Key
● Cold climates
● Cool temperate climates
● Dry climates
● Warm temperate climates
● Tropical climates

▼ Debundja in Cameroon is in the tropics. Temperatures are hot and the climate is humid. A slight drop in temperature in the fall brings a very rainy season.

▼ Riyadh in Saudi Arabia is in a tropical zone. It is always hot, and daily temperatures never fall below 68°F/20°C. It is in a desert region with hardly any rainfall.

▶ Scientists divide the world into three main climatic regions. To the north and south are the cold regions within the Arctic and Antarctic Circles. The tropics are the hot regions north and south of the Equator. Their outer boundaries are marked by the Tropic of Cancer in the north, and the Tropic of Capricorn in the south. Between these hot and cold regions lie the temperate regions where climates vary greatly.

▼ Many things influence climate, and height above sea level is one of them. The air grows colder the higher up you go. A mountain may have many different climates. Mount Kenya is in the tropics. As you would expect, the climate is tropical around the base. However, higher up, it becomes temperate. Higher still it grows colder and trees will not grow. At the top, the peak is covered with snow all the year round— even in midsummer.

Cold currents

Warm currents

▲ The oceans affect the world's climate. The sea stores the sun's heat, and keeps coastal temperatures more stable than inland. The oceans also have other effects. Warm currents, such as the Gulf Stream, bring extra warmth to the coastal regions in their path. Cold currents bring cooler weather to coastal regions.

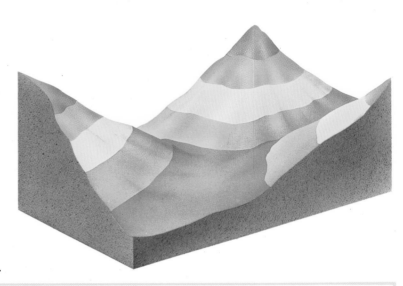

Rainfall and humidity

Rain falls when the moisture in a cloud cools and condenses. The drops of moisture grow too big to remain in the air and fall as rain.

These projects show how to measure the rainfall in your area, and how to measure the level of humidity (the amount of moisture in the air).

Making a rain gauge

You will need a glass jar, a larger straight-sided tin and a plastic funnel. The funnel should fit as tightly as possible into the rim of the tin. It should not overlap at the top. If it is a bit too small, pack foam rubber around the rim for a good, tight fit.
Fill the tin with water to a depth of 20 millimeters.
Now pour the water into the jar. Glue a strip of paper to the side of the jar, and mark off the water level. Now divide the distance from this mark to the base of the jar into 20 equal parts. Each part will now represent one millimeter of rain when it falls.
Empty out the water and put the jar, with the funnel, into the tin. Place your rain gauge in the open and write down the level of rainfall every day.

Making a hygrometer

A hygrometer is an instrument for measuring humidity. You need two identical household thermometers with the degrees in Centigrade.
Fix one thermometer to a piece of board. This is the dry bulb thermometer.
The other thermometer needs a wet bulb. Fix a hollow bootlace around the bulb. Fit the thermometer to the board, with the end of the lace dangling into a jar of water. Water will travel up the lace and around the bulb.
In dry weather, the water around the bulb will evaporate, and there will be a large difference between the readings on your two thermometers.
In wet weather, less water will evaporate giving a higher reading.
To find the level of humidity, find the dry bulb reading in the column running across the top of the table (below). Subtract the wet bulb reading to find the difference. Find the difference in the column running down the side of the table. Now run down from the top column and across from the side column and find the point at which they meet. This tells you the humidity.
For example, if your dry bulb reading is between 18° and 19°, and the wet bulb reading is 5° lower, the humidity is 61%.

Difference between wet and dry bulb in degrees C	Dry bulb temperatures				
	15-16°	16-17°	17-18°	18-19°	19-20°
1	88%	90%	91%	92%	92%
1.5	83%	85%	86%	87%	88%
2	77%	81%	82%	83%	84%
2.5	74%	77%	78%	79%	80%
3	67%	72%	74%	75%	77%
3.5	64%	68%	70%	71%	73%
4	60%	63%	66%	68%	70%
4.5	55%	60%	62%	64%	66%
5	50%	55%	58%	61%	63%
5.5	47%	52%	55%	57%	60%
6	45%	47%	51%	53%	57%
6.5	40%	44%	47%	50%	53%
7	37%	41%	44%	48%	50%
7.5	34%	37%	40%	44%	48%

The world's vegetation

There are several different plant zones on the earth which are similar to the climate zones. This is because climate has a great effect on which plants can grow in different areas. Temperature, rain and soil are important. Without soil, the earth's surface would have no plants. Soil is very small pieces of rocks and minerals mixed with decayed plants and animals. These decayed materials are called humus. Soils with a lot of humus in them are rich and fertile so that plants and crops grow well in them.

In areas near the Equator, heavy rain washes minerals and humus out of the soil. This means the soil is not good for farming but thick forests grow there because of the heat and heavy rain. Further away from the Equator where it only rains in one half of the year the vegetation is mainly grassland with some trees. This type of region is called savanna and it is found in many parts of Africa.

Areas with temperate climates have great varieties of vegetation. The plants include deciduous forests and, in the north, coniferous forests. A deciduous tree loses its leaves in winter while a coniferous tree is evergreen. This means that it has leaves all the year round.

Between the icy regions around the North Pole and the coniferous forests is an area called the tundra. No trees grow on the tundra but there is some thin vegetation. There is no tundra area around the South Pole.

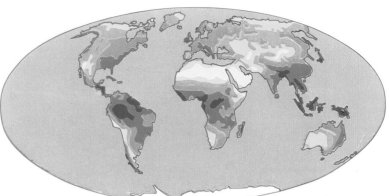

▲ This map shows average yearly rainfall. The amount of rainfall greatly affects plant life. Trees need plenty of moisture. Few grow in the dry tropical Sahara. However, trees grow tall in wet tropical rainforests. Deciduous trees need moderate rainfall.

Average yearly rainfall	Inches		Millimeters
	Over 196.8	●	Over 5000
	78.7	●	2000
	39.3	●	1000
	19.6	○	500
	11.8	○	300
	Under 3.9	○	Under 100

▲ Coniferous trees bear seeds in cones. Examples include pine, spruce and fir. Their leaves are thin. Most conifers keep them all year. They can survive in cold climates which would kill a deciduous tree. Conifers grow quickly, and new forests are often planted for timber.

▲ Deciduous trees shed their leaves in winter. Deciduous forests grow in temperate climates where rain falls fairly evenly throughout the year. The trees include chestnut, beech, oak, maple, ash and lime. Willows are deciduous and grow very well on damp waterside banks.

▼ Grasslands are regions where the rainy season is fairly short. While the rain falls, vegetation flourishes. However, the long dry season tends to kill off the larger plants. Few trees survive, but the roots of sturdy grasses are not harmed. Grasslands include the prairies and pampas of America and the African savanna.

▲ Tropical forests are always hot and wet. The vegetation grows and flowers all year round. The trees tend to grow tall, with broad leaves at the top. Their long stems are often entwined by creepers growing up towards the sunlight. Fungi often grow on the cool and shaded forest floor. Many exotic birds and animals live here.

Key

- Mediterranean forest and scrub
- Savanna
- Tropical rain forest
- Monsoon forest
- Dry tropical scrub
- Desert
- Scrub, steppe and semi-desert
- Deciduous and broadleaf forest
- Coniferous forest
- Tundra and ice

▲No vegetation can grow in the true polar regions. The climate is much too cold. This is Port Lockroy in the Antarctic.

▲ This is the Alaskan tundra in the fall. The climate is too cold for trees to grow, but grasses and other plants may survive.

▲ Mount Ararat in Turkey rises from a high steppe. A few trees may take root and survive the dry summer and cold winter.

▲ Tropical scrublands are hot, dry regions where there is just enough rain to support desert vegetation such as coarse grasses and cacti.

▲ Temperate forests grow on the north coast of Algeria. Further south lies the Sahara where there are few trees and no forests.

▲ The North American prairies are grasslands. Few trees grow here, but the fertile soil is good for grazing cattle and growing corn.

▲ Certain regions of the Sahara are true deserts. They are hot and dry, and absolutely nothing can take root in the shifting sands.

The world's crops

Many raw materials and kinds of food come from the earth's plants. Since earliest times, people have gathered nuts, berries and plants for food, used bark and tree roots for dyes and medicine, and fibers and leaves for making houses and cloth.

Wood is the most important plant product. People have used it for building, and for making tools, toys and paper. Forests cover almost two thirds of the surface of the earth. There are two main types of forest – the coniferous forests in the far north and south, and the deciduous forests of the temperate and tropical lands.

The wood from the coniferous forests in northern Europe and Asia is used for making paper and furniture. The woods from the tropical forests, which are called hardwoods, include mahogany, ebony and teak.

Grass also has many uses. Some people still wear grass skirts and grass is used to make the walls and roofs of houses in many parts of the world. Bamboo is a woody kind of tropical grass. Its stems are used for building, making furniture, tools and the fibers are used in making some kinds of paper and in weaving.

Rubber is another major product obtained from trees. Rubber trees grow naturally in the forests of South America. The great plantations of south-east Asia developed from plants taken from the Amazon basin.

▼ Wood is valuable both as a fuel and a building material. It can be carved and shaped to make beams, beds or boats. Wood is also crushed to pulp and pressed to make paper and cardboard.

▼ Rubber is made from the sap of rubber trees. This is a special type of sap called latex. It is stretchable, solid and waterproof. It is valuable for many goods including tires and waterproof fabrics and rubber bands.

▲ Cotton grows as a low shrub in hot climates throughout the world. Since ancient times, people have twisted and woven the fiber to make thread, fabrics, and many kinds of clothing.

▼ Wheat is a cereal plant whose seeds grow as edible grain. It was one of the first crops which early man learnt to sow and harvest. The grains are crushed to make flour. Flour is the basic material in bread.

◀ Sugar is a substance containing a mixture of carbon, hydrogen and oxygen – sugary foods are called carbohydrates. Sugar is present in many plants, especially sugar cane and sugar beet, a root vegetable.

◄ Rice is the seed of a grass-like plant. It first grew wild in the marshlands of Asia's great rivers. The ancient Chinese learnt how to grow it over 4,000 years ago. The plant needs a hot climate and plenty of moisture.

► Coffee beans come from a plant which only grows well in rich soil in hot, damp climates. The Arabs were the first to use coffee to make a drink. The habit spread to Europe and North America in the seventeenth century.

◄ Coconut is the fruit of the coco palm. It grows throughout the tropics. The fruit produces food and palm oil. The shell can be carved to make cups and bowls.

► Cassava is a plant which produces sweet, starchy roots. Brazilian Indians have grown it for centuries and it is now grown elsewhere in the tropics. It is a valuable food and also used to make laundry starch.

◄ Tea grows as a bushy tree. The ancient Chinese were the first to produce a drink from its leaves. The taste for tea spread to Japan and India. It reached Europe and North America in the seventeenth century.

Making peppermints

Sugar beet and sugar cane must be refined before sugar can be used in cooking. There are many types of sugar. Confectionery sugar is used in this recipe. You need 1lb (500g) sugar; 1 egg white; $\frac{1}{8}$ pint (75ml) thick cream; peppermint essence.

1. Sift the sugar into a bowl. Now add the egg white and cream to the sugar.

2. Stir the mixture well so that it is smooth. Then add a few drops of peppermint essence until it tastes good.

3. Dust a board with sugar and roll out the paste. When the paste is quite thin, cut it into rounds or shapes with a cutter.

4. Put the peppermints on a wire rack to dry for at least 12 hours. After this time they will be ready to eat.

The seas and oceans

There are five oceans in the world – the Pacific, which is the largest, the Atlantic, the Indian, the Arctic and the Antarctic. They cover almost three quarters of the earth's surface. Land, particularly peninsulas and islands, divides the oceans into seas. The islands of the West Indies, for example, separate the Caribbean Sea from the Sargasso Sea in the North Atlantic Ocean.

The ocean floor is made up of shelves, slopes and deeps. The continental shelf is the shallow part of the oceans around the continents. The ocean floor gradually slopes away from the continental shelf to the ocean deeps. The deeps off the coast of Japan reach down to over 34,000 feet (10,300 meters). There are also huge mountain ranges, such as the Mid-Atlantic Ridge, on the ocean floor. These mountains were formed in the same way as mountains on land but they are hidden under water.

The oceans and seas are always moving because of waves, currents and tides. Waves are made by winds blowing across the surface of the water. Ocean currents can be either cold or warm and they have an important effect on climate. Tides are regular rises and falls of the sea. They happen when the gravity of the moon attracts and pulls the sea water slightly towards it. Tides vary in different parts of the world but they always happen twice in every 24 hours 50 minutes. This is the time it takes for the moon to orbit the earth.

Pacific Ocean

Sea   Land

◀ Geographers tend to look at the continents when they study the earth. However, the oceans cover much more of the earth's surface than the continents do. If you look at the globe from the Pacific side, you can hardly see any land at all. The seas cover about 71 per cent of the earth's surface. The ocean bed goes down much deeper below sea level than the mountains rise above it.

Coastline
Sea level
Active volcanic island
Ocean ridge
Continental shelf
Land
Volcanic islands (dormant or extinct)
Atoll with a lagoon
Volcanic pipe
Magma
Sedimentary layers of rock
Deep sea shelf
Abyss

▲ This picture shows a section of the ocean bed. It is divided into four main zones – the continental shelf, the continental slope, the deep sea shelf, and the abyss. These zones do not slope down evenly to the middle of the oceans. The ocean bed contains ridges, trenches, and some great mountain ranges below sea level.

Trawlers fish in the waters of the continental shelf. People drill for oil in these zones too. Special craft have been designed to reach the deepest levels of the abyss. In some places, the peaks of underwater ranges form reefs and islands. The skeletons of tiny sea creatures form coral after many years. This may build up around the crater of a volcanic island. As the island sinks, the coral forms a shallow lagoon called an atoll.

◀ The oceans move with the tides. The waves on the surface are caused by winds. On calm days far out at sea, the shape of the waves tends to be fairly regular and they are evenly spaced. The highest points are called the crests. The lowest points are called the troughs.

◀ As the waves approach a large mass of land, the ocean bed tends to shelve less steeply. There is not enough water ahead of a wave to complete the shape of the crest. The front of the crest begins to fall away sharply. The crest may almost overlap the trough ahead.

◀ When the wave reaches the coast, water surges up the beach. Since it cannot keep traveling onward, it falls back and meets the next wave as it advances. It slides back under the advancing crest. Nothing now supports the weight of the wave's crest and so it breaks.

▲ Surfing is a popular sport, especially in countries with long ocean beaches where high waves build up far from the shoreline.

The surfer tries to catch a wave before the crest breaks. The forward-moving face of the wave travels inshore at high speed.

Warm currents | Cold currents

▲ Ocean currents are major movements of water in the oceans. They may be warm or cold – the Gulf Stream is warm. It keeps European harbors ice-free in winter.

◀ **Tides**
The moon exercises a strong gravitational pull on the oceans. The sun's influence is less great because it is so much further away. So-called spring tides are the highest tides. They occur at new and full moon. At these times, the sun, moon and earth are in a direct line. The sun and moon's gravitational pulls act together pulling the oceans most strongly.

The lowest tides are called neap tides. These occur at the moon's first and third quarters — times when exactly a quarter, or three quarters of the moon can be seen at night. At these times the sun and moon are at right angles to the earth. They are out of phase, so they do not exercise such a direct gravitational pull on the oceans and the tides are low.

Floating in salt water
Have you noticed that it is easier to float in the sea than in a swimming pool? This is because sea water is salty. The more salt there is in water the more things float in it. To prove this, take a drinking straw and plug one end with modeling clay.

Now fill a glass jar with water and float the straw in it.

With a pen mark off the water level on the straw so that you can see how much it floats in ordinary water.
To see how much more the straw floats in salt water, add two large spoonfuls of salt to the jar. Stir it in well and then put in the straw. You will see how much more it floats.

Travel and communications

There are three main kinds of transport – land, water and air. All these are vital for carrying people, food, raw materials and goods from one place to another. Countries in North America and Western Europe have advanced transport systems. The world's poorer countries do not have such good communications and they often rely on primitive methods for transport.

The earliest way of carrying things about was on the backs of people or animals. Horses, camels, elephants, yaks, llamas, donkeys and mules are useful animals either for carrying goods and people or for working in the fields and pulling carts. The best way to travel across snow and ice in the Arctic regions is on a dog-sledge.

Railroads were invented in the nineteenth century in Britain and they soon spread to the rest of the world. A fairly cheap way of transporting heavy goods is by rail, but today many people and industries use highways and roads instead.

Another important way of moving products and materials is by sea, rivers and canals. The type of boat used on a canal is called a barge. Container ships are easy to load and unload as all the goods are pre-packed in crates. The fastest form of transport is by air. There are now airports all over the world and people who want to travel quickly go by airplane. Traveling by air is becoming much more popular, especially with vacationers.

◄Cars zoom round the 'octopus', a clover-leaf highway in Caracas. Motor cars were developed by inventors in Europe and the United States in the late nineteenth century. They have transformed our way of life since then. However, rising fuel costs may mean that many people will give up owning a car.

▼ Trains are still a vital form of overland transport. The first steam train service ran between Stockton and Darlington in England. It opened in 1825. Modern trains often run on electricity. New, high-speed passenger services run between major cities.

▼People still perform many important carrying tasks in poor countries. Goods may be put on the head so that the whole of the body takes their weight. Horses and donkeys are the oldest beasts of burden used by man. They were probably used first by the ancient Egyptians over 6,000 years ago.

◄ There are very few cars in China. Most people use bicycles to get about. They can also be adapted for carrying light cargoes.

Major shipping routes

► Camels like this one in Israel are well suited to desert travel. They can go without water for many days, and their broad hooves do not sink into the sand. There are two main types. The dromedary has one hump. The Bactrian camel has two.

◄Aircraft offer the fastest form of transport. However, they are not as suitable as ships or trains for carrying heavy cargoes.
Two Americans called Wilbur and Orville Wright made the first true aircraft powered by motor, in 1903. Modern aircraft, like the one shown here are powered by jets.

► Aircraft have replaced ships as the main way for passengers to cross the oceans. However, ships like this container vessel can carry much bulkier cargoes.
Sailing ships have been used since ancient times. The first steamship was built in 1783. Diesel engines came later. Nuclear energy now powers some modern ships.

▼ Large trucks have many advantages over trains for carrying goods overland. They are not faster, but they are more adaptable. The goods do not have to be unloaded and reloaded at a station. 'Big rigs' like this can carry container goods straight to a dock for loading onto a ship. However, these large trucks can cause problems such as air pollution to the environment.

Major air routes

This map shows the main sea lanes and aircraft routes around the world.

The shrinking globe

Today, the world often seems smaller than it is because people can speed from one continent to another in just a few hours. In fact, the time it takes to travel from place to place has become more important than actual distances.

In the middle of the nineteenth century, sailing boats took one to three months to cross the Atlantic Ocean. Steam ships later completed the same journey in about 10 days. The fastest way to cross the Atlantic now is by supersonic passenger jet. Concorde, for example, takes only $3\frac{1}{2}$ hours to fly from New York to London. This is half the time taken by other aircraft.

The airplane has also speeded up postal services throughout the world. Letters can arrive in another country within a few days of being mailed. It is also possible to communicate directly with people without traveling. The international telephone system links almost all parts of the world, and teleprinters and computers enable people to send messages over great distances. This is useful for anyone who has business dealings abroad. Another reason the world seems quite small is that television pictures, by using satellites, can show events as they actually happen on the other side of the world.

504 hours 1860

Clipper

Steamer

DC-4

Concorde

◀ When the clipper sailing ship was designed in the nineteenth century, it was the fastest sea transport in the world. However, it was later replaced by the steamer, which was driven by steam turbines and not by sail. The DC-4 used to be the fastest passenger plane in the world, but the supersonic Concorde is the fastest today.

288 hours 1906

24 hours 1963

3½ hours Today

◀ These globes are all at the same angle showing the Atlantic Ocean and how long the journey from London to New York has taken over the years. They vary in size because the less time it takes to go from one place to another, the smaller the world seems to be. In the 1800s the only way of crossing the Atlantic Ocean was by ship. The clipper sailing ship was the fastest kind, but even this took over three weeks to make the journey. One of the major uses of the clipper was to carry tea from Asia to England. The introduction of the steamer as a means of transport meant that traveling time was nearly halved in the early part of this century. Most steam ships were designed to carry passengers and mail. The invention of airplanes meant that it took even less time for people to cross the Atlantic. Today it can take only 3½ hours.

▲ Many satellites orbit the earth. They pick up sound and television signals from one place and send them down to relay stations in other places. This is how events can be shown on television while they are happening on the other side of the world. Satellites are also used to help weather-forecasters predict the weather.

▶ In 1876 Alexander Graham Bell invented the telephone. Since then it has been improved and people can now talk to each other over great distances.

▲ The teleprinter is a machine on which printed messages can be sent and received. It has a keyboard like a typewriter and the messages are sent by telegraph. Teleprinters are generally used in offices and not in private houses. Some ships have teleprinters as well.

COUNTRIES OF THE WORLD

The key explains what the symbols on the maps of the different countries mean. They show where the main farming and industrial areas are, and where the main crops and mineral resources can be found. The symbols are in four colors — blue for animals and animal farming, green for plants and vegetation, red for minerals and mining, and purple for industry and tourism. The maps also show the main mountains, rivers, towns, roads and railroads.

The facts and figures panel gives the most important information about the country — its population, area, language, capital and currency. You can easily compare the facts about different countries.

- ● Towns with over 1,000,000 people
- ● Towns with under 1,000,000 people
- ▲ Mountains
- ⌒ Railways
- ⌒ Major roads
- Wheat
- Corn/Maize
- Rice
- Cereal crops — oats, barley, rye etc
- Citrus fruits
- Grapes, mainly for making wine

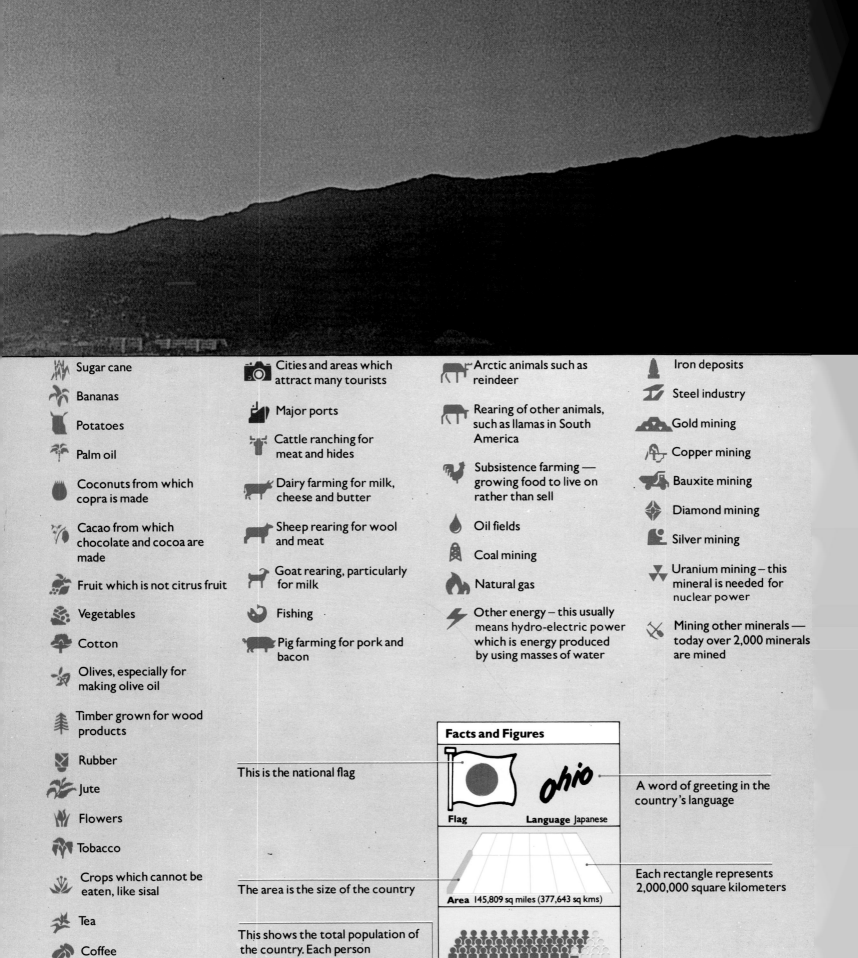

Sugar cane	Cities and areas which attract many tourists
Bananas	Major ports
Potatoes	Cattle ranching for meat and hides
Palm oil	Dairy farming for milk, cheese and butter
Coconuts from which copra is made	Sheep rearing for wool and meat
Cacao from which chocolate and cocoa are made	Goat rearing, particularly for milk
Fruit which is not citrus fruit	Fishing
Vegetables	Pig farming for pork and bacon
Cotton	
Olives, especially for making olive oil	
Timber grown for wood products	
Rubber	
Jute	
Flowers	
Tobacco	
Crops which cannot be eaten, like sisal	
Tea	
Coffee	
Groundnuts	
Spices	
Industrial areas	
Shipbuilding	

Arctic animals such as reindeer	Iron deposits
Rearing of other animals, such as llamas in South America	Steel industry
Subsistence farming — growing food to live on rather than sell	Gold mining
Oil fields	Copper mining
Coal mining	Bauxite mining
Natural gas	Diamond mining
Other energy – this usually means hydro-electric power which is energy produced by using masses of water	Silver mining
	Uranium mining – this mineral is needed for nuclear power
	Mining other minerals — today over 2,000 minerals are mined

Facts and Figures

This is the national flag

Flag

ohio

Language Japanese

A word of greeting in the country's language

The area is the size of the country

Area 145,809 sq miles (377,643 sq kms)

Each rectangle represents 2,000,000 square kilometers

This shows the total population of the country. Each person represents 3,000,000 people in real life – so half a person equals 1,500,000 people

Population 115,920,000

An example of the money used in the country

Yen

Currency

Tokyo

Capital

This shows where abouts the capital is

Looking at Europe

Europe is the world's second smallest continent. It covers an area of 3,850,000 square miles (9,972,000 sq kms). This is about one million square miles larger than Australia.

Despite its small area, Europe is very densely populated. Its population of 660 million is 47 times larger than Australia's of 14 million.

Europe is surrounded by seas to the north, west and south. The only land boundary is with Asia in the east. The coastline of Europe is very irregular because deep seas and inlets divide the land into peninsulas and islands. In the south, Spain and Portugal form one peninsula and Italy another. In the north, the Scandinavian countries also form peninsulas.

There are many great rivers in Europe. These include the Rhine which flows into the North Sea and the Danube which runs into the Black Sea. The five main mountain ranges are the Pyrenees, Alps, Apennines, Carpathians and the mountains of Scandinavia. The nearness to the sea greatly modifies Europe's climate, especially in the west where the warm Gulf Stream makes the climate milder.

In Europe there are many countries and most have their own language. More than 70 languages are spoken in Europe. Some of Europe's boundaries are political, others follow mountain ranges and river valleys.

▼The most densely populated area of Europe is an arc sweeping down from northern Britain to southern Italy. It includes north-eastern France, Belgium, Holland, Denmark, West and East Germany, Poland, Czechoslovakia and Hungary. Much of this is made up of lowland industrial and farming regions, broken up by hills and mountain ranges: the Alps, Apennines and Carpathians.

Spain, Portugal, Greece and the Balkan countries are less densely populated. Here, many centers of population are around the coasts, away from the mountainous terrain inland.

In the north, Iceland, Norway, Finland and Sweden are much more thinly populated. Together, they make up almost a third of Europe's land mass. However, much of the land is mountain, forest or tundra. Most Swedes, Finns and Norwegians live on the Baltic coast.

West Germany has a population of over 61 million people. This makes it the most populated country in Europe. Next come Italy (57 million), the United Kingdom (56 million), and France (53 million). There are nine cities in Europe with populations of over 2 million people. London is the largest.

Inhabitants

per sq mile	per sq km
Under 16	Under 6
16-256	6-100
256-512	100-200
Over 512	Over 200

Key

Timber		Sheep	
Cereals		Dairy	
Potatoes		Pigs	
Fruit		Farming	
Flowers		Reindeer	
Wheat		Coal	
Olives		Iron	
Non food products		Steel	
Grapes/Wine		Minerals	
Corn/Maize		Oil	
Citrus fruit		Natural gas	
Tobacco		Silver	
Rice		Energy	
Port		Uranium	
Industry		Bauxite	
Shipbuilding		Gold	

▼ Europe is heavily industrialized. However, agriculture is still important, especially in the south. The forests of Scandinavia provide much timber, and fishing is important on the Atlantic coast. Oil and natural gas have been found beneath the North Sea, and coal is still vital to Europe's industries. Europe's great seaports have always been thriving centers of world trade. Inland, goods are carried by many roads, railways, rivers and canals.

Reykjavik

ICELAND

Hammerfest

SWEDEN

FINLAND

FAEROE ISLANDS

Norwegian Sea

Gulf of Bothnia

NORWAY

Oslo

Helsinki

SHETLAND ISLANDS

ORKNEY ISLANDS

Stockholm

HEBRIDES

GOTLAND

UNITED KINGDOM

Glasgow Edinburgh

Belfast

North Sea

DENMARK

Baltic Sea

Dublin

IRELAND Liverpool

Cork

Copenhagen

Gdansk

Birmingham

EAST GERMANY

Hamburg

R. Vistula

Cardiff

HOLLAND

Amsterdam

Berlin

Warsaw

R Thames

London

Antwerp

Essen

Bonn

Leipzig

R. Elbe

POLAND

R. Oder

SOVIET UNION

Atlantic Ocean

CHANNEL ISLANDS

Brussels

BELGIUM

English Channel

Le Havre

Brest

R. Seine

FRANCE

R. Meuse

Frankfurt

WEST GERMANY

Prague

Krakow

Carpathian Mountains

Paris

Stuttgart

CZECHOSLOVAKIA

R. Rhine

R Danube

Nantes

R. Loire

Bay of Biscay

Basle

Berne

Munich

Vienna

Bordeaux

Vaduz

AUSTRIA

Budapest

Massif Central

Lyon

SWITZERLAND

Innsbruck

HUNGARY

Bilbao

Geneva

Alps

R Sava

RUMANIA

SPAIN

R Douro

R. Garonne

Pyrenees

Turin

Milan

Trieste

Venice

Zagreb

Bucharest

R Danube

Madrid

R Ebro

Marseille

Nice

R Po

Belgrade

Varna

Lisbon

R. Tagus

Barcelona

CORSICA

Tiber

Florence

YUGOSLAVIA

BULGARIA

PORTUGAL

R Guadalquivir

Rome

ITALY

Adriatic Sea

Sofia

Balkans

BALEARIC ISLANDS

SARDINIA

Tyrrhenian Sea

Naples

Apennines

ALBANIA

Tirana

Thessaloniki

Strait of Gibraltar

CORFU

GREECE

Aegean Sea

Palermo

SICILY

Ionian Sea

Athens

Mediterranean Sea

Iraklion

CRETE

Scale

0   500 miles

0   500 kms

British Isles

The British Isles are two large islands – Great Britain and Ireland – and many smaller islands. They are the most westerly part of Europe except Iceland. Great Britain consists of three countries – England, Scotland and Wales. Ireland is divided into the Republic of Ireland (or Eire) and Northern Ireland. Great Britain and Northern Ireland together are called the United Kingdom.

The northern part of Great Britain is more mountainous than the southern part. The main mountain ranges are the Grampians in Scotland, the Pennines in England, and the Cambrian Mountains in Wales.

England is the most densely populated country and has many important industrial areas. London is the capital and is the center of the road and railroad system. It is one of the world's most important industrial and commercial cities.

Scotland is divided into highland and lowland areas. The scenery is often spectacular in the highland area which includes many islands around the coast. In the south are the two main cities – Edinburgh, the capital, and Glasgow, the industrial center. Oil from the North Sea is an important new industry.

Wales is the smallest country. It is mountainous and most of the population live in the industrial southern area. Cardiff is the capital.

Ireland is often called the 'Emerald Isle' because of its green fields. It is shaped like a bowl with a rim of mountains around the coast and a low-lying central plain. Dublin is the capital of Eire and Belfast of Northern Ireland. The Shannon is the longest river in the British Isles. It is 224 miles (358 kms) long. The largest lake in the British Isles – Lough Neagh – is in Northern Ireland. Eire is mainly a farming country but industry and tourism are becoming more important. It exports meat and dairy products.

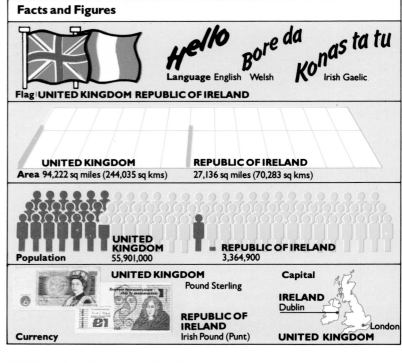

Facts and Figures

Flag | UNITED KINGDOM   REPUBLIC OF IRELAND

Language English   Welsh   Irish Gaelic

UNITED KINGDOM	REPUBLIC OF IRELAND
Area 94,222 sq miles (244,035 sq kms)	27,136 sq miles (70,283 sq kms)

Population   UNITED KINGDOM 55,901,000   REPUBLIC OF IRELAND 3,364,900

Currency   UNITED KINGDOM Pound Sterling   REPUBLIC OF IRELAND Irish Pound (Punt)

Capital   IRELAND Dublin   London   UNITED KINGDOM

▼ Oil was found under the North Sea bed in 1970. Oil production is now very important to Britain's economy.

▲ This map shows the counties in the British Isles. There are 46 in England, 26 in the Republic of Ireland, 8 in Wales, 6 in Northern Ireland and 12 regions and island areas in Scotland.

◀ A Scottish piper plays the bagpipes. Bagpipes were also used in other countries but became most popular in Scotland, Northumberland and Ireland, where they are still played today.

▶ Castle Stewart stands in the Firth of Lorne — the mouth of the Lorne river — on Scotland's west coast. It is near the resort of Oban.

▲ Whisky is distilled in Scotland. Malt and barley are two main ingredients in this important Scottish product. After distilling, the whisky matures in casks.

◀ This cottage with its thatched roof and whitewashed walls is typical of the west coast of Ireland. Many of the people who live here are farmers. They often divide up their fields with stone walls.

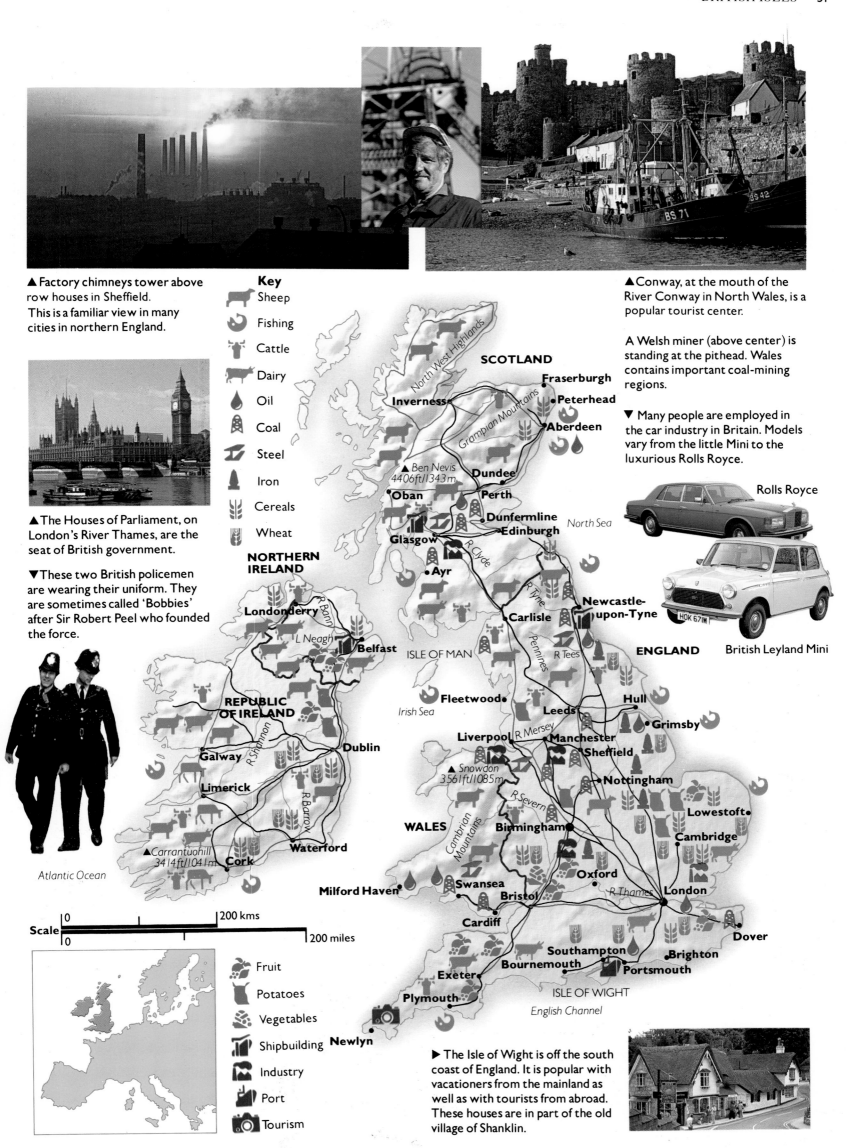

▲ Factory chimneys tower above row houses in Sheffield. This is a familiar view in many cities in northern England.

▲ The Houses of Parliament, on London's River Thames, are the seat of British government.

▼ These two British policemen are wearing their uniform. They are sometimes called 'Bobbies' after Sir Robert Peel who founded the force.

Atlantic Ocean

Key
- Sheep
- Fishing
- Cattle
- Dairy
- Oil
- Coal
- Steel
- Iron
- Cereals
- Wheat

Scale
0 ___ 200 kms
0 ___ 200 miles

- Fruit
- Potatoes
- Vegetables
- Shipbuilding
- Industry
- Port
- Tourism

▲Conway, at the mouth of the River Conway in North Wales, is a popular tourist center.

A Welsh miner (above center) is standing at the pithead. Wales contains important coal-mining regions.

▼ Many people are employed in the car industry in Britain. Models vary from the little Mini to the luxurious Rolls Royce.

Rolls Royce

British Leyland Mini

SCOTLAND
- Fraserburgh
- Inverness
- Peterhead
- Aberdeen
- North West Highlands
- Grampian Mountains
- ▲ Ben Nevis 4406ft/1343m
- Dundee
- Oban
- Perth
- Dunfermline
- Edinburgh
- North Sea
- Glasgow
- R Clyde
- Ayr

NORTHERN IRELAND
- Londonderry
- R Bann
- L Neagh
- Belfast
- ISLE OF MAN
- Carlisle
- R Tyne
- Newcastle-upon-Tyne
- **ENGLAND**
- Pennines
- R Tees

REPUBLIC OF IRELAND
- Galway
- R Shannon
- Dublin
- Limerick
- R Barrow
- ▲Carrantuohill 3414ft/1041m
- Cork
- Waterford
- Irish Sea
- Fleetwood
- Hull
- Leeds
- Grimsby
- Liverpool
- R Mersey
- Manchester
- Sheffield
- ▲ Snowdon 3561ft/1085m
- Nottingham
- **WALES**
- Cambrian Mountains
- R Severn
- Birmingham
- Lowestoft
- Cambridge
- Oxford
- Swansea
- Bristol
- R Thames
- London
- Cardiff
- Dover
- Milford Haven
- Exeter
- Southampton
- Bournemouth
- Brighton
- Portsmouth
- Plymouth
- ISLE OF WIGHT
- Newlyn
- *English Channel*

▶ The Isle of Wight is off the south coast of England. It is popular with vacationers from the mainland as well as with tourists from abroad. These houses are in part of the old village of Shanklin.

France

France is the second largest country in Europe after the Soviet Union. Three of France's boundaries are with seas – the English Channel in the north-west, the Bay of Biscay in the west and the Mediterranean Sea in the south. France also has boundaries with Belgium, Luxembourg, West Germany, Switzerland, Italy and Spain. The boundaries with Switzerland and Italy follow the Jura and the Alps. The boundary with Spain follows the Pyrenees.

Mont Blanc in south-east France is the highest mountain in France and in the whole of Europe. It is 15,771 feet (4,807 meters) high. The country's largest upland area is the Massif Central. France has four large rivers – the Seine, the Loire, the Garonne and the Rhône. The main ports in France are Le Havre on the Atlantic and Marseille on the Mediterranean. Paris is the capital of France and is a big center of communications for France and Europe. In Paris there are many main railroad terminals and three international airports.

One quarter of all French people make their living from farming. France produces fruit and cheese as well as one third of all the world's wine. France is also an important industrial country. Industry is found mainly in the north and east where there are coal and iron deposits. Lille is a big industrial city. France exports motor vehicles, chemicals, machinery and textiles.

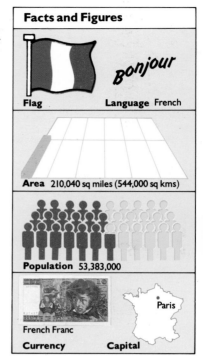

Facts and Figures

Flag   Language French

Area 210,040 sq miles (544,000 sq kms)

Population 53,383,000

French Franc

Currency   **Capital**   Paris

▲ The Eiffel Tower in Paris attracts many tourists. It is made of iron and stands 948 feet (400 meters) high. There is a radio station and a television aerial at the top.

► This chateau is in the Loire valley. It was built in the fifteenth century and is separated from the land by a moat. Moats were built around most chateaus for protection.

◄ Antibes is a popular resort on the Riviera, a region along the Mediterranean in France and Italy. It is also a port and center of a flower growing area.

▲ Mont Blanc is in the Alps on the border between France and Italy. It is the highest mountain in Europe. There is a seven mile (11.3kms) tunnel under the mountain linking France and Italy.

► France is famous all over the world for its food and chefs. Most chefs must go through years of training at one of the many cooking schools before they are allowed to work in the top restaurants.

▼ The French enjoy eating as much as they enjoy cooking. There are many outdoor cafés in Paris where people spend hours sitting, talking and eating.

◄ Bread is eaten with almost every meal in France. There are many types of bread. Here a baker is carrying out the long loaves known as baguettes.

▲ One of France's most popular exports is wine. Many different types of wine are produced. Here workers are treading on the grapes to turn them into wine.

► The city of Nantes lies on the Loire river and has been a trading port since Roman times. Many products are produced here and sent all over the world.

◄ The Dordogne river joins the Garonne river north of Bordeaux to form the Gironde. The valley is popular as a tourist attraction and there are many vineyards here.

► The Michelin tire man is recognized the world over. Tires are an important French product and they are known for their high quality.

▲ This French racing car is a Renault. The French make many cars both for racing and for ordinary use.

◄ This Citroën is known as the 'Deux Chevaux' because it has a two horsepower engine.

Scale

0   200 kms

0   200 miles

Key

- Cereals
- Grapes/Wine
- Potatoes
- Fruit
- Vegetables
- Olives
- Corn/Maize
- Port
- Industry
- Tourism
- Shipbuilding
- Fishing
- Dairy
- Pigs
- Sheep
- Coal
- Oil
- Minerals
- Bauxite
- Iron
- Energy

English Channel

BELGIUM

Dunkerque

Lille

Amiens

LUXEMBOURG

Ardennes

R Meuse

Le Havre

Metz

R Moselle

Caen

Nancy

Strasbourg

Brest

Paris

R Rhine

Atlantic Ocean

Rennes

R Seine

Mulhouse

Le Mans

R Loire

Nantes

Tours

Dijon

WEST GERMANY

R Saône

Jura Mountains

L Geneva
(Lac Leman)

La Rochelle

Limoges

Clermont-Ferrand

Lyon

Mont Blanc 15771ft/4807m

Bay of Biscay

Grenoble

SWITZERLAND

Massif Central

R Dordogne

R Rhône

Alps

Bordeaux

ITALY

R Garonne

R Tarn

Montpellier

MONACO

Bayonne

Toulouse

Nice

Marseille

Bastia

Pyrenees

Perpignan

Toulon

SPAIN

Mediterranean Sea

CORSICA

Ajaccio

The Low Countries

The Netherlands, Belgium and Luxembourg are often grouped together as the Low Countries. This is because they lie in a lowland region near the North Sea.

The Netherlands is also known as Holland and the people who live there are called the Dutch. The Netherlands is a flat land with many canals and windmills. Much of it lies below sea level. The Dutch have built dykes to keep back the sea. They have also built dams to prevent flooding by the rivers Rhine and Maas. The Dutch grow flowers, vegetables and fruits and make cheeses like Edam and Gouda. They also produce radios, textiles and electronic goods. Rotterdam is the major industrial port in the Netherlands, and Amsterdam is the capital. The government of the Netherlands works from The Hague.

Belgium is south of the Netherlands. The River Meuse divides the country into two main areas. In the south-east is a wooded upland area called the Ardennes. To the north and west is good farmland where arable crops are grown. Dairy farming is also important in this area. French and Flemish are the two Belgian languages. In the capital city, Brussels, people speak both these. The River Schelde flows through the port of Antwerp in the north. Ostend is a car ferry port.

Although they are small countries, the Netherlands and Belgium have the most dense population in Europe. The Grand Duchy of Luxembourg lies to the south-east of Belgium. This is a very small country which has an important steel industry and rich farmlands.

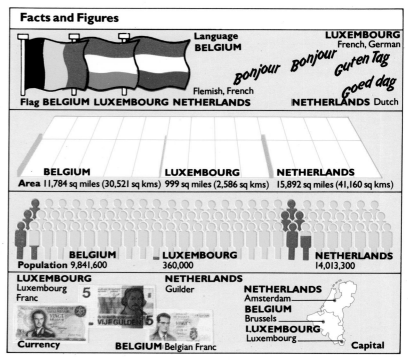

Facts and Figures

Language		**LUXEMBOURG** French, German
BELGIUM	*Bonjour Bonjour*	*Guten Tag*
		Goed dag
Flag BELGIUM LUXEMBOURG NETHERLANDS	Flemish, French	**NETHERLANDS** Dutch

BELGIUM	**LUXEMBOURG**	**NETHERLANDS**
Area 11,784 sq miles (30,521 sq kms)	999 sq miles (2,586 sq kms)	15,892 sq miles (41,160 sq kms)

BELGIUM	**LUXEMBOURG**	**NETHERLANDS**
Population 9,841,600	360,000	14,013,300

LUXEMBOURG Luxembourg Franc	**NETHERLANDS** Guilder	**NETHERLANDS** Amsterdam
		BELGIUM Brussels
		LUXEMBOURG Luxembourg
Currency	**BELGIUM** Belgian Franc	**Capital**

▶ Delft, in South Holland, is a very old city. It is famous for china, tiles and pottery.

◀ Visitors to the capital of Holland may take a boat trip on one of its many canals. Amsterdam is built on a network of canals and there are more than 1,000 bridges. There are two universities and the city is also a center of science.

▼ Nearly one half of the land in Holland is below sea level. There are huge engineering projects to keep the sea out. Ijsselmeer Dyke (formerly the Zuiderzee) was built in 1932. Gradually the land behind the dyke is being reclaimed.

Making a windmill
Cut out a piece of card in the shape shown. Place an unsharpened pencil on the back and tape it down. Draw and cut out the arms of the windmill on another bit of card.

Using a paper fastener, secure the arms to the big piece of card. Put a small piece in between the two so the arms will move freely in the wind.

▲ Haarlem is the center of the bulb-growing industry. Holland earns 485 million guilders a year from exports of bulbs.

▲ Dairy farming is very important in Holland. Windmills were once used to pump up water from the low-lying polders to stop them from flooding.

◀ The best-known Dutch cheeses are Gouda and Edam.

◀ The headquarters of the Common Market are in Brussels, the capital of Belgium. Brussels is a very old city on the Senne river in central Belgium. It is also an important industrial center. It produces electronic equipment, machine tools, rubber and lace.

◀ The Ardennes, in south-east Belgium, rise to 2,300 feet (700 meters). Two main rivers, the Meuse and the Sambre, flow through the woods and valleys.

▶The waterways of Bruges give it the name 'Venice of the North.' It is said to be the best preserved medieval city in Europe. There are winding cobbled streets and gabled houses. Bruges is famous for lace.

▼ Ostend is the largest holiday resort on the Belgian coast. It is also a fishing port. It is connected with Bruges and Ghent by canals. A ferry port is here too.

▼ Antwerp, on the River Schelde, is the major port of Belgium.

THE NETHERLANDS

North Sea

Leeuwarden
Groningen

Ijmuiden
Haarlem
Amsterdam

Ijsselmeer

R Ijssel

Hengelo

Den Haag
(The Hague)

R Lek

Utrecht
Arnhem

Rotterdam
R Waal
Nijmegen

Breda

Eindhoven

Ostende
(Ostend)

Brugge (Bruges)

Antwerpen
(Antwerp)

Gent
(Ghent)

R Schelde

Bruxelles
(Brussels)

Liège

Namur

R Meuse

Mons

Charleroi

BELGIUM

R Maas

WEST GERMANY

FRANCE

LUXEMBOURG

Luxembourg

Esch-sur-Alzette

Key

 Wheat

 Flowers

 Vegetables

 Fruit

 Cereals

 Industry

 Tourism

 Port

 Dairy

 Pigs

 Cattle

 Farming

 Coal

Steel

Iron

Natural gas

Oil

Scale

0

0

200 kms

200 miles

West Germany

West Germany extends from the North Sea and Baltic in the north to the Alps in the South. It has borders with nine countries – Denmark in the north, the Netherlands, Belgium, Luxembourg and France in the west, East Germany and Czechoslovakia in the east and Switzerland and Austria in the south.

In the north is the North German Plain. This flat, lowland area is used for growing wheat, rye, potatoes and sugar beet. The central area includes the Harz and Sauerland mountains, the Rhine valley and the Ruhr area. This area is densely populated.

The upland plain of Bavaria has rich farmlands. To the south of Munich, the capital, are the Alps which form the border with Austria.

The Rhine is the largest river in West Germany and the most important river in Europe. It rises near St Gotthard in Switzerland and flows for 800 miles (1,280 kms) to the North Sea. Many important German cities stand on the Rhine. These include Bonn, Düsseldorf, Mainz and Cologne. The Rhine valley is famous for its beautiful scenery and castles. Many wines come from the Rhine valley and they are also made on some of the Rhine's tributaries especially the Moselle.

West Germany is the greatest industrial country in Europe. The main industrial area is around the River Ruhr. The main towns include Dortmund, Duisburg and Essen. Frankfurt is the financial center of the country. The two main ports are Bremen and Hamburg on the North Sea. West Germany also has an important canal system. The country's non-industrial products include many kinds of beer.

West Germany is a federal republic. 'Federal' means that the country is divided into different states. Each of the 10 states has its own capital and government. The capital of the whole country is Bonn.

Facts and Figures

Flag

Language German

Area 96,004 sq miles (248,651 sq kms)

Population 61,321,700

Deutsche Mark
Currency

Bonn
Capital

▼ After 1945 Germany was split into East and West Germany. Another name for West Germany is the Federal Republic of Germany. The country has 10 federal states, each with its own government.

▲The south Rhineland, which contains the Eifel and Hunsruck Mountains, is mainly agricultural. Cereals are grown in the Hunsruck Highlands and there are also famous vineyards here.

◄The Germans drink more beer than any other nationality. There are many hand-made beer mugs, all of different designs. The Munich Beer Festival is famous throughout the world. Many people go to it each year.

▲ The Bavarian Alps in the southeast are on the border with Austria. Berchtesgaden is a popular resort with vacationers. There is good skiing nearby.

▶ This stretch of the River Rhine is particularly famous for its castles and vineyards. The fine wines which are made here are exported to countries all over the world.

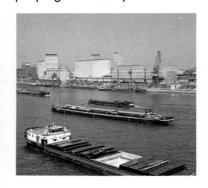

▲ Mannheim is a major Rhine port and industrial town. The Rhine carries more traffic than any other waterway. It is navigable by ocean-going vessels as far as Mannheim.

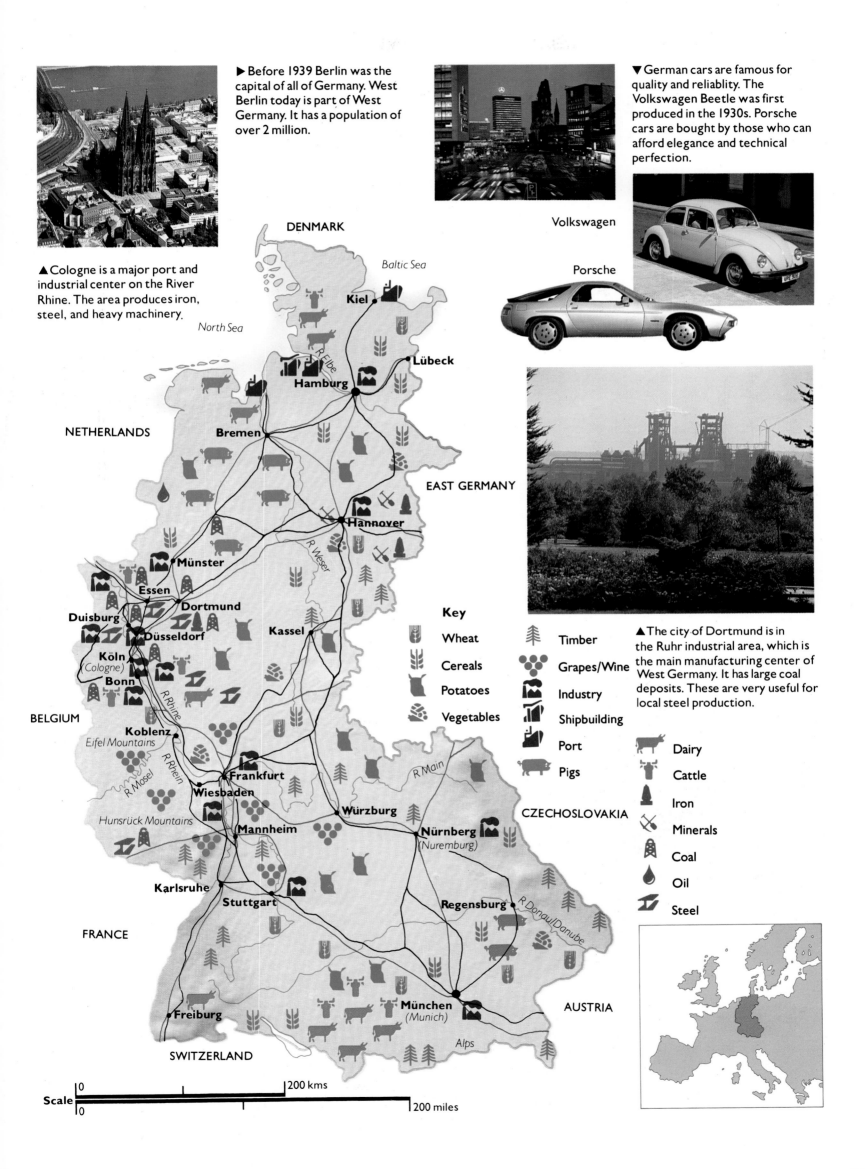

▶ Before 1939 Berlin was the capital of all of Germany. West Berlin today is part of West Germany. It has a population of over 2 million.

▼ German cars are famous for quality and reliablity. The Volkswagen Beetle was first produced in the 1930s. Porsche cars are bought by those who can afford elegance and technical perfection.

Volkswagen

Porsche

▲ Cologne is a major port and industrial center on the River Rhine. The area produces iron, steel, and heavy machinery.

DENMARK

Baltic Sea

North Sea

Kiel

R Elbe

Hamburg

Lübeck

NETHERLANDS

Bremen

EAST GERMANY

Hannover

R Weser

Münster

Essen

Dortmund

Kassel

Duisburg

Düsseldorf

Köln
(Cologne)

Bonn

BELGIUM

Koblenz

Eifel Mountains

R Rhine

R Mosel

R Rhein

Frankfurt

Wiesbaden

Hunsrück Mountains

Mannheim

Würzburg

R Main

Nürnberg
(Nuremburg)

CZECHOSLOVAKIA

Karlsruhe

Stuttgart

Regensburg

R Donau/Danube

FRANCE

Freiburg

München
(Munich)

AUSTRIA

Alps

SWITZERLAND

Key

Wheat		Timber	
Cereals		Grapes/Wine	
Potatoes		Industry	
Vegetables		Shipbuilding	
		Port	
		Pigs	

Dairy

Cattle

Iron

Minerals

Coal

Oil

Steel

▲ The city of Dortmund is in the Ruhr industrial area, which is the main manufacturing center of West Germany. It has large coal deposits. These are very useful for local steel production.

Scale

| 0 | | | 200 kms |
| 0 | | | 200 miles |

Scandinavia, Finland and Iceland

Northern Europe is made up of Finland, Iceland and Norway, Sweden and Denmark. These last three countries are sometimes called Scandinavia. The Arctic Circle passes through the northern parts of Norway, Sweden and Finland and it just touches the northern coasts of Iceland. North Cape in Norway is the most northerly point on the European mainland.

Norway is a long, narrow country with many mountains, glaciers and fjords. A fjord is a narrow inlet on the coast with steep sides like cliffs. Because of its fjords, Norway has the most jagged coastline in the world. It also has over 150,000 small rocky islands called skerries. Most Norwegians live in the south-east near Oslo, the capital. Fishing is a major industry and all the large cities in Norway are seaports.

Sweden lies to the east of Norway. This is another long country and it stretches for over 1,000 miles (1,600 kms) from north to south. Like Norway, Sweden has many forests. Its main industries are timber, paper, iron ore and steel. Stockholm, the capital, Gothenburg and Malmo are the largest cities in Sweden.

Denmark is a flat country to the south-west of Sweden. It is separated from Sweden by a narrow strip of water called The Sound. Denmark is made up of many islands and the Jutland peninsula. The capital, Copenhagen is on the largest island, Zealand. Fishing, shipping and tourism are all important in Denmark. Danish farm products such as bacon, butter and cheese are known throughout the world.

Finland is to the east of Sweden across the Gulf of Bothnia. Southern Finland is made up of thousands of tiny islands and a great number of lakes. Timber is the most important industry here. The capital is Helsinki. The northern part of Finland, Norway and Sweden is called Lapland. The people who live here are called the Lapps and they herd reindeer.

Iceland is the most westerly country in Europe. It is an island with many volcanoes, geysers and glaciers. Fishing is the main industry and the capital is Reykjavik.

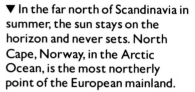

▲ There are about 30,000 Lapps in northern Scandinavia. Lapps follow their herds and use the reindeer for both food and transport.

▼ In the far north of Scandinavia in summer, the sun stays on the horizon and never sets. North Cape, Norway, in the Arctic Ocean, is the most northerly point of the European mainland.

▼ Geirangerfjord on the west coast of Norway is a typical fjord. It winds along for many miles with high mountains and cascading waterfalls on either side. Boats sail from a village at the head of the fjord around the coast.

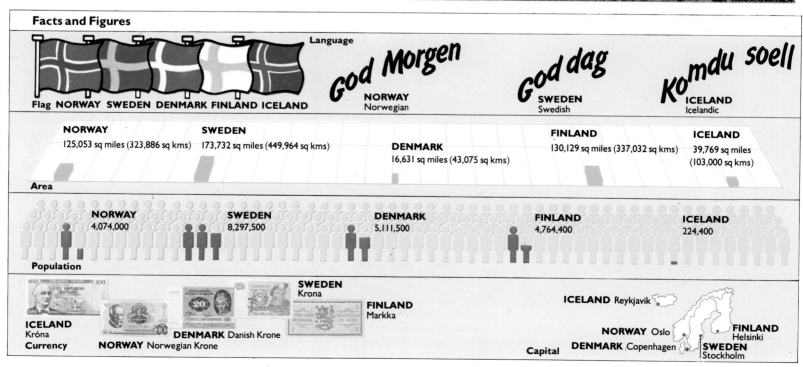

Facts and Figures

Flag NORWAY SWEDEN DENMARK FINLAND ICELAND

Language

God Morgen
NORWAY
Norwegian

God dag
SWEDEN
Swedish

Komdu soell
ICELAND
Icelandic

NORWAY 125,053 sq miles (323,886 sq kms)	**SWEDEN** 173,732 sq miles (449,964 sq kms)	**DENMARK** 16,631 sq miles (43,075 sq kms)	**FINLAND** 130,129 sq miles (337,032 sq kms)	**ICELAND** 39,769 sq miles (103,000 sq kms)

Area

NORWAY 4,074,000	**SWEDEN** 8,297,500	**DENMARK** 5,111,500	**FINLAND** 4,764,400	**ICELAND** 224,400

Population

ICELAND Króna
Currency **NORWAY** Norwegian Krone
DENMARK Danish Krone
SWEDEN Krona
FINLAND Markka

ICELAND Reykjavik
NORWAY Oslo
DENMARK Copenhagen
Capital
FINLAND Helsinki
SWEDEN Stockholm

▼ Iceland is an island just south of the Arctic Circle. At Lake Myvatn in the north of the island, there are many geysers and hot springs caused by volcanic activity. The Icelanders use the hot water from the springs as a cheap form of heating both private houses and public buildings .

◀ Timber is one of Sweden's main exports. Trees are felled using modern equipment. The logs are floated downstream to the timber plant where they are turned into wood products for export. Matches, paper and pine furniture are just some of these.

▶ Pork is Denmark's biggest export. It produces more than half the Danish farmers' income. Over 10 million pigs go to bacon factories each year.

Key

🌲 Timber	🏭 Port	🦌 Reindeer	
🌾 Cereals	🏭 Industry	⚡ Energy	
🌾 Wheat	🚢 Shipbuilding	Steel	
Potatoes	Fishing	Iron	
Vegetables	Dairy	Coal	
	Pigs	Minerals	
	Sheep	Copper	

Scale
0 — 200 kms
0 — 200 miles

SWEDEN
NORWAY
FINLAND
DENMARK
ICELAND
SOVIET UNION

Tromsø
Narvik
Kiruna
Mount Kebnekaise 6946ft/2117m
Luleå
Oulu
R Kemi
R Oulu
Vaasa
Tampere
Turku (Abo)
Helsinki (Helsingfors)
Trondheim
Östersund
Sundsvall
Gulf of Bothnia
Bergen
Stavanger
Oslo
Örebro
Stockholm
Norrköping
Baltic Sea
Kristiansand
Skagerrak
Göteborg (Gothenburg)
Jönköping
Ålborg
Kattegat
Århus
Esbjerg
København (Copenhagen)
Helsingborg
Fredericia
Odense
Malmö
North Sea
Siglufjördur
Akureyri
Reykjavík
Keflavík
R Thjorsa
R Glåma
R Otra
R Lågen
R Dal
R Ljusnan
R Indal
R Ångerman

The Alpine Countries

Much of Switzerland and Austria are in the Alps. They are the most mountainous countries in Europe. Many visitors go to see the beautiful scenery with its mountain peaks, deep valleys and lakes. Switzerland and Austria are good countries for mountain climbing and skiing. One of the most famous mountains in Switzerland is the Matterhorn. It is 14,690 feet (4,478 meters) high.

Important roads and railroad lines run through the Alps. The Simplon Tunnel and Simplon Pass link Switzerland and Italy and the Brenner Pass runs through Austria to Italy. The longest road tunnel in the world is the Alberg Tunnel in Austria. It is almost 9 miles (14 kms) long.

The capital of Switzerland is Berne. The regions of Switzerland are called cantons. In Switzerland most people speak German, but French and Italian are also important languages. Basle is Switzerland's only port. It stands on the River Rhine where the borders of Switzerland, France and Germany meet. Barges come up the river to Basle. The largest city is Zürich which is the business and industrial center. The Swiss produce cheese, chocolate, clocks, watches and toys.

In Austria people speak German. Austria produces brown coal, iron ore, oil, timber and paper. Graz and Linz are industrial cities. Salzburg and Innsbruck are tourist centers. Vienna is the capital of Austria. It is called the crossroads of Europe because many roads and railroads meet there.

The small country of Liechtenstein lies between Austria and Switzerland. It is only 15 miles (24 kms) long and 5 miles (8 kms) wide. The population is 24,000 and the capital is Vaduz.

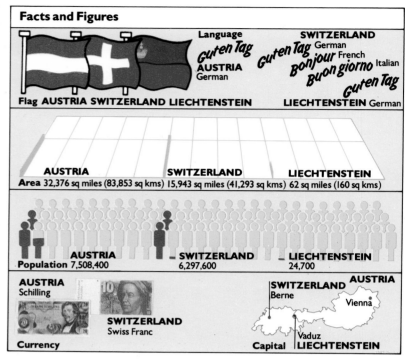

Facts and Figures

	AUSTRIA	SWITZERLAND	LIECHTENSTEIN
Flag			
Language	German	German, French, Italian	German
	Guten Tag	*Guten Tag, Bonjour, Buon giorno*	*Guten Tag*
Area	32,376 sq miles (83,853 sq kms)	15,943 sq miles (41,293 sq kms)	62 sq miles (160 sq kms)
Population	7,508,400	6,297,600	24,700
Currency	Schilling	Swiss Franc	
Capital	Vienna	Berne	Vaduz

◄Cuckoo clocks are on display in this Swiss tourist store. They are shaped like chalets (wooden Alpine cottages).

▼The summit of the Matterhorn rises above the surrounding peaks. In 1865, an English mountaineer called Edward Whymper became the first to reach the summit. Four of his seven-man party fell to their deaths on the way down but this has not deterred others.

◄A farmer brings his cattle to market in Switzerland. Dairy produce is used to make cheeses and chocolates. Alpine cattle wear bells around their necks in case they should get lost in the mountains' wooded slopes and valleys.

▶Women wrap sweets in a Swiss chocolate factory. The Swiss make chocolate of the finest quality, and their brand names are famous throughout the world.

◄Swiss Emmental cheese comes from the valley of the Emme river. Here, Emmental is stored in a cheese cellar.

◄Cheeses are named according to region. Emmental and Gruyère contain distinctive 'holes' formed by air bubbles.

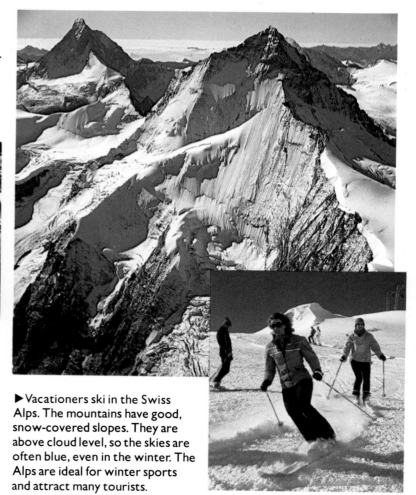

▶Vacationers ski in the Swiss Alps. The mountains have good, snow-covered slopes. They are above cloud level, so the skies are often blue, even in the winter. The Alps are ideal for winter sports and attract many tourists.

CZECHOSLOVAKIA
WEST GERMANY
LIECHTENSTEIN
SWITZERLAND
L Constance
Basle
FRANCE
Zürich
Innsbruck
Neuchâtel
Berne
R Rhein
Vaduz
Lausanne
R Rhône
Genève
L Geneva (Lac Leman)
Alps
Locarno
Lugano
ITALY
Matterhorn 14690ft/4478m

R Inn
Linz
R Donau/Danube
Salzburg
Wien *(Vienna)*
Leoben
HUNGARY
Grossglockner 12461ft/3789m
Graz
R Drau
AUSTRIA
Klagenfurt
YUGOSLAVIA

Key

Timber		Pigs	
Wheat		Sheep	
Fruit		Coal	
Grapes/Wine		Iron	
Cereals		Steel	
Potatoes		Oil	
Vegetables		Natural gas	
Industry		Minerals	
Tourism		Uranium	
Dairy		Energy	

Scale 0 — 200 kms / 0 — 200 miles

◀ A man works a cash dispenser outside a Swiss bank. Switzerland is peaceful and prosperous. People feel safe banking their money there. As a result, it is a world banking center.

▶ Barges are docked in Basle's harbor. The city is an important inland port and center for trade and industry. The surrounding region is good farming country.

▼ The State Opera House in Vienna is one of the city's famous historic buildings.
Austria's capital has attracted artists and musicians for many years. The composers Brahms and Mahler worked here. Johann Strauss made the city famous with his series of Viennese waltzes which are still popular today.

Making a cheese fondue
This is a very popular Swiss meal. Rub garlic around a ceramic dish and put it over a spirit burner with a low flame. Now mix 1lb (500g) grated Gruyère cheese and two glasses of wine in the dish. Stir it all gently until it melts. This makes enough fondue for four people. Eat it by dipping chunks of bread on long forks into the cheese.

Italy

Italy is a long and narrow peninsula that juts into the Mediterranean Sea. In the north it has borders with France, Switzerland, Austria and Yugoslavia. Italy is shaped rather like a large riding boot. In the south-west the Strait of Messina, which is only 2 miles (3.2 kms) wide, separates the island of Sicily from the mainland. Although it is like a triangle in shape, Sicily is sometimes described as a 'football' about to be kicked by the Italian 'boot'. Sicily is the largest island in the Mediterranean.

In the north of Italy are the Alps and south of these mountains is the Po river valley. This is a very large lowland with rich soil. Almost half the population of Italy live in the Po valley. South of the valley, the Apennine Mountains stretch down Italy from north to south. Southern Italy has a number of volcanoes and suffers from earthquakes. Mount Etna is a volcano in Sicily which is 10,958 feet (3,340 meters) high. Another famous Italian volcano is Mount Vesuvius near Naples which is 4,000 feet (1,219 meters) high.

Most of the Italian industry and farming is done in the north of the country. Rice, tomatoes, sugar beet and wheat (which is used for making pasta) are all grown in the Po valley. The dairy industry is also important and the Italians make many cheeses including Gorgonzola. Turin is the center of Italy's motor-car industry and Milan is the country's main business center.

Tourism is an important Italian industry. Tourists visit the many historic cities such as Venice, Florence and the capital, Rome.

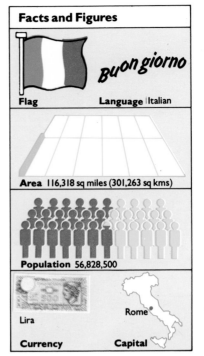

Facts and Figures

Flag

Language | Italian

Area 116,318 sq miles (301,263 sq kms)

Population 56,828,500

Lira

Currency

Rome

Capital

▲ Italy is divided into 20 regions which are divided into another 94 provinces. San Marino and Vatican City are independent small states.

▼ Cars are a major export for Italy, and also a major source of employment for many people. The Fiat company is one of the oldest car manufacturers in Italy.

▲ Saint Mark's church in Venice was built in the ninth century as a shrine for the bones of Saint Mark.

◀ The city of Venice is built on a marshland beside the Adriatic Sea. Many waterways and canals run through the city and are used for transportation instead of roads. A gondola is a boat which is used on the canals to carry people and goods from place to place.

Cooking spaghetti
Spaghetti is very popular in Italy. To cook it first bring salted cold water to the boil. To keep the spaghetti from breaking, don't drop it in all at once, but lower it slowly into the boiling water. Eating spaghetti can be messy unless you eat it the way the Italians do. Grab a bunch of spaghetti with a fork and then roll it around the fork, using a spoon as a support. With some luck, the spaghetti will stay on the fork until it reaches your mouth!

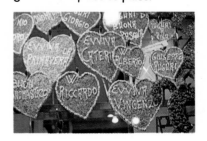

▲ The bakery shops of Milan are often filled with these special cakes with names written on them.

Key

- Grapes/Wine
- Wheat
- Citrus fruit
- Vegetables
- Rice
- Tourism
- Industry
- Port
- Sheep
- Dairy
- Oil
- Natural gas
- Iron
- Steel

SWITZERLAND

AUSTRIA

Mont Blanc
15771ft/4807m

FRANCE

Torino (Turin)
Milano (Milan)
Verona
R Piave
YUGOSLAVIA
Trieste
Venezia (Venice)
R Po
Genova (Genoa)
Bologna
Adriatic Sea
La Spezia
Ligurian Sea
R Arno
Firenze (Florence)
Livorno (Leghorn)
Ancona
R Tevere/Tiber
Roma (Rome)
Apennine Mountains
Foggia
Olbia
Sassari   SARDINIA
Napoli (Naples)
Mount Vesuvius
4000ft/1219m
Bari
Tyrrhenian Sea
Potenza
Salerno
Taranto
Brindisi
Cagliari
Catanzaro
Strait of Messina
SICILY   **Messina**
Ionian Sea
Palermo
Mount Etna
10958ft/3340m
Reggio di Calabria
Catania

Scale
0 — 200 kms
0 — 200 miles

▲ This picture shows the formal gardens behind the Pope's residence in the Vatican City. This is a small triangular state which is independent of Italy. The Pope is its absolute ruler. Above everything else, the Vatican is the seat of government for the Roman Catholic Church. Apart from the papal offices, the Vatican City also houses the famous Sistine Chapel. This is the private chapel of the Popes of Rome. The chapel is decorated with many frescoes and mosaics, but the greatest work in the chapel is the ceiling.

▼ Vesuvius is a large active volcano situated near the Bay of Naples. An eruption in 79 AD buried the city of Pompeii in lava. The last eruption occurred in 1944.

▶ These farmers are threshing wheat in fields in northern Italy. This is an important agricultural area and many crops grow here.

▼ Tuscany is a province on the north-west coast of Italy. It is known for its famous Chianti vineyards.

◀ This is the west front of the Duomo — or cathedral — in Milan. It was begun in 1386 and people then expected it to be the largest church in existence. Today, it is the third largest cathedral in Europe.

Spain and Portugal

The south-western peninsula of Europe is called the Iberian Peninsula. The main countries here are Spain and Portugal, but there are also the small areas of Gibraltar in the south and Andorra in the eastern Pyrenees.

The Pyrenees form the border with France in the north-east. This mountain range makes communications difficult and many of the passes are snow-bound in winter. The peninsula is also bounded by the Atlantic in the north and west and the Mediterranean in the south and east. Punta Marroqui, the most southerly point of Europe, is only 6 miles (10kms) from the coast of Africa.

Spain is the third largest country in Europe. In its center is a dry upland area called the Meseta. This reaches an average height of 2,000 feet (610 meters) and is very hot in summer and cold in winter. The highest mountain in Spain is in the Sierra Nevada and is 11,421 feet (3,480 meters) high.

Spain is an agricultural country. It produces wine, sherry, oranges and other fruit. The country has always been split into regions which each have their own capitals. Barcelona, the second largest city, is the capital of Catalonia. The capital of the Basque region in the north is Bilbao. Many of the regions also have their own language or dialect. For example, Catalan is spoken in Catalonia and Basque in the Basque region.

Madrid is the largest city in Spain and its capital. It is in the center of the country and is also the center of all the main roads and railroads.

Portugal borders on the Atlantic in the west. Shipping and tourism have always been important. Portugal, like Spain, is also agricultural. Its products include cork and wine. Port, a type of strong wine, is produced around the city of Porto which is the second largest city in Portugal. Lisbon is the largest city and the country's capital. The southern region is called the Algarve. It is an important tourist area.

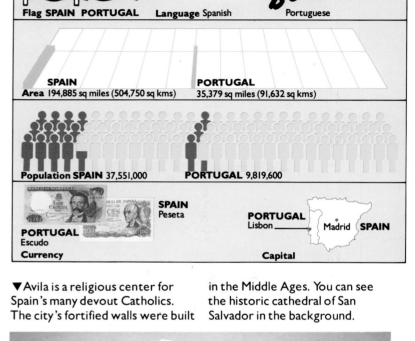

Facts and Figures

Flag SPAIN PORTUGAL **Language** Spanish Portuguese

Buenos dias
Bom dia

SPAIN
Area 194,885 sq miles (504,750 sq kms)

PORTUGAL
35,379 sq miles (91,632 sq kms)

Population SPAIN 37,551,000 **PORTUGAL** 9,819,600

SPAIN Peseta
PORTUGAL Escudo
Currency

PORTUGAL Lisbon
Madrid **SPAIN**
Capital

▼Avila is a religious center for Spain's many devout Catholics. The city's fortified walls were built in the Middle Ages. You can see the historic cathedral of San Salvador in the background.

▶ The Sierra Nevada is a mountain range near Spain's Mediterranean coast. There are olive groves on its southern slopes.

▼Dancers perform the flamenco. This Spanish dance involves clapping and stamping of feet.

▶ Benidorm is a popular tourist resort on Spain's Mediterranean Costa Blanca (the White Coast). The towering modern hotels take vacationers from all over Europe.

◀Citrus fruits such as lemons and oranges grow in groves in southern Spain. They need plenty of sunshine and well-drained soil.

▼Cork comes from the bark of cork trees like this one in Portugal. Cork is waterproof. Air trapped inside allows it to float.

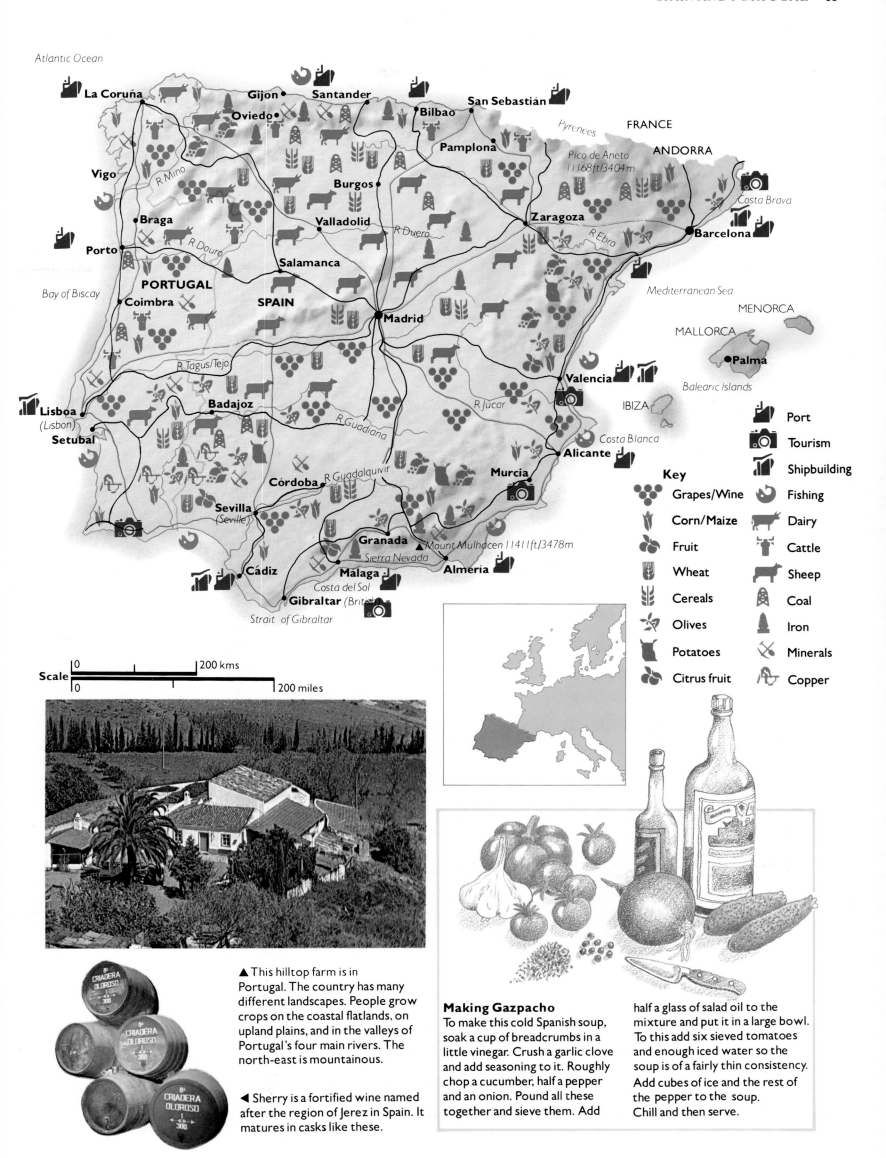

Atlantic Ocean

La Coruña
Gijon • Santander
Oviedo • Bilbao
San Sebastián
Pyrenees FRANCE
Vigo
Pamplona ANDORRA
R Mino
Pico de Aneto
11168ft/3404m
Braga
Burgos
Costa Brava
Porto Valladolid R Duero Zaragoza
R Douro R Ebro
Barcelona
Salamanca
PORTUGAL
Coimbra Mediterranean Sea
Bay of Biscay SPAIN Madrid
MENORCA
MALLORCA
R Tagus/Tejo Valencia Palma
Balearic Islands
Lisboa Badajoz IBIZA
(Lisbon) R Jucar
Setubal R Guadiana Costa Blanca
Alicante
Córdoba R Guadalquivir Murcia
Sevilla
(Seville) Granada Mount Mulhacen 11411ft/3478m
Sierra Nevada Almería
Cádiz Malaga
Costa del Sol
Gibraltar (British
Strait of Gibraltar

Key

Port
Tourism
Shipbuilding
Grapes/Wine · Fishing
Corn/Maize · Dairy
Fruit · Cattle
Wheat · Sheep
Cereals · Coal
Olives · Iron
Potatoes · Minerals
Citrus fruit · Copper

Scale
0 — 200 kms
0 — 200 miles

▲ This hilltop farm is in
Portugal. The country has many
different landscapes. People grow
crops on the coastal flatlands, on
upland plains, and in the valleys of
Portugal's four main rivers. The
north-east is mountainous.

◄ Sherry is a fortified wine named
after the region of Jerez in Spain. It
matures in casks like these.

CRIADERA
OLOROSO

Making Gazpacho
To make this cold Spanish soup,
soak a cup of breadcrumbs in a
little vinegar. Crush a garlic clove
and add seasoning to it. Roughly
chop a cucumber, half a pepper
and an onion. Pound all these
together and sieve them. Add

half a glass of salad oil to the
mixture and put it in a large bowl.
To this add six sieved tomatoes
and enough iced water so the
soup is of a fairly thin consistency.
Add cubes of ice and the rest of
the pepper to the soup.
Chill and then serve.

Eastern Europe

Poland, East Germany, Czechoslovakia and Hungary are all in the east of Europe. The largest of these countries is Poland. In the north of Poland is a low plain. This rises to a plateau in the south where the Carthusian and Sudeten mountains form a border with Czechoslovakia. The main crop grown in Poland is rye. Potatoes, sugar beet, vegetables, milk and cheese are also produced. Poland has many coal and metal mines and large chemical and textile industries. The capital of Poland is Warsaw which stands on the River Vistula.

The Oder and Neisse rivers separate Poland from East Germany. This is another low-lying country. The land is higher in the south-east where the border with Czechoslovakia follows the Ore Mountains. In the west and south-west there is a man-made boundary between East and West Germany. Most of East Germany's industries, which are based on chemicals and steel, are in the south. Some industrial goods are also made in the city of Dresden in the south-east. Leipzig is East Germany's largest city after Berlin, the capital.

Czechoslovakia is a long country of mountains, basins and valleys. It takes its name from the Czechs and the Slovaks who are the people who live there. Czechoslovakia is mainly a farming country but it also has many minerals such as coal, iron and copper. The timber, glass and porcelain industries are important as well. Prague, the capital, stands on the Vltava river. The country's other main centers are Brno, its second largest city, Bratislava, the old capital of Slovakia, and Ostrava, an important industrial town. Pilsen is famous as it is the place where lager beer was first brewed.

Hungary is a lowland country and, like Czechoslovakia, away from the sea. Its main rivers are the Danube and the Tisza. The lowlands produce good crops of grain, sugar beet, vegetables, tobacco and fruits. Hungary is a farming country but it also has a mining industry. The capital is Budapest, which is really two cities linked by a number of bridges. Buda, on the west bank of the Danube, is the old fortress town, and Pest, on the other bank, is the newer city.

▼The spires of St Vitus' Cathedral tower above the Hradcany Palace in Prague. The historic city is famous for its architecture, but Prague is also a bustling modern capital with over one million inhabitants. The bridge links the old city with the industrial center over the Vltava river.

▶A world clock stands in East Berlin's Alexanderplatz. It shows the time in the main places in the world. Berlin is the capital of the German Democratic Republic – or East Germany.

▼The mountainous borderlands of Czechoslovakia are sparsely populated. The church plays an important part in the daily life of the village people.

Facts and Figures

Flag HUNGARY POLAND GERMAN DEMOCRATIC REPUBLIC	**CZECHOSLOVAKIA**		

Language			
POLAND Polish *Dobry den*	**GERMAN DEMOCRATIC REPUBLIC** German *Guten Tag*	**CZECHOSLOVAKIA** Czech *Dzien dobry*	

Area

HUNGARY 35,920 sq miles (93,032 sq kms)	**POLAND** 120,725 sq miles (312,677 sq kms)	**GERMAN DEMOCRATIC REPUBLIC** 41,826 sq miles (108,328 sq kms)	**CZECHOSLOVAKIA** 49,375 sq miles (127,881 sq kms)

Population

HUNGARY 10,698,800	**POLAND** 35,048,700	**GERMAN DEMOCRATIC REPUBLIC** 16,751,400	**CZECHOSLOVAKIA** 15,184,300

Currency

POLAND Zloty	**GERMAN** Mark	**HUNGARY** Forint	**CZECHOSLOVAKIA** Koruna

Capital

GERMAN DEMOCRATIC REPUBLIC Berlin	**POLAND** Warsaw	**CZECHOSLOVAKIA** Prague	**HUNGARY** Budapest

▲Farm workers operate a threshing machine in Poland. Rye and wheat are the country's main cereal crops. Poland lies on a low plain between the much larger countries of the Soviet Union and East Germany. It is mainly an agricultural country but there is shipbuilding at Gdansk and coal mining in the south.

66

Key

- Potatoes
- Wheat
- Vegetables
- Non-food products
- Cereals
- Fruit
- Timber
- Grapes/Wine
- Industry
- Port
- Shipbuilding
- Dairy
- Pigs
- Sheep
- Cattle
- Coal
- Iron
- Steel
- Minerals
- Copper
- Natural gas
- Oil
- Gold
- Bauxite

Scale

0 ——— 200 kms
0 ——— 200 miles

Map labels: Baltic Sea, Gulf of Gdańsk, R Elbe, Rostock, Gdynia, Gdańsk, Szczecin (Stettin), EAST GERMANY, Berlin, Magdeburg, R Oder, Poznań, POLAND, Bialystok, Halle, Dessau, Leipzig, R Wisla/Vistula, R Bug, Warszawa (Warsaw), Dresden, Zwickau, Wrocław, Łódz, Lublin, WEST GERMANY, Walbrzych, Kielce, Częstochowa, Sudeten Mountains, Praha (Prague), Plzen, Katowice, Kraków, CZECHOSLOVAKIA, Ostrava, Brno, Kosice, AUSTRIA, SOVIET UNION, Bratislava, Miskolc, R Tisza, Budapest, Debrecen, HUNGARY, Pecs, Szeged

▲ This scene shows the interior of a home in Budapest. Hungary is a farming country with strong traditions. The bold and colorful design of the tablecloth is a traditional pattern.

▲ Fish soup with coarse bread is traditional fare at Hungarian inns. The soup is flavored with paprika, a favorite spice in Hungary. It gives food a bright red color. Paprika is also used to spice goulash, a stew made from beef and onions, which is Hungary's national dish. It is eaten all over the world.

◄ Fruit is displayed at a state orchard in Hungary. As elsewhere in Eastern Europe, much farming land is owned by the state, rather than by individual landowners.

Decorating Easter eggs
It is a traditional Polish custom to decorate eggs at Easter. First, hardboil an egg and allow it to cool. Then paint one half of the egg and put it in an egg cup so it can dry. Now paint the other half. When the egg is painted all over, decorate it with your own designs using a small brush and different colored paints.

The Balkans

The Balkans is a name for the countries of Rumania, Bulgaria, Yugoslavia, Greece, Albania and the European part of Turkey. The area is very mountainous. The word 'Balkan' comes from the Turkish for mountain and the area is named after the Balkan Mountains which cross Bulgaria from east to west. Other Balkan mountain ranges are the Rhodope in Bulgaria, the Pindus in Greece, the Dinaric Alps in Yugoslavia and the Carpathian and Transylvanian Alps in Rumania.

The Danube is the area's major river and many of the Balkan cities stand on the Danube or its tributaries. Belgrade, the capital of Yugoslavia, is on the Danube and the capital of Bulgaria, Sofia, is close to one of its many tributaries, the Iskâr. Bucharest, the capital of Rumania, is situated in the Wallachia Plain which is partly formed by the Danube valley.

Many of the mountains are made of limestone. In Greece the mountains continue into the Aegean Sea as lines of islands which are like stepping stones across the sea to Turkey. Crete is the largest of the many Greek islands and the fourth largest in the Mediterranean.

Athens is the capital of Greece. Its port on the Aegean is called Piraeus. Shipping and tourism are major industries. Currants and tobacco are important Greek crops. Greece also produces wine. One of the most famous types of Greek wine is called retsina.

Yugoslavia means 'south Slavia' and is a union of the southern Slavic peoples – the Serbs, Croats, Slovenes and Macedonians. It is the largest of the Balkan countries and is mainly agricultural. However, in the last 30 years industry has developed a lot. Many of Yugoslavia's cities have grown in size. The main cities are Belgrade, the capital, Zagreb, and Ljubljana.

Both Rumania and Bulgaria have coasts on the Black Sea. They grow corn, wheat and tobacco. Albania is the smallest and poorest Balkan country. Its capital is Tirana.

Throughout the Balkans the main types of livestock are sheep, goats and poultry. The donkey is still a very important means of transport for both people and all types of farm products and crops.

◀ The Rhodope Mountains in the south of Bulgaria form the border with Greece. Woodworking and the wool and textile industries are the main occupations. Here a local folk music group are playing the bagpipes.

▶ A shepherd brings his flock through the Rugovska Kusora gorge in Yugoslavia. These mountains form the border between Yugoslavia and Albania. They are the highest part of the Dinaric Alps. There are caves, canyons, gorges and lakes throughout the mountains here.

▲ Sheep farming is important in Rumania. Women wash raw wool in a stream before using it to make clothes.

◀ Rumania's main crops are wheat, corn, sugar beet, barley, sunflower seeds and tobacco. Much wine is also produced.

Facts and Figures

Language

yia sou **GREECE** Greek

Buna **RUMANIA** Rumanian

Flag ALBANIA BULGARIA GREECE RUMANIA YUGOSLAVIA

Area

ALBANIA 11,100 sq miles (28,748 sq kms)

BULGARIA 42,823 sq miles (110,912 sq kms)

GREECE 50,962 sq miles (131,990 sq kms)

RUMANIA 91,700 sq miles (237,500 sq kms)

YUGOSLAVIA 98,766 sq miles (255,804 sq kms)

Population

ALBANIA 2,758,000

BULGARIA 8,822,600

GREECE 9,360,000

RUMANIA 21,953,000

YUGOSLAVIA 22,083,000

Currency

GREECE Drachma

YUGOSLAVIA Dinar

RUMANIA Leu

BULGARIA Lev

Capital

YUGOSLAVIA Belgrade
ALBANIA Tirana
RUMANIA Bucharest
BULGARIA Sofia
GREECE Athens

▲ Greece has many olive groves and is the third largest producer in the world of olive oil. It produces over 150,000 metric tons each year and exports most of it.

▶ The Acropolis is a rocky hill in the center of Athens, Greece. It is the site of the ancient part of Athens. Today, Athens is a modern industrial city with a population of over 2.5 million. It is the capital of Greece.

▲ This busy street is in the town of Berat, in central Albania. It is a mountainous country with only 2.5 million people, but it has the fastest growing population in Europe.

▶ Sikinos is an island in the Aegean Sea. The steep hillsides are farmed in steps. Only one quarter of Greek land is fertile.

◀ Dubrovnik is an important Yugoslavian port and tourist resort. It is a beautiful city with many medieval buildings.

◀ Tobacco is grown in southern Yugoslavia. The tobacco leaves are hung out to dry after being harvested.

Mount Olympos 9570ft/2917m

Key

Corn/Maize	Olives	Port	Minerals
Cotton	Fruit	Cattle	Oil
Potatoes	Tobacco	Sheep	Iron
Vegetables	Citrus fruit	Pigs	Bauxite
Wheat	Grapes/Wine	Dairy	Copper
Timber	Industry	Goats	Coal
Rice	Tourism	Fishing	Gold
			Natural gas

Scale 0   200 kms
0   200 miles

Looking at Asia

Asia is the largest continent in the world. The whole of the smallest continent, Australia, would fit into Asia six times. More people live in Asia than in any other continent. Over 2,000 million people live there. Most of them live in China, India, Malaysia, Indonesia and Japan. Very few people live in Mongolia, Siberia and the deserts of south-west Asia. The continent stretches from the Arctic Ocean in the north to the Indian Ocean in the south and from the Ural Mountains in the west to the Pacific Ocean in the east.

In the south of Asia there are several large peninsulas. A peninsula is like a finger of land which juts out into the sea. Malaya is a long narrow peninsula and India a larger, wider one. In central Asia there are the high mountains of the Himalayas. Mount Everest in the Himalayas is the highest mountain in the world. It is 29,028 feet (8,848 meters) high and stands on the borders between Nepal and Tibet, which is part of China.

North of the Himalayas are large upland areas called plateaus. Many of these are deserts like the Gobi Desert in Mongolia. Further north still are the steppes of Siberia. These are huge flat areas with few trees. Asia also includes important island groups such as Japan, the Philippines and Indonesia.

The longest river in Asia is the Yangtse Kiang. It flows for 3,200 miles (5,120 kms) from the center of China to the Pacific Ocean.

▶ It is easiest to think of Asia as five separate subcontinents—south-west Asia, the Soviet Union, China, the Indian subcontinent and south-east Asia.
There are immense differences in climate and landscape from the tropical Pacific islands to Arctic Siberia; from the sands of Arabia to industrial Japan.
Communications have always been limited by the great natural barriers.

Inhabitants
per sq mile	per sq km
Under 16	Under 6
16-256	6-100
256-512	100-200
Over 512	Over 200

◀ China and India are the two most heavily populated countries in the world. China has 960 million people and India 638 million. Together, their people make up over three quarters of Asia's total population. Many live in the fertile valleys of the great rivers Huang Ho, Yangtse Kiang and Ganges. However, much of Asia is sparsely populated, and there are vast regions which are almost deserted — the Himalaya Mountains, the steppes of Siberia, the Arabian and Gobi Deserts. Mongolia's population averages less than one person per square mile/kilometer. China's average is 100 times greater than this.

Arctic Ocean

East Siberian Sea

Laptev Sea

Kara Sea

Bering Sea

Key

Rice
Citrus fruit
Fruit
Tea
Wheat
Corn/Maize
Groundnuts
Cereals
Coffee
Bananas
Cotton
Sugar cane
Industry
Cattle
Fishing
Sheep
Pigs
Oil
Minerals
Iron
Coal
Natural gas
Gold
Bauxite

UNION OF SOVIET SOCIALIST REPUBLICS

R Lower Tunguska

R Lena

Sea of Okhotsk

Gorky

Perm'

Ural Mountains

R Ob

R Angara

Sverdlovsk

R Yenisey

Omsk

R Irtys

Vladivostok

JAPAN

Sea of Japan

Aral Sea

Ulan Bator

Mukden

NORTH KOREA

Tokyo

Osaka

Tashkent

MONGOLIA

Pyong-yang

Hiroshima

Gobi Desert

Peking

Seoul

Tientsin

SOUTH KOREA

AFGHANISTAN

CHINA

R Hwang Ho

Yellow Sea

Kabul

Islamabad

Lahore

Nanking

Shanghai

East China Sea

PAKISTAN

Himalayas

Chengtu

Chungking

Karachi

NEPAL

New Delhi

Katmandu

BHUTAN

R Yangtse

Taipei

Lucknow

Varanasi

R Ganges

TAIWAN

BANGLADESH

Canton

Calcutta

Dacca

Macau

Hong Kong

Bombay

Chittagong

Mandalay

Hanoi

INDIA

R Irrawaddy

BURMA

LAOS

Hyderabad

Bay of Bengal

Vientiane

R Krishna

Western Ghats

Rangoon

THAILAND

R Mekong

VIETNAM

Bangalore

Madras

Bangkok

KAMPUCHEA

South China Sea

Manila

PHILIPPINES

Pacific Ocean

SRI LANKA

Phnom Penh

Ho Chi Minh City

Colombo

Gulf of Siam

Indian Ocean

BRUNEI

Penang

MALAYSIA

Strait of Malacca

Kuala Lumpur

SINGAPORE

BORNEO

Java Sea

INDONESIA

Djakarta

Timor Sea

Scale

0 — 1000 miles

0 — 1000 kms

Soviet Union

The Union of Soviet Socialist Republics is the largest country in the world. It covers one eighth of the world's total land surface. It has a large population; only China and India have more inhabitants. The country is often called Russia, but Russia is in fact only one of the 15 republics which make up the Union of Soviet Socialist Republics or Soviet Union. An important part of the Soviet Union is in Europe, but most of the country is in northern Asia.

In Europe, the Soviet Union has borders with Norway, Finland, Poland, Czechoslovakia, Hungary and Rumania. In Asia it borders on Turkey, Iran, Afghanistan, China and Mongolia. The country extends west from Poland to the Pacific Ocean where Vladivostock is a major port. Icebreakers keep it open in winter.

Much of the Soviet Union has a very cold climate, especially in Siberia which is in the north and east. Siberia is three times larger than Europe. In the south the Soviet Union has a hot climate where it borders on the deserts of central Asia.

The Soviet Union is an industrial country, but farming, mining and forestry are also important. Wheat and sugar beet are two main crops. Oil, timber and iron ore are among the country's chief resources.

Most of the country's population lives in a triangular area linking the cities of Leningrad, Odessa and Sverdlovsk. Moscow is in the middle of this area.

▶ Lake Baikal in Siberia is frozen from November to May. Cars can cross the ice, which is 2.5 feet (70 cms) thick. It is about 5,000 feet (1,524 meters) deep, so it is the deepest freshwater lake in the world.

▼ Children from a village near the lake build a snow fortress.

Facts and Figures

Flag — Language Russian

Area 8,649,500 sq miles (22,402,200 sq kms)

Population 262,400,000

Moscow

Capital

▶ St Basil's Cathedral stands in Red Square, Moscow. The Kremlin, the Soviet seat of government, is nearby. Moscow has nearly 8 million people and is one of the biggest cities in the world.

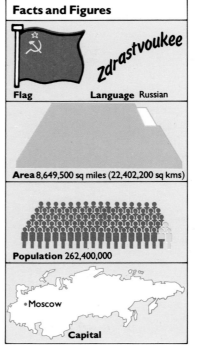

▲ The Soviet Union is made up of 15 separate socialist republics. Russia is the largest republic. Armenia is the smallest.

Key

- 🌲 Timber
- 🌾 Wheat
- 🌾 Cereals
- 🥔 Potatoes
- 🌾 Rice
- 🍇 Fruit
- 🌿 Cotton
- 🌱 Vegetables
- 🏭 Port
- 🏭 Industry
- 🦌 Reindeer
- 🐑 Sheep
- 🐂 Cattle
- 🐄 Dairy
- 🐟 Fishing

Scale
0 — 200 kms
0 — 200 miles

▲ These are traditional wooden dolls from Russia. They are painted in bright colors to show Russian national costume. Each one is hollow, so that a smaller one will fit inside.

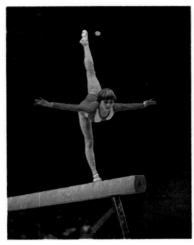

▶ Sport is an important part of life in the Soviet Union. Children may specialize in sports from an early age, and gymnastics are especially popular. Yelena Davydova is an Olympic gold medalist. She is seen here performing at the 1980 Olympics which were held in Moscow.

АБВГЛЕЖЗИКЛЛ
МНОПРСТ УФХЦЧ
ШЪ Ы Э ЮЯ

You can see from the alphabet written out above that Russian letters are very different to your own. However, the date on the stamp – issued to celebrate a space mission – shows that the same numbers are used in the Soviet Union as in your country.

▶ The Soviet Union exports iron, steel and machinery. This factory is producing tractors for the Russian market.

▼ Kiev, the capital of the Ukraine, is an important industrial center. It produces cameras, airplanes and fibers.

East Siberian Sea

R Kolyma

Bering Sea

R Aldan

Sea of Okhotsk

R Lena

Yablonovy Range

Chabarovsk

Sea of Japan

Irkutsk

cha
506 m

MONGOLIA

Vladivostok

Coal

Iron

Steel

Copper

Uranium

Gold

Oil

▲ Tashkent, the capital of Uzbekistan, is one of the oldest cities in central Asia. The town has many houses of historic interest. It also has many modern buildings now and is a scientific and industrial center. It is sometimes called the city of white gold because cotton is the main crop in Uzbekistan. Tashkent has a population of 1.5 million and is the fourth largest city in the USSR.

South-west Asia

The countries in south-west Asia are Afghanistan, Iran, Turkey, Iraq, Syria, Jordan, Lebanon, Israel, Saudi Arabia, Kuwait and the countries of southern Arabia. The seas around this area are the Persian Gulf, Red Sea and the Gulf of Aden in the south. In the north is the Caspian Sea which is an inland sea. Here too is the Black Sea which is joined to the Mediterranean Sea by the Dardanelles and the Bosporus. The large Turkish city of Istanbul is on the Bosporus and a bridge across the Bosporus links Europe and Asia.

The Suez Canal connects the Mediterranean with the Red Sea. This is a man-made waterway which was opened in 1869. It is important because the only other way ships can travel from the east to Europe is around the southern tip of Africa which is called the Cape of Good Hope.

Much of south-west Asia is desert country and has a hot climate. There are many high mountains, especially in Turkey, Iran and Afghanistan. Water is scarce and many of the rivers run dry. The main rivers are the Tigris and Euphrates. They flow from the high mountains in eastern Turkey through Syria and Iraq to the Persian Gulf which lies between Saudi Arabia and Iran.

Farming is a major activity, but water is always needed and so oases are important. There are many sheep, goat and camel herders in south-west Asia. This area is one of the world's main producers of oil. Saudi Arabia, Iraq, Iran and Kuwait are the most important countries for this. The oil flows by pipeline to the ports and tankers on the coasts of the Mediterranean and Persian Gulf.

Saudi Arabia is the center of the religion called Islam. People who believe in Islam are called Moslems. Mecca is an important place for Moslem pilgrims. The main language in south-west Asia is Arabic. Israel has a different religion and language. Most of the people are Jewish and speak Hebrew. Farsi is spoken in Iran.

The island of Cyprus is also part of south-west Asia. The population is made up of both Greeks and Turks. The capital is Nicosia and Famagusta is an important port. The country's main export is citrus fruit.

◀ The mosque of Sultan Ahmed I is one of several beautiful temples in Istanbul. A mosque is a temple where Moslems gather to pray. They kneel in the direction of Mecca, birthplace of the prophet Mohammed. The towers at the side are called minarets.

▼ Cotton pickers gather their crop in Turkey. The raw cotton grows as a downy fiber around the seed-head. The fiber is twisted and woven to form cloth. The hulls of the seeds are used in fertilizers. Cardboard can be made out of part of the stalks.

▼ An oil rig rises above the desert landscape of Abu Dhabi. Abu Dhabi is one of the main Arab states on the Persian Gulf. Oil was first discovered in Abu Dhabi in 1960. All of the states are hot, barren lands. Oil now brings them great wealth and power. They have few other products.

Facts and Figures

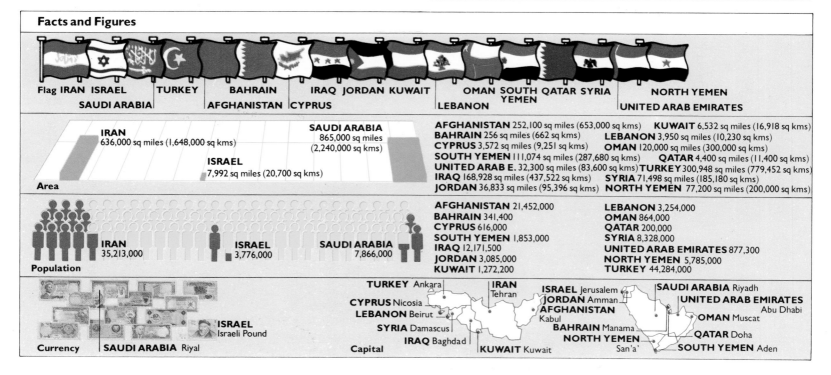

Flag IRAN ISRAEL TURKEY BAHRAIN IRAQ JORDAN KUWAIT OMAN SOUTH YEMEN QATAR SYRIA NORTH YEMEN
SAUDI ARABIA AFGHANISTAN CYPRUS LEBANON UNITED ARAB EMIRATES

Area

IRAN 636,000 sq miles (1,648,000 sq kms)
SAUDI ARABIA 865,000 sq miles (2,240,000 sq kms)
ISRAEL 7,992 sq miles (20,700 sq kms)

AFGHANISTAN 252,100 sq miles (653,000 sq kms)
BAHRAIN 256 sq miles (662 sq kms)
CYPRUS 3,572 sq miles (9,251 sq kms)
SOUTH YEMEN 111,074 sq miles (287,680 sq kms)
UNITED ARAB E. 32,300 sq miles (83,600 sq kms)
IRAQ 168,928 sq miles (437,522 sq kms)
JORDAN 36,833 sq miles (95,396 sq kms)
KUWAIT 6,532 sq miles (16,918 sq kms)
LEBANON 3,950 sq miles (10,230 sq kms)
OMAN 120,000 sq miles (300,000 sq kms)
QATAR 4,400 sq miles (11,400 sq kms)
TURKEY 300,948 sq miles (779,452 sq kms)
SYRIA 71,498 sq miles (185,180 sq kms)
NORTH YEMEN 77,200 sq miles (200,000 sq kms)

Population

IRAN 35,213,000
ISRAEL 3,776,000
SAUDI ARABIA 7,866,000

AFGHANISTAN 21,452,000
BAHRAIN 341,400
CYPRUS 616,000
SOUTH YEMEN 1,853,000
IRAQ 12,171,500
JORDAN 3,085,000
KUWAIT 1,272,200
LEBANON 3,254,000
OMAN 864,000
QATAR 200,000
SYRIA 8,328,000
UNITED ARAB EMIRATES 877,300
NORTH YEMEN 5,785,000
TURKEY 44,284,000

Currency
ISRAEL Israeli Pound
SAUDI ARABIA Riyal

Capital
TURKEY Ankara
CYPRUS Nicosia
LEBANON Beirut
SYRIA Damascus
IRAQ Baghdad
IRAN Tehran
ISRAEL Jerusalem
JORDAN Amman
AFGHANISTAN Kabul
BAHRAIN Manama
NORTH YEMEN San'a'
KUWAIT Kuwait
SAUDI ARABIA Riyadh
UNITED ARAB EMIRATES Abu Dhabi
OMAN Muscat
QATAR Doha
SOUTH YEMEN Aden

Black Sea

Istanbul
Samsun
Bursa
Ankara
TURKEY
Izmir
Erzurum

Caspian Sea
SOVIET UNION

Tabriz
R Tigris
Qolleh-ye Damavand
(18369ft/5599m)
Mashhad

Adana
Gaziantep
Mediterranean Sea
Levkosia (Nicosia)
CYPRUS
LEBANON
Halab
SYRIA
R Euphrates
Kirkuk
Tehran
IRAN
Kabul
Herat
AFGHANISTAN

Tripoli
Dimashq
(Damascus)
Baghdad
Kandahar

Beirut
Haifa
ISRAEL
Tel Aviv
Jerusalem
IRAQ
Dezful
Esfahan
Kerman
R Helmond

'Amman

JORDAN
Kuwait
Abadan
Kuwait
Shiraz
PAKISTAN

EGYPT
KUWAIT

Persian Gulf

Al-Manamah
BAHRAIN
Doha
QATAR
Dubai
Gulf of Oman

Al-Hufuf
Ar-Riyad
(Riyadh)
UNITED ARAB
EMIRATES
Muscat

Red Sea
Al-Madinah
(Medina)
OMAN

Juddah
(Jiddah)
SAUDI ARABIA

Makkah
(Mecca)

Arabian Sea

SOUTH YEMEN

San'a'
NORTH YEMEN

Aden
Gulf of Aden

▼ A girl from Kermanshah in Iran sits in a field of raw wool. The province is a flourishing center for farming and making textiles.

◄ A camel train approaches a village in north-western Iran. The region lies on the ancient trade routes which once linked Asia with Europe.

▼ A bargeman transports rush matting throught a marshy estuary of the Tigris and Euphrates rivers. In ancient times the people of the area made huge boats from rushes and sailed them out to sea.

▶ Women of Shiraz in Iran weave at their loom. Iran produces some of the most beautiful carpets in the world.

Scale
0 — 200 kms
0 — 200 miles

Key

Olives		Cattle	
Grapes/Wine		Goats	
Wheat		Sheep	
Vegetables		Farming	
Tobacco		Fishing	
Rice		Animal Farming	
Citrus fruit		Coal	
Cotton		Iron	
Fruit		Minerals	
Cereals		Copper	
Port		Oil	
Industry		Gold	

The Indian Subcontinent

More people live in India than in any other country in the world except China. The high Himalayan Mountains separate India from the rest of Asia. There are two small countries – Nepal and Bhutan – in these mountains. To the south of the Himalayas in India many people live on the plain of the River Ganges. The main upland area of India is called the Deccan.

India has a tropical climate. Most of the country's rain falls during the monsoon which takes place from June to September.

Farming is very important in India. But India still has to import much of its food as it cannot grow enough to feed everyone. Wheat, millet, rice and cotton are the main crops. Tea is grown in Assam province and exported to many countries. There are a large number of cows in India which are used for pulling plows and carts. They are not killed because the main religion of India forbids the killing of cows as they are sacred.

Cotton and textiles are important industries. India also has many iron ore and coal mines. India's largest cities are Calcutta, Madras and Bombay, which are all ports, and New Delhi, which is the capital.

Pakistan became a separate state in 1947. Most of its people are Moslems. Karachi, which is at the mouth of the River Indus, is Pakistan's largest city and its port. The capital is a new city called Islamabad. Bangladesh separated from Pakistan in 1971. Its capital is Dacca and its people are also Moslem.

Sri Lanka is an island country which lies off the southeast coast of India. Its old name was Ceylon. Tea, rubber and coconuts are its products. Colombo is the capital.

▲ Benares (now called Varanasi) is one of the world's oldest cities and an important religious center in India. Hindu pilgrims come from all over the country to bathe here in the sacred waters of the Ganges.

▶ Yaks graze in the foothills of the Himalayas, in Nepal. This immense mountain range includes Mount Everest, the highest peak in the world (29,028 feet, 8,848 meters).

◀ Islamabad – the city of Islam – was built to replace Karachi as Pakistan's capital. Building work started in 1960.

▶ The Taj Mahal in India is one of the world's most beautiful buildings. It was built by a Mogul emperor as a memorial to his favorite wife.

Facts and Figures

Flag BANGLADESH BHUTAN INDIA SRI LANKA PAKISTAN NEPAL

Language BANGLADESH Bengali INDIA Hindi

Supropat *Namastey*

BANGLADESH 55,598 sq miles (143,998 sq kms)

BHUTAN 17,800 sq miles (46,100 sq kms)

SRI LANKA 25,332 sq miles (65,610 sq kms)

PAKISTAN 307,374 sq miles (796,095 sq kms)

NEPAL 56,136 sq miles (145,391 sq kms)

Area INDIA 1,269,420 sq miles (3,287,782 sq kms)

PAKISTAN 75,620,000 **BANGLADESH** 86,643,000

Population INDIA 638,388,000 **BHUTAN** 1,269,000 **SRI LANKA** 14,184,000 **NEPAL** 13,420,000

BANGLADESH Taka

INDIA Rupee

Currency PAKISTAN Pakistan Rupee SRI LANKA Sri Lanka Rupee

NEPAL Katmandu **BHUTAN** Thimphu
PAKISTAN Islamabad **BANGLADESH** Dacca
INDIA New Delhi
Capital **SRI LANKA** Colombo

► Tea pluckers gather their crop in Darjeeling, India. The leaves are picked by hand and heated to dry them out. Brands of tea are named according to the region they come from.

▼ Sacred cows wander freely through a poor district of Calcutta. Killing them is forbidden, although their milk can be drunk.

► Sikhs are members of a religious community which grew up in the Punjab in northern India. Sikh men wear turbans, and are supposed never to cut their hair or beards. However, many sikhs prefer to remain clean shaven and do not grow a beard.

▲ This Indian girl is dancing in bare feet, as is customary. She uses her hands to express feelings.

▼ Villagers shop in a vegetable market near Delhi, India. Food is generally bought in open markets.

SOVIET UNION

AFGHANISTAN

PAKISTAN

Islamabad • **Rawalpindi**

Lahore

IRAN

Karachi

R Indus

Hyderabad

Arabian Sea

Himalayas

NEPAL   CHINA

BHUTAN

Mount Everest 29028ft/8848m

Katmandu   **Thimphu**

New Delhi

R Brahmaputra

Lucknow

R Ganges

Varanasi (Benares)

Dacca

BURMA

Calcutta

Chittagong

BANGLADESH

INDIA

R Narmada

Nagpur

Bombay

R Godavari

R Mahanadi

Hyderabad

R Krishna

Scale   0   200 kms
0   200 miles

Mangalore

Bangalore

Madras

Bay of Bengal

Colombo   **SRI LANKA**

Indian Ocean

Key

Rice	Industry	
Wheat	Goats	
Corn/Maize	Animal farming	
Tea	Cattle	
Cotton	Fishing	Oil
Sugar cane	Sheep	Natural gas
Cereals	Coal	Copper
Jute	Iron	Gold
Rubber	Steel	Energy
Coconuts	Minerals	Diamonds

China

More people live in China than in any other country in the world. Its population is over 950 million. Only the Soviet Union and Canada are larger in area than China. The correct name for the country since 1949 has been the Chinese People's Republic. This includes Manchuria, Inner Mongolia, Sinkiang and Tibet. Taiwan, which used to be called Formosa, is a separate country. The small area of Hong Kong in the south is British. Macao, which is even smaller, is controlled by Portugal.

In China many people live in the valley of the Yangtse Kiang, the hill country of the south, and in the plain of the Hwang Ho or Yellow River. These are also important farming areas. In the cooler areas of the north, wheat, cotton, corn and tobacco grow. In the hotter south, rice, sugar cane and soya beans are the main crops.

There are over 20 cities in China with populations of over a million people. These include Shanghai which is a large port and Peking which is the capital.

The Chinese are famous for their porcelain, silk and paper-making. Mining is also important. In Manchuria, coal and steel are the main industries.

Mongolia, North Korea and South Korea lie to the north and east of China. Herding cattle is Mongolia's main type of farming. The capital is Ulan Bator. North Korea has large deposits of iron ore and other minerals. The capital is Pyong-yang. South Korea grows rice and produces silk, fruit and wine. Seoul is the capital.

▲ The Great Wall of China stretches 1500 miles (2400 kms) across northern China. It was built in ancient times to keep out nomadic peoples from the north. Many tourists now visit the Great Wall each year.

NEPAL

Mount Everest 29028 ft

▶ The Chinese grow rice in fields known as paddy fields. First, the paddy is plowed over. Water buffalo are often used to do this work. Then the field is fertilized, smoothed and flooded.

▶ People grow the seedlings elsewhere. Then they plant the seedlings by hand in neat rows in the flooded paddy. The plants grow in the water. The paddy is drained before harvesting. Rice is a very important crop in China.

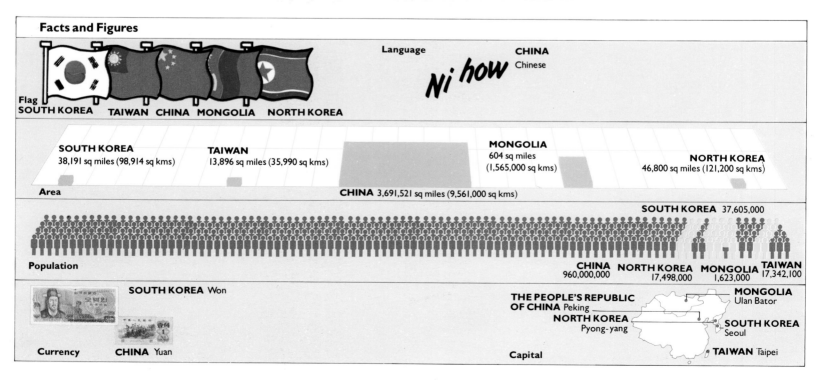

Facts and Figures

Flag
SOUTH KOREA TAIWAN CHINA MONGOLIA NORTH KOREA

Language

CHINA Chinese

Ni how

SOUTH KOREA 38,191 sq miles (98,914 sq kms)	**TAIWAN** 13,896 sq miles (35,990 sq kms)		**MONGOLIA** 604 sq miles (1,565,000 sq kms)	**NORTH KOREA** 46,800 sq miles (121,200 sq kms)

Area   CHINA 3,691,521 sq miles (9,561,000 sq kms)

SOUTH KOREA 37,605,000

Population

CHINA 960,000,000   NORTH KOREA 17,498,000   MONGOLIA 1,623,000   TAIWAN 17,342,100

SOUTH KOREA Won

Currency   CHINA Yuan

THE PEOPLE'S REPUBLIC OF CHINA Peking
NORTH KOREA Pyong-yang

MONGOLIA Ulan Bator
SOUTH KOREA Seoul
TAIWAN Taipei

Capital

◀ A Chinese textile worker weaves silk at her loom. The Chinese learnt how to make silk over 4,000 years ago. Silk fiber is produced by the silkworm when it makes its cocoon. People spin and weave the fiber into cloth.

▶ A woman carts hay in Mongolia. Here farmers grow wheat and oats, and nomads drive their herds over the dry hills.

SOVIET UNION

R Selenge

•Ulaanbaatar
(Ulan Bator)

MONGOLIA

•ulumuqi
(Urumqi)

INNER MONGOLIA

Beijing
(Peking)
R Huang Ho

●Tianjin
(Tientsin)

●Harbin

Shenyang

NORTH KOREA

Pyong-yang

●Luda
(Dairem) Seoul●
Inch'on●   ●Pusan

SOUTH KOREA

CHINA

•Lanzhou

R Changjiang/Yangtse

●Lasa
(Lhasa)

ahmaputra

BHUTAN

INDIA

R Lancang/Mekong

●Chengdu

Chongqing
(Chungking)

●Nanjing
(Nanking)

●Shanghai

●Wuhan

●Taipei

TAIWAN

Kunming

Guangzhou
(Canton)

●Kowloon
●Hong Kong
Macao●

BURMA

VIETNAM

LAOS

HAINAN

	Rice		Shipbuilding
	Tea		Fishing
	Sugar cane		Pigs
	Rubber		Sheep
	Tobacco		Cattle
	Timber		Reindeer
	Jute		Animal farming
	Cotton		Coal
	Wheat		Iron
	Groundnuts		Steel
	Fruit		Minerals
	Vegetables		Oil
	Industry		Copper
	Port		

Scale
0   200 kms
0   200 miles

◀ These neon signs in Kowloon, Hong Kong, advertise goods both in English and Chinese. Hong Kong is a British colony. The people are mostly Chinese but many people from western Europe and the United States now live there.

◀ Dancers take part in a dragon carnival. The dragon is an important figure in Chinese tales and festivals. It is thought of as a friendly creature rather than a fierce one.

Japan

Japan is a group of islands lying off the coast of northeast Asia. The Sea of Japan separates them from the mainland. The four main islands are called Honshu, Shikoku, Kyushu and Hokkaido. Honshu is the largest – it is almost as large as England, Scotland and Wales put together. There are also hundreds of small islands, many of which are uninhabited.

More than three quarters of Japan is mountainous. Many of the mountains are volcanoes. The most famous is Mount Fujiyama, which is the highest in the country. Earthquakes and earth tremors occur often. Japan has a jagged coastline and there are many natural harbors.

Japan is a very crowded country. Most of the people live in the plains along the coast and in the large cities such as Tokyo, the capital, Osaka and Yokohama.

Japan is known throughout the world for its industry. Although it must import oil, coal and iron ore, Japan manufactures ships, cars, motorcycles, radios, televisions and cameras. Rice is Japan's main food crop. Other crops are tea and tobacco. Fishing, silkworm farming and pearl diving are also important.

Facts and Figures

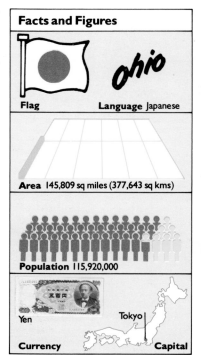

Flag	Language Japanese

Area 145,809 sq miles (377,643 sq kms)

Population 115,920,000

Yen — Currency

Tokyo — Capital

▲ Flying kites is a national pastime in Japan. By tradition, kites flying over a house at night will ward off evil spirits.

▶ Japan has a thriving motor industry. The names of firms such as Datsun, Honda, Toyota and Suzuki are well known throughout the world. Japanese autos, motorcycles and trucks have a reputation for low prices and running costs.
Other important exports include high precision instruments such as computers, wristwatches and hi-fi equipment. Nikon cameras are famous. The girl (far right) is working at the factory in Tokyo.

Wood

Paper

Paper glued over wood

String

Make a kite

Take some strong but thin paper (about 1 yard/meter square). Draw a diamond shape as in the picture and cut it out. Fit four pieces of light wood along the sides of the kite for the frame. Glue the ends together and then glue the paper over the frame. Glue two more pieces of wood across the center of the kite to strengthen the frame. Attach a string for flying the kite. Finally, add a tail made from string and tissue paper.

▶ The tea ceremony is a traditional way of entertaining guests. It was introduced from China by Buddhists in the fifteenth century.

▼ Ancient and modern exist side by side in Japan. Here, the 'bullet train' speeds past Mount Fujiyama. The line runs between Tokyo and Osaka. It provides the fastest train service in the world.

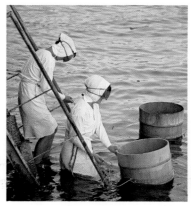

▲ Pearl fishers in Japan wear face masks and white clothing. The cultivation of pearls is a major industry.

▶ Noh plays are a traditional form of drama in Japan. The plays are short and include music, singing, dancing and mime. The main characters wear face masks.

◀ Shoppers throng the streets of Tokyo. This is the capital of Japan and a seaport. The total population of this city is over 9 million people.

▲ A girl presents herself at a Shinto temple. Children are supposed to do this at the ages of three, five and seven. She is dressed in a silk kimono.

Key

- 🌲 Timber
- 🥬 Vegetables
- 🍎 Fruit
- 🌾 Cereals
- 🌱 Rice
- 🥔 Potatoes
- ⚓ Port
- 🚢 Shipbuilding
- 🏭 Industry
- 🐟 Fishing
- 🐄 Dairy
- 🐂 Cattle
- 🐓 Farming
- ⛏ Coal
- ⚒ Minerals
- Iron
- Gold
- Copper
- Steel

▲ Many Japanese make regular pilgrimages to Shinto shrines like this one in Kyoto. Shinto is Japan's national faith. It stresses reverence for ancestors, family virtues and cleanliness.

HOKKAIDO

Sea of Okhotsk

Sapporo

Kushiro

Muroran

Sea of Japan

Sendai

HONSHU

R. Shinano

R. Tone

R. Kitakami

Tokyo

Yokohama

Kyoto

Nagoya

Mount Fujiyama
12388ft/3776m

Kobe

Osaka

Wakayama

Hiroshima

R. Asahi

Kitakyushu

Fukuoka

Nagasaki

SHIKOKU

Pacific Ocean

Kagoshima

KYUSHU

Scale

| 0 | 200 kms |
| 0 | 200 miles |

South-east Asia

The countries in south-east Asia are Malaysia, Singapore, Brunei, Kampuchea, Thailand, Laos, Vietnam and Burma.

Malaysia includes Malaya which is the southern part of the Kra or Malay peninsula and the areas of Sabah and Sarawak in northern Borneo. Rubber plantations cover over half of Malaya which is the largest producer of rubber in the world. Tin is also very important here. The capital of Malaysia is Kuala Lumpur.

Singapore is a small island off the southern coast of Malaya. The Straits of Johore separate Singapore from the mainland although there is a causeway link across the straits. The city of Singapore is a great trading center of south-east Asia. The port of Singapore handles most of Malaysia's foreign trade.

On the island of Borneo, the small country of Brunei lies between Sabah and Sarawak. Brunei's main source of wealth is oil. Thailand is an important rice producing country. It also produces rubber and tin. In the northern hills elephants are used to bring teak and other kinds of wood out of the forests. The capital of Thailand is Bangkok. It stands at the mouth of the Menam river. The city has many temples and canals which in Thailand are called klongs.

Kampuchea (which used to be called Cambodia), Laos and Vietnam also grow rice. Rice grows in paddy fields and there are many in the Red River valley in northern Vietnam and along the Mekong which runs through Kampuchea and Vietnam. But the country which grows more rice than any other in the world is Burma. There are many paddy fields around the mouth of the Irrawaddy river.

◄ These women are crossing a field of young rice in Thailand. The country's central region is a flat and fertile plain, ideal for rice-growing. The crop needs both warmth and moisture to flourish. Thailand's paddy fields are irrigated by rivers and specially dug canals. Rice makes up a large part of the Thai diet.

▶ Elephants are often used to carry logs of teak from the forested mountains of northern Thailand. Although they are huge animals they are easy to train. Here, as in India, elephants have proved highly intelligent beasts of burden. They can learn to obey many different commands and perform a wide variety of tasks.

▶ This pump is at the Seria oil field in Brunei. The country has other oil fields beneath the sea, which are being worked offshore. Oil and natural gas are Brunei's main exports; rubber is also produced. The main food crops that are grown here are cassava and rice.

▲ Basketware is on display at this floating market in Bangkok. Thailand's capital is a great trading center. Many of its people live in boats, or in waterside houses on stilts. People have used the klongs – or canals – as a way of getting about for many centuries.

Facts and Figures

Flag BURMA KAMPUCHEA LAOS MALAYSIA THAILAND VIETNAM BRUNEI SINGAPORE

Language

Menglaba BURMA Burmese

Sawasdee THAILAND Thai

chao VIETNAM Vietnamese

Area

BURMA 261,288 sq miles (676,577 sq kms)

KAMPUCHEA 69,898 sq miles (181,035 sq kms)

LAOS 91,400 sq miles (236,800 sq kms)

MALAYSIA 127,316 sq miles (329,747 sq kms)

VIETNAM 127,207 sq miles (329,465 sq kms)

BRUNEI 2,226 sq miles (5,765 sq kms)
SINGAPORE 238 sq miles (616 sq kms)

THAILAND 209,411 sq miles (542,373 sq kms)

Population BURMA 34,361,000

KAMPUCHEA 4,500,000

LAOS 3,633,000

MALAYSIA 12,736,600

THAILAND 45,000,000

VIETNAM 51,883,000

BRUNEI 201,300
SINGAPORE 2,362,700

Currency BURMA Kyat

MALAYSIA Ringgit

SINGAPORE Singapore Dollar

THAILAND Baht

BRUNEI Brunei Dollar

Capital

BURMA Rangoon
THAILAND Bangkok
MALAYSIA Kuala Lumpur

VIETNAM Hanoi
LAOS Vientiane
KAMPUCHEA Phnom Penh

◀A woman taps a rubber tree on a Malayan plantation. Diagonal cuts are made in the trees, and the sap is collected in small bowls. The sap contains a substance called latex which is treated, dried and pressed into sheets of rubber for export.

▶The Shwee Dragon pagoda is a Buddhist temple in Rangoon, capital of Burma. Most Burmese people are Buddhists. The monks wear saffron-colored robes called pongyis.

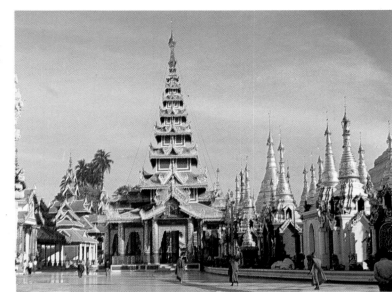

▲ Much of Malaysia is bordered by the sea, and fish is an important part of the people's diet. It is generally brought ashore in slender sailing boats like these. As most of the fish that is caught is eaten by the Malaysians themselves, very little is exported.

Key

- 🌿 Rice
- 🌾 Corn/Maize
- 🌱 Tea
- 🌿 Cotton
- 🌾 Sugar cane
- 🌷 Rubber
- 🥥 Coconuts
- 🌴 Palm oil
- 🌲 Timber
- ⚓ Port
- 🏭 Industry
- 🐄 Animal Farming
- 🦢 Fishing
- 🐖 Pigs
- ⛽ Coal
- ⛏ Minerals
- 💧 Oil
- ⚒ Iron
- ⛰ Gold

INDIA

BANGLADESH

Mount Victoria 10016ft/3053m ▲

R Chindwin

R Irrawaddy

R Salween

Mandalay

Sittwe

BURMA

Bay of Bengal

CHINA

R Red Hong

R Black Da

LAOS

Louang Prabang

Hanoi

Gulf of Tonkin

Chiang Mai

Vientiane

THAILAND

R Chao Phraya

R Mekong

South China Sea

Da-nang

VIETNAM

Rangoon

Tavoy

Andaman Sea

Krung Thep (Bangkok)

KAMPUCHEA

Phnom Pénh

Nha-trang

Gulf of Thailand

Ho Chi Minh City (Saigon)

Pinang (George Town)

MALAYSIA

R Pahang

Kuala Lumpur

Scale | 0 — 200 kms
0 — 200 miles

SINGAPORE • Singapore

MALAYSIA

Bandar Seri Begawan

BRUNEI

SABAH

R Baram

SARAWAK

Kuching

R Rajang

INDONESIA

Indonesia and the Philippines

Indonesia is a large country in south-east Asia. There are more than 13,600 islands in Indonesia which lies between the Pacific and Indian Oceans. Over 900 of the islands have no-one living on them. The main islands are Java, Sumatra, Kalimantan and Celebes. Djakarta on the island of Java is the capital of Indonesia.

The islands of Indonesia lie on both sides of the Equator and they have a hot, wet climate. The country is mountainous and there are many volcanoes. The most famous of these is Krakatoa which is in the Sunda Straits between Java and Sumatra.

There are large plantations where the tropical forests have been cleared. Here rubber, tea, coffee, tobacco and sugar cane grow. Rice and cassava are important types of food in Indonesia. These crops grow on the coastal plains. Spices, copra and palm oil are also important.

Many teak and ebony trees grow in the forests of Indonesia. The wood is used to make expensive furniture. Indonesia also has many oil wells and tin mines.

The Philippines is a group of 7,000 islands to the north of Indonesia. The largest islands are Luzon and Mindanao. The capital is Manila which is on the island of Luzon. The islands are mountainous and volcanic eruptions and earthquakes are common. The main products are tobacco, timber, pineapples, palm oil and sugar cane.

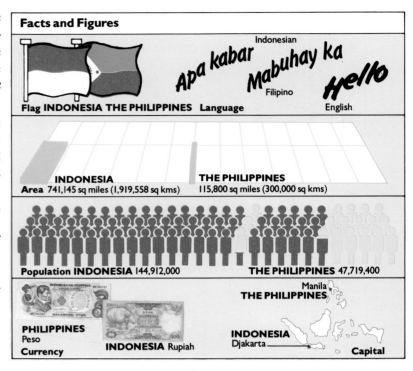

Facts and Figures

Flag INDONESIA THE PHILIPPINES   Language

Apa kabar (Indonesian)   *Mabuhay ka* (Filipino)   *Hello* (English)

INDONESIA
Area 741,145 sq miles (1,919,558 sq kms)

THE PHILIPPINES
115,800 sq miles (300,000 sq kms)

Population INDONESIA 144,912,000   THE PHILIPPINES 47,719,400

PHILIPPINES Peso   INDONESIA Rupiah   Currency

THE PHILIPPINES   Manila

INDONESIA   Djakarta   Capital

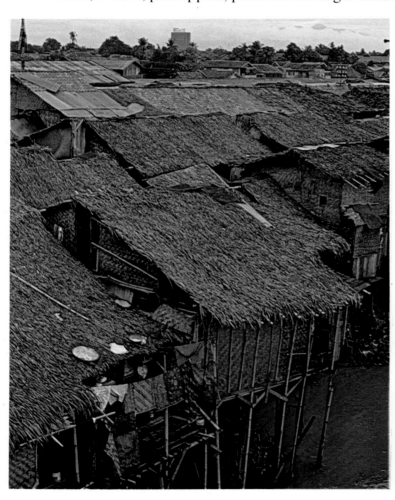

▲Djakarta is at the mouth of the Chiliwong river. Many canals and waterways run through the city. Some houses are built on stilts. However, Djakarta is also a modern capital, with many car factories and textile mills. Its port handles most of Indonesia's foreign trade.

▶ Dancing girls perform in traditional costume on the island of Bali. The island people have developed high forms of music, dancing, theater and architecture. Bali also has great natural beauty. It is now one of Indonesia's main tourist centers.

▲ A clothworker makes batik in Djakarta. This way of making patterned material is a speciality of Indonesia. Wax protects the pattern when the fabric is dyed.

▲ The Javanese are famous for their traditional wooden puppets. They are worked by rods from below. The puppeteer hides behind a screen, twisting and tilting the rods to achieve a wide variety of movements.

◀ Bell-shaped stone carvings decorate the steps of the great temple of Borobudur in central Java. The temple was built as a Buddhist shrine more than a thousand years ago. Today, most of Indonesia's people are Moslems.

▲ The Dyaks of Borneo are a very primitive people. The interior has many regions of jungle and mountain which have never been fully explored by outsiders. Wars still break out between tribes, and headhunters still exist. Some Dyaks live along the coast as well.

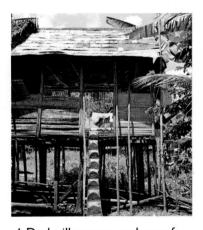

▲ Dyak villages are made up of long houses. Many families may live in one long house, and each has its own chief. The people live by fishing and hunting. They also grow crops such as rice and yams.

▲ On the Philippine island of Luzon there are ancient rice terraces. The system of paddies and channels is over 2,000 years old. It was built by the primitive Igorot people. Most of the islanders are of Malay origin. They are known as Filipinos.

▲Villagers dry peanuts on Bali. The island has volcanoes, but there is also a fertile plain. Here, rice, fruit, coffee and vegetables are grown. Pigs and cattle are also raised for sale abroad.

Key

Tobacco	Groundnuts
Corn/Maize	Spices
Rice	Industry
Coconuts	Port
Timber	Fishing
Sugar cane	Gold
Palm oil	Coal
Coffee	Minerals
Rubber	Oil

LUZON
PHILIPPINES
Manila Quezon City
South China Sea
Iloilo
Cebu
Pacific Ocean
Davao

Medan
SUMATRA
MALAYSIA
Padang
Pontianak
BORNEO (KALIMANTAN)
Palembang
SULAWESI (CELEBES)
Indian Ocean
Bandjarmasin
Djakarta Java Sea
Semarang Ujung Pandang
Bandung
Surabaja INDONESIA
JAVA
WEST IRIAN (NEW GUINEA)
R. Digul
TIMOR
Timor Sea

Scale
0 200 kms
0 200 miles

Looking at Africa

Africa is the world's second largest continent. Only Asia is larger. It is over 5,000 miles (8,000 kms) from Cape Vert in the west to Cape Guardafui in the east. This is almost as far as the greatest length of the continent from Tangier in the north to Cape Agulhas in the south.

Unlike the coasts of Europe and Asia, Africa has few large bays or gulfs and its shape is fairly regular. Off the coasts of Africa are some small, volcanic islands. These include the Canary Islands in the north and St Helena in the south. Madagascar is off the east coast. It is one of the world's largest islands.

The Equator passes through the center of Africa. It is the only continent which both the Tropic of Cancer and Tropic of Capricorn pass through.

The main mountain ranges are the Atlas Mountains in the north-west, the Drakensberg Mountains in the south-east and the highlands of East Africa. The rest of the continent is made up of plateaus with a narrow plain around the coast.

The River Nile flows north from the highlands of East Africa to the Mediterranean Sea. It is the longest river in Africa and one of the longest in the world. The River Zaire is the second longest in Africa.

In East Africa the Great Rift Valley stretches for thousands of miles. Africa's largest lake is Lake Victoria in East Africa. The Sahara Desert separates northern from central and southern Africa. The people in the north are mainly Arabs and in the south they are mainly negroes.

Inhabitants

per sq mile	per sq km
Under 16	Under 6
16-256	6-100
256-512	100-200
Over 512	Over 200

◄ Africa has a total population of 451 million people. Much of the continent is thinly populated. The people live mostly in a few major areas of settlement.

In the north, the main center of population is a narrow strip running along the coast of the Mediterranean Sea. The valley of the lower Nile is also thickly populated. The rest of North Africa is covered by the Sahara Desert where few people live. South of the Sahara, the main concentration of people is in West Africa. Nigeria holds about 75 million people — far more than any other African country. Other major population centers include the East African coast and plateau, Cape Town and Johannesburg.

Scale

0   1000 miles
0   1000 kms

◄ Most Africans work on the land. Cacao and groundnuts are some main agricultural products sold for export. Compared with Europe and North America, there are few industrial centers. However, important fields of oil and natural gas have been found in West Africa and the Sahara. In addition, southern Africa produces many precious gems and minerals.

Key

- Cotton
- Palm oil
- Grapes/Wine
- Citrus fruit
- Fruit
- Olives
- Rice
- Sugar cane
- Non-food products
- Bananas
- Coffee
- Cereals
- Groundnuts
- Cacao
- Corn/Maize
- Wheat
- Port
- Industry
- Dairy
- Sheep
- Fishing
- Oil
- Iron
- Coal
- Minerals
- Energy
- Uranium
- Natural gas
- Diamonds
- Bauxite
- Gold
- Copper

Mediterranean Sea

Algiers
Tunis
TUNISIA
Tripoli
Benghazi
LIBYA
Suez Canal
Alexandria
Cairo
Suez
EGYPT
Libyan Desert
Aswan
Red Sea

NIGER
Sahara Desert
Agades
CHAD
SUDAN
R Nile
Port Sudan
Gulf of Aden
L Chad
Kano
N'Djamena
Khartoum
R Blue Nile
DJIBOUTI
Djibouti
NIGERIA
R Chari
R White Nile
Addis Ababa
SOMALI REPUBLIC
Ibadan
CENTRAL AFRICAN REPUBLIC
Bangui
ETHIOPIA
CAMEROON
Douala
Yaoundé
EQUATORIAL GUINEA
Likasi
UGANDA
Mogadishu
Libreville
Port Gentil
GABON
CONGO
Mbandaka
Kisangani
Kampala
KENYA
Nairobi
Brazzaville
R Zaire
ZAIRE
RWANDA
L Victoria
BURUNDI
Kinshasa
Mombasa
CABINDA
TANZANIA
Zanzibar
Luanda
L Tanganyika
Dar-es-Salaam
ANGOLA
Lobito
Huambo
L Malawi
COMORO ISLANDS
Lubumbashi
Kitwe
MOZAMBIQUE
Ndola
Lilongwe
ZAMBIA
MALAWI
Lusaka
Blantyre
R Zambezi
Salisbury
Beira
SOUTH WEST AFRICA (NAMIBIA)
Bulawayo
Antananarivo
Windhoek
BOTSWANA
MADAGASCAR
Gaborone
Kalahari Desert
Pretoria
Maputo
Johannesburg
SWAZILAND
R Orange
Bloemfontein
LESOTHO
Durban
SOUTH AFRICA
Indian Ocean
Cape Town
Cape of Good Hope
East London
Port Elizabeth

Northern Africa

The large Sahara Desert stretches across northern Africa. It is the largest desert in the world and covers over 3,500,000 square miles (9,100,000 sq kms). The Sahara takes up over one quarter of Africa and is almost as large as the United States.

Sand dunes cover only a small part of the Sahara. Most of the ground is rocky. A hot, dusty wind called the khamsin blows from the desert to the Mediterranean. Khamsin is the Arabic for 50. The Arabs say that this wind blows for 50 days from April to June.

The camel is still an important type of transport in the Sahara. Some roads now also cross the desert. In the past, the trip from Morocco to West Africa by camel took two months. Today you can cross the desert by car or bus in five days. There are many fertile oases in the Sahara where crops, like dates, grow. It is also rich in iron ore, petroleum and natural gas.

The high Atlas Mountains are found in Morocco, Algeria and Tunisia. There is farming along the coasts as well as large cities and ports such as Casablanca, Oran, Algiers and Tunis.

Libya and Egypt lie to the east of Tunisia and Algeria. They also have coastlines on the Mediterranean. Most of Libya is desert and the country is rich in oil. The population of Libya is only 2.5 million. Egypt is also a desert country, but its population is much bigger. Over 35 million people live there, mainly along the River Nile. Cairo is the capital of Egypt and the largest city in Africa.

The main countries of the southern Sahara are Mauritania, Mali, Niger, Chad and the Sudan. Except for the Sudan, their populations are very small. They export groundnuts. Groundnut is another name for peanut.

▲ An ancient desert settlement sprawls down a hillside in the Algerian Sahara. A district or settlement is known as a Beni.

◄ A Moroccan woman passes a stall selling vegetables, in Marrakesh near the Atlas Mountains. She is veiled according to Moslem custom. Marrakesh is a historic trading center.

▲ Marrakesh is famous for its leatherwork. Here, skins are tanned in vats to make leather.

◄ Youngsters herd cattle and goats near Tenes in northern Algeria. Many Algerians are of mixed Arab and Berber origins. Most are Moslems. Algeria has two main regions: north and south. The north is more fertile. The south is a large, thinly populated desert region.

◄ The Tuareg are a proud Berber people of the Sahara. Unlike other Moslems, the men wear veils and the women do not.

Facts and Figures

Language	ALGERIA, EGYPT, LIBYA, MOROCCO, THE SUDAN, MAURITANIA, TUNISIA — *Salam* Arabic
	Ahlan wa sahlan ALGERIA Algerian

Flag ALGERIA EGYPT LIBYA MOROCCO THE SUDAN CHAD NIGER MALI MAURITANIA TUNISIA

Area

EGYPT 385,201 sq miles (997,667 sq kms)
MOROCCO 181,330 sq miles (699,970 sq kms)
THE SUDAN 966,757 sq miles (2,503,890 sq kms)
ALGERIA 896,592 sq miles (2,322,164 sq kms)
LIBYA 675,000 sq miles (1,749,000 sq kms)
CHAD 495,755 sq miles (1,284,000 sq kms)
NIGER 458,075 sq miles (1,186,408 sq kms)
MALI 478,832 sq miles (1,240,142 sq kms)
MAURITANIA 398,000 sq miles (1,030,700 sq kms)
TUNISIA 63,379 sq miles (164,150 sq kms)

Population

ALGERIA 18,245,000
LIBYA 3,014,100
THE SUDAN 17,865,000
EGYPT 41,065,000
MOROCCO 19,470,000
CHAD 4,309,000
NIGER 5,126,000
MALI 6,290,000
MAURITANIA 1,420,000
TUNISIA 6,201,000

Capital

TUNISIA Tunisian Dinar
LIBYA Libyan Dinar
EGYPT Pound
ALGERIA Dinar
MOROCCO Dirham
THE SUDAN Pound
CHAD CFA Franc
MAURITANIA Nouakchott
MALI Bamako
TUNISIA Tunis
ALGERIA Algiers
MOROCCO Rabat
EGYPT Cairo
LIBYA Tripoli
THE SUDAN Khartoum
CHAD N'Djamena
NIGER Niamey

Scale

| 0 | | 200 kms |
| 0 | | 200 miles |

Atlantic Ocean

Mediterranean Sea

Tanger (Tangier)
Alger (Algiers)
TUNISIA
Oran
Tunis
Rabat
Tripoli
Casablanca
Benghazi
Alexandria
Suez Canal
MOROCCO
Ghardaïa
Cairo
El Aaiún
ALGERIA
LIBYA
EGYPT
Red Sea
WESTERN SAHARA
Aswan
Sahara Desert
Sahara Desert
R Nile
MAURITANIA
MALI
Emi Koussi 11200ft/3415m
Port Sudan
Nouakchott
NIGER
CHAD
SUDAN
R Niger
Khartoum
L Chad
SENEGAL
Niamey
R Blue Nile
Bamako
N'Djamena
R White Nile
ETHIOPIA
UPPER VOLTA
NIGERIA
GUINEA
CAMEROON
CENTRAL AFRICAN REPUBLIC
ZAIRE

Key

Citrus fruit
Cotton
Grapes/Wine
Sugar cane
Olives
Cereals
Industry
Palm oil
Non-food products
Fishing
Rice
Groundnuts
Dairy
Cattle
Uranium
Oil
Natural gas
Iron

◄ A Bedouin rides past the ancient pyramids of Egypt. The first pyramids were built over 4,000 years ago as burial tombs for the pharaohs (kings of ancient Egypt). The Bedouin are basically a nomadic desert people. However, some now live in more permanent settlements and villages.

►An Arab dhow plies the Nile near Aswan in Egypt. Dhows are vessels with triangular sails. Two great dams near Aswan store water for irrigation and hydro-electricity.

◄ A village woman of Egypt draws water from the Nile. The great river's banks have been cultivated for thousands of years. Regular flooding provides irrigation. The waters also bring down sediment which enriches the land. Many crops are grown along the Nile's fertile banks. These include cotton, rice, wheat and dates.

Making a headdress

In very hot climates people have to protect themselves from the powerful rays of the sun. This is why many people who live in such climates wear loose-fitting, flowing clothes which help to keep them cool. Many types of headdress are worn in northern Africa to shade people's heads and necks from the sun. You can make your own Arab-style headdress with a piece of cloth, such as a dish towel. Put it on your head so that one side comes over your forehead and the rest hangs over your shoulders. Tie a cord or thin belt around your forehead to secure the cloth.

West and Central Africa

There are many countries in West and Central Africa. The largest are Ghana, Nigeria, Ivory Coast, Cameroon and Zaire. All the countries except Upper Volta and the Central African Republic have coastlines on the Atlantic. Gambia, Benin and Togo are long and narrow in shape. All the countries are tropical and have equatorial forests and grasslands.

Zaire is the largest of these countries. The River Zaire flows through it. Tropical rain forests cover most of Zaire and the Congo Republic. This area also has many copper, diamond, gold and uranium mines. But most of the people still keep to their old way of life and work as farmers. In the rain forest about 100,000 pygmies live. Pygmies have a primitive way of life.

There are hot humid rain forests along the coast of the Gulf of Guinea. This coast has many different names – the Grain Coast, Ivory Coast, Gold Coast and Slave Coast. These names refer to the products which Europeans and Arabs have taken from this coast in the past.

Away from the coasts there are grasslands called savanna. Unlike the rain forests, the grasslands have a dry season. Nearer to the Sahara, in the north, thorn bushes and scrub vegetation grow.

The Niger is the second largest river in West Africa. It enters the sea in Nigeria. Nigeria has many tin mines. It also produces palm oil and cacao from which cocoa and chocolate are made.

The largest producer of cacao in the world is Ghana. In Ghana there are also many bauxite mines. The metal aluminum is made from bauxite.

▼ These are ancient dye pits in Kano, Nigeria. The mud-walled city has been a trading center for centuries. Modern Kano is a thriving commercial city with around 500,000 inhabitants.

◀ A woman from Bida decorates pottery. Bida is a town lying in the west of central Nigeria. It has long been famous for its local crafts. Like other Nigerian towns, it was visited by Arab traders long ago, who introduced the Moslem religion.

▼ A pygmy family poses in a rain-forest clearing in Zaire. They hunt game with spears and nets. Their hut is made from dried banana fronds.

◀ The great Akosombo Dam in Ghana has helped to create an immense man-made lake. The dam was completed in 1965, and blocks the Volta river in the Ajena gorge. Water is stored here to irrigate the land. It also produces hydro-electricity for the aluminum industry, one of the most important in Ghana.

MAURITANIA

Dakar SENEGAL

GAMBIA MALI

Banjul

Bissau GUINEA

GUINEA-BISSAU

Conakry Kan

Freetown

SIERRA LEONE

Monrovia

LIBERIA

Atlantic Ocean

Facts and Figures

GHANA	NIGERIA	ZAIRE	BENIN	CENTRAL AFRICAN REPUBLIC	CONGO	GABON	THE GAMBIA	GUINEA	GUINEA-BISSAU	IVORY COAST	LIBERIA SENEGAL SIERRA LEONE	TOGO UPPER VOLTA
Flag			CAMEROON									

Area

GHANA 92,098 sq miles (238,533 sq kms)
NIGERIA 356,700 sq miles (923,800 sq kms)
ZAIRE 905,365 sq miles (2,344,885 sq kms)

GUINEA-BISSAU 13,948 sq miles (36,125 sq kms)
IVORY COAST 124,504 sq miles (322,463 sq kms)
CENTRAL AFRICAN REP. 241,305 sq miles (624,977 sq kms
LIBERIA 37,757 sq miles (97,790 sq kms)
SIERRA LEONE 27,699 sq miles (71,740 sq kms)
UPPER VOLTA 105,869 sq miles (274,200 sq kms)
CONGO REPUBLIC 132,047 sq miles (342,000 sq kms)

SENEGAL 75,955 sq miles (196,722 sq kms)
TOGO 21,925 sq miles (56,785 sq kms)
BENIN 43,475 sq miles (112,600 sq kms)
CAMEROON 179,588 sq miles (465,054 sq kms)
GABON 103,347 sq miles (267,667 sq kms)
THE GAMBIA 4,016 sq miles (10,403 sq kms)
GUINEA 94,926 sq miles (245,857 sq kms)

Population

GHANA 11,103,000
ZAIRE 27,519,000
NIGERIA 74,595,000

GUINEA-BISSAU 777,200
IVORY COAST 7,205,000
CENTRAL AFRICAN REPUBLIC 2,305,000
LIBERIA 1,716,900
SIERRA LEONE 3,305,000
UPPER VOLTA 6,617,000
CONGO REPUBLIC 1,454,000

SENEGAL 5,518,000
TOGO 2,409,000
BENIN 3,435,000
CAMEROON 7,980,700
GABON 1,300,200
THE GAMBIA 584,500
GUINEA 4,887,000

Currency NIGERIA Naira GHANA Cedi ZAIRE Zaire

Capital

THE GAMBIA Banjul
SENEGAL Dakar
GUINEA Conakry
GUINEA-BISSAU Bissau
SIERRA LEONE Freetown
LIBERIA Monrovia
GHANA Accra
TOGO Lomé
BENIN Porto Novo
UPPER VOLTA Ouagadougou
IVORY COAST Abidjan
NIGERIA Lagos
CENTRAL AFRICAN REPUBLIC Bangui
CAMEROON Yaoundé
GABON Libreville
CONGO REPUBLIC Brazzaville
ZAIRE Kinshasa

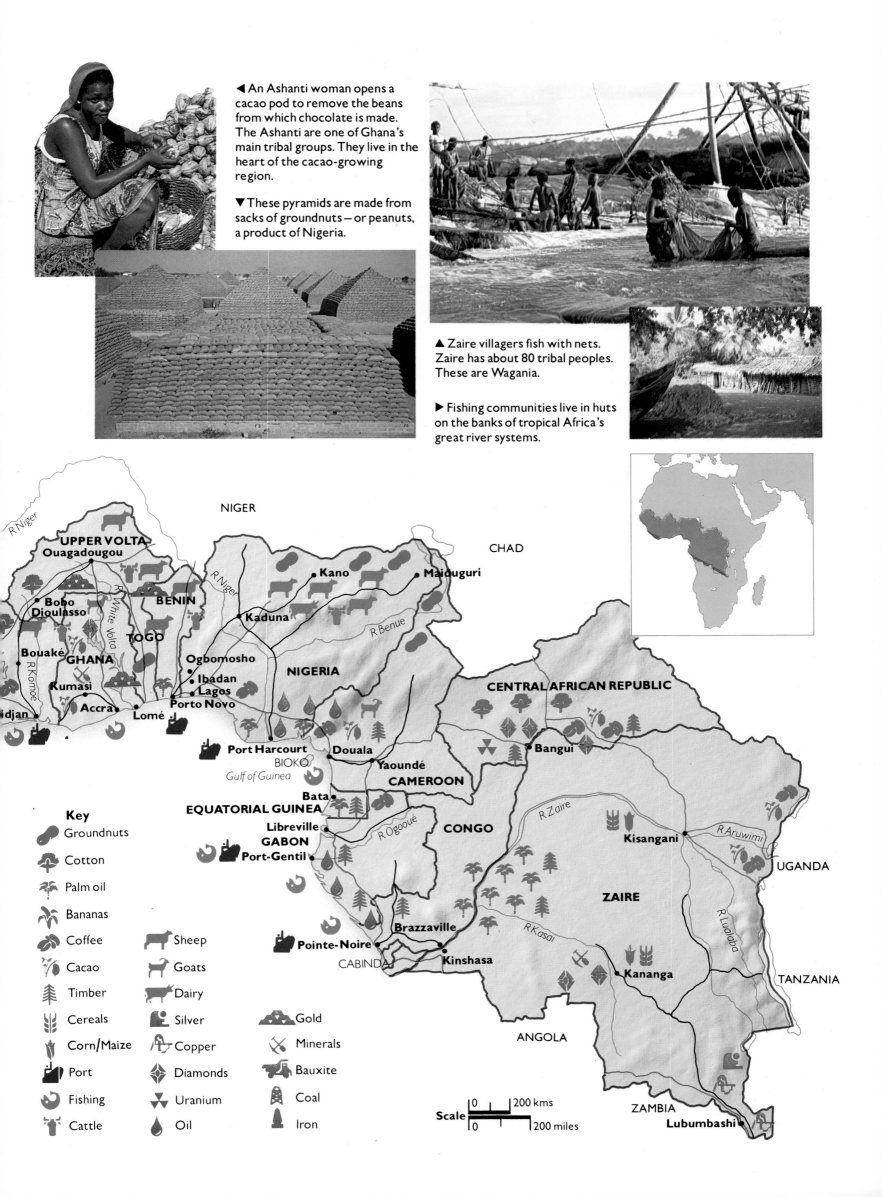

◀ An Ashanti woman opens a cacao pod to remove the beans from which chocolate is made. The Ashanti are one of Ghana's main tribal groups. They live in the heart of the cacao-growing region.

▼ These pyramids are made from sacks of groundnuts — or peanuts, a product of Nigeria.

▲ Zaire villagers fish with nets. Zaire has about 80 tribal peoples. These are Wagania.

▶ Fishing communities live in huts on the banks of tropical Africa's great river systems.

Key

- Groundnuts
- Cotton
- Palm oil
- Bananas
- Coffee
- Cacao
- Timber
- Cereals
- Corn/Maize
- Port
- Fishing
- Cattle
- Sheep
- Goats
- Dairy
- Silver
- Copper
- Diamonds
- Uranium
- Oil
- Gold
- Minerals
- Bauxite
- Coal
- Iron

NIGER

UPPER VOLTA
Ouagadougou

Bobo
Dioulasso

BENIN

TOGO

GHANA

Bouaké

Kumasi

Accra

Lomé

Porto Novo

Ogbomosho

Ibadan

Lagos

Kaduna

Kano

Maiduguri

NIGERIA

CHAD

Port Harcourt

BIOKO

Gulf of Guinea

Douala

Yaoundé

CAMEROON

Bata

EQUATORIAL GUINEA

Libreville

GABON

Port-Gentil

CENTRAL AFRICAN REPUBLIC

Bangui

CONGO

R Ogooué

R Zaire

Kisangani

R Aruwimi

UGANDA

ZAIRE

Brazzaville

R Kasai

R Lualaba

Pointe-Noire

CABINDA

Kinshasa

Kananga

TANZANIA

ANGOLA

ZAMBIA

Lubumbashi

R Niger

White Volta

R Komoe

R Benue

Scale   0   200 kms
         0   200 miles

Eastern Africa

The main countries in East Africa are Kenya, Uganda, Tanzania, Ethiopa and Somalia. Smaller countries in this area are Rwanda, Burundi and Djibouti.

All of East Africa is in the tropics. The Equator passes through Kenya and Uganda. However, most of the countries are high and mountainous and so they have cooler climates than in West Africa. The two highest African mountains are in East Africa, Mount Kilimanjaro and Mount Kenya. Mount Kilimanjaro is 19,340 feet (5,895 meters) high and it lies in Tanzania.

The people of Kenya and most of eastern and southern Africa are called the Bantu. The population of Kenya is over 15 million and it includes many Asian, Arab and European people. Coffee, tea, cotton and sisal grow in Kenya. Nairobi is the capital. The main port is Mombasa. Kenya has many good beaches and famous wildlife parks which many visitors go to each year.

Uganda is an inland country. Its capital is Kampala. It produces cotton, sisal, tobacco and copper. A railroad line runs from Kampala to Nairobi and Mombasa. The old countries Tanganyika and Zanzibar together form Tanzania. The capital and port of Tanzania is Dar-es-Salaam. It is a farming country and its main crops are cassava, yams, wheat and spices such as cloves.

Rwanda and Burundi are small farming countries. Ethiopia is Africa's most mountainous country. Many rivers, such as the Blue Nile, flow from these mountains. The capital is Addis Ababa. Somalia is a desert land. Cotton growing and fishing for tunny and mother-of-pearl are important industries. The capital is Mogadishu.

▲ Mount Kilimanjaro towers above the surrounding countryside. It has two peaks which are linked by a sloping ridge. The graceful animals are impala, part of the antelope family.

▶ The giraffe, lion, elephant, gazelle and zebra are just some of the animals native to Africa which are now in danger of becoming extinct. Game and Safari parks have been set up to protect these animals from hunters. Elephants are most often hunted for their ivory tusks. Ivory traders sell them for vast sums of money. Other animals are hunted for their skins.

Facts and Figures

Flag ETHIOPIA KENYA TANZANIA UGANDA BURUNDI DJIBOUTI RWANDA SOMALIA

Language
Jambo Swahili TANZANIA KENYA

subuh wanaagsán Somali SOMALIA

Area

ETHIOPIA	KENYA	TANZANIA	UGANDA	
471,800 sq miles (1,221,900 sq kms)	224,081 sq miles (580,367 sq kms)	364,886 sq miles (945,050 sq kms)	93,104 sq miles (241,139 sq kms)	BURUNDI 10,747 sq miles (27,834 sq kms) DJIBOUTI 8,900 sq miles (23,000 sq kms) RWANDA 10,169 sq miles (26,338 sq kms) SOMALIA 246,300 sq miles (638,000 sq kms)

Population ETHIOPIA 30,017,000 KENYA 15,780,000 TANZANIA 16,308,000 UGANDA 13,224,900

BURUNDI 4,176,000
DJIBOUTI 242,000
RWANDA 4,820,000
SOMALIA 3,542,000

Capital

ETHIOPIA Birr
UGANDA Shilling
KENYA Shilling
RWANDA Franc
BURUNDI Franc
SOMALIA Shilling
TANZANIA Shilling

DJIBOUTI Djibouti City
ETHIOPIA Addis Ababa
SOMALIA Mogadishu
UGANDA Kampala
RWANDA Kigali
BURUNDI Bujumbura
KENYA Nairobi
TANZANIA Dar-es-Salaam

▶ A laborer cuts sisal in Kenya. Sisal is a type of hemp. Cords and twine are made from the leaves, most of this is exported.

▼ A plowman drives his team in the highlands of Ethiopia. Few trees are left in these regions. Many of the forests have been cleared by farmers working the poor soil.

◀ A doctor treats Masai in a mobile clinic. The Masai are a proud, nomadic people who drive their herds across the bushlands of Kenya and Tanzania. They live off the meat and milk of their livestock.

▲ Kenyan fishermen use basketwork traps to catch their fish. The traps have tapering entrances, so the fish cannot get out again.

Cotton
Coffee
Corn/Maize
Wheat
Sugar cane
Tea
Tobacco
Rice
Coconuts
Bananas
Cereals

Dairy
Cattle
Sheep
Goats
Diamonds
Copper

▲ A woman pounds corn in Rwanda. The country is poor and most people live in small villages. Maize is the basic diet of many villagers. Cassava, sweet potatoes and pulses are also grown here.

▶ A Masai woman prepares to take part in a dance called the muchungwa. She wears traditional ear-rings, necklace and make-up.

Scale

| 0 | 200 kms |
| 0 | 200 miles |

Asmera

DJIBOUTI
Djibouti
Gulf of·Aden
R Blue Nile
SOMALI REPUBLIC
Dire Dawa
Hargeysa
Addis Ababa
R Omo
ETHIOPIA
R Shebele

L Turkana

UGANDA
KENYA
Kampala
Mogadishu
RWANDA
L Victoria
Kigali
Mwanza
▲ Mount Kenya 17058ft/5199m
Nairobi
Indian Ocean
BURUNDI
Bujumbura
Kilimanjaro 19340ft/5895m
Mombasa
L Tanganyika
Tanga
TANZANIA
Dar-es-Salaam
ZAMBIA
R Ruvuma
MOZAMBIQUE

Southern Africa

The main countries in southern Africa are Angola, Zambia, Zimbabwe, Botswana, Mozambique, South-West Africa and the Republic of South Africa.

In the north of the area, there are tropical grasslands. In Zimbabwe cattle rearing is important. There are also many mineral mines. Zimbabwe exports gold and asbestos. In Zambia there are large copper and zinc mines. An important railroad runs through Angola. It takes the copper from the mines in Shaba province in Zaire to the port of Lobito on the coast.

South-West Africa, which is also called Namibia, and Botswana are much drier countries. The long and narrow Kalahari Desert is in Botswana. There are many mines in Botswana and South-West Africa which produce diamonds, nickel and tin.

The Republic of South Africa is the most southerly country in Africa. The population is about 24 million. Of these over 15 million are Bantu Africans, 4 million are Europeans and over 5 million are Asians. There are many racial problems in South Africa.

Farming and cattle raising are important in South Africa, but it is also a mining country. Gold mines around Johannesburg employ many people. Diamonds are exported from Kimberley. There are also iron, copper, and asbestos mines. Johannesburg is the largest city in South Africa.

▲ Smoke rises from a Bantu village in Lesotho. The round huts are a traditional kind of dwelling.

▶ The Victoria Falls are on the border between Zambia and Zimbabwe. This great cascade is formed as the Zambezi river plunges over a great gorge one mile (1.6 kms) wide.

▲ South Africa produces more gold than any other country. Its annual production accounts for about two thirds of the world's total. The gold is cast in bars like these.

◀ These Zambian miners work in a copper mine. Copper is Zambia's main export. The country is poor and depends heavily on the copper industry. But many Zambians work the land. They live on small farms, growing just enough food to feed themselves and their families. This is called subsistence farming.

Facts and Figures

Language

Goeiemôre — Afrikaans — NAMIBIA, SOUTH AFRICA

English — MALAWI, SWAZILAND, LESOTHO, ZAMBIA, BOTSWANA, SOUTH AFRICA

Hello

Dumelang — Setswana — BOTSWANA

Kinahe — Bantu dialect — ZAMBIA, ANGOLA, ZIMBABWE, MOZAMBIQUE, SOUTH AFRICA

Flag

ANGOLA, BOTSWANA, SOUTH AFRICA, MOZAMBIQUE, ZAMBIA, ZIMBABWE, LESOTHO, MALAWI, NAMIBIA, MADAGASCAR, SWAZILAND

Area

ANGOLA 481,353 sq miles (1,246,700 sq kms)
MOZAMBIQUE 308,642 sq miles (799,380 sq kms)
SOUTH AFRICA 438,173 sq miles (1,133,759 sq kms)
ZIMBABWE 150,685 sq miles (390,272 sq kms)
BOTSWANA 222,000 sq miles (576,000 sq kms)
ZAMBIA 290,586 sq miles (752,614 sq kms)
LESOTHO 11,720 sq miles (30,355 sq kms)
MADAGASCAR 226,658 sq miles (587,041 sq kms)
MALAWI 45,747 sq miles (118,484 sq kms)
NAMIBIA 318,251 sq miles (824,268 sq kms)
SWAZILAND 6,704 sq miles (17,364 sq kms)

Population

ANGOLA 6,901,000
BOTSWANA 792,000
MOZAMBIQUE 12,000,000
SOUTH AFRICA 24,116,000
ZAMBIA 5,649,000
ZIMBABWE 7,140,000
LESOTHO 1,216,800
MADAGASCAR 9,048,000
MALAWI 5,561,821
NAMIBIA 980,000
SWAZILAND 494,500

Currency

SWAZILAND Lilangeni
LESOTHO Maloti
ZAMBIA Kwacha
SOUTH AFRICA Rand
BOTSWANA Pula
ZIMBABWE Zimbabwe Dollar

Capital

MALAWI Lilongwe
ANGOLA Luanda
ZAMBIA Lusaka
NAMIBIA Windhoek
BOTSWANA Gaborone
LESOTHO Maseru
ZIMBABWE Salisbury
MADAGASCAR Antananarivo
MOZAMBIQUE Maputo
SWAZILAND Mbabane
SOUTH AFRICA Pretoria

▶ A river San lays his net in Botswana. The San are a people of southern Africa, known to whites as Bushmen. The San are basically a nomadic people. Some now live in settlements, but others still roam the bushlands in small hunting bands.

▼ The great Table Mountain dominates the skyline of Cape Town. You can reach the top by cable car. There is a very good view of the cape from the summit.

▲ Herero women pose for a photograph in Botswana. The Herero are a Bantu people famous for their great cattle herds. Many still live in small farming communities, but others are now living in larger settlements.

▲ A San tribesman hunts with bow and arrow in Namibia. The arrow is tipped with poison. The San have learnt to survive in the Kalahari Desert. They camp in rock shelters and kill what game they can find.

Scale

0 ——— 200 kms
0 ——— 200 miles

Key

- 🫘 Coffee
- 🌽 Corn/Maize
- 🌿 Cotton
- 🥬 Vegetables
- 🌾 Non-food products
- 🌱 Tobacco
- 🍃 Tea
- 🌾 Rice
- 🌾 Wheat
- 🍎 Fruit
- 🍇 Grapes/Wine
- 🌾 Sugar cane
- 🏭 Industry
- ⚓ Port
- 🐟 Fishing
- 🐄 Dairy
- 🐂 Cattle
- 🐑 Sheep
- 🐐 Goats
- 🛢 Oil
- ◈ Diamonds
- 🔺 Iron
- ⚒ Copper
- ⛏ Coal
- ⛏ Gold
- ▽ Uranium

ZAIRE

ANGOLA
Luanda
Lobito
Huambo
R.Kwanza

MALAWI   TANZANIA

ZAMBIA
Ndola
Lusaka
R.Luangwa
R.Zambezi
Lilongwe
Blantyre
R.Lugenda

Livingstone
Salisbury

MOZAMBIQUE

ZIMBABWE
Bulawayo
Beira

SOUTH-WEST AFRICA (NAMIBIA)
Windhoek

BOTSWANA
Kalahari Desert
Gaborone
R.Limpopo

Pretoria
Johannesburg
Maputo

SWAZILAND

Bloemfontein
Kimberley
Maseru

SOUTH AFRICA

Orange River

LESOTHO
Durban

East London
Port Elizabeth
Cape Town

MADAGASCAR
Mahajanga
Antananarivo
R.Betsiboka
Toliary

Looking at Australasia

Australasia is made up of Australia, New Zealand and the islands of the southern and western Pacific. It would fit into Asia almost seven times and it is the only continent which is made up entirely of islands. It is also the only continent in the world that does not join directly onto the mainland of any other continent.

Australasia lies on the opposite side of the globe from Europe and the eastern United States. Because of this Australia is sometimes nick-named the 'down-under' country.

The largest island in the continent is Australia which is also the largest island in the world. The rest of Australasia is made up of New Zealand, the many small islands in the Pacific Ocean and the eastern half of New Guinea. The islands in the Pacific Ocean are called Oceania. The islands are extremely scattered. This means that air and sea transport are very important.

European settlers went to live in Australia and New Zealand in the eighteenth and nineteenth centuries. There are fewer European settlers in Oceania. The native people of Australia are called Aborigines. In New Zealand the native people are the Maoris.

The whole continent has a small population. It has only 0.02% of the world's population but covers 6% of the world's land surface. In Australia there are only 3 people to every square mile. In the United States there are 25 and in Great Britain 250 people to the same area.

▼ Australasia is a continent of sharp contrasts. The populated regions of Australia and New Zealand are highly industrialized. Their farming is efficient, and the two countries export meat, grain and dairy produce on a world scale. The other Pacific islands are not so developed and they produce little for export. Distances between the islands are immense. Some have become centers for international air travel. The Pacific islanders are great sea-farers themselves. They have traveled thousands of miles in their wooden boats.

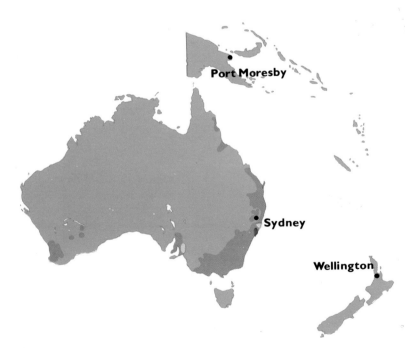

▲ The total population of Australasia is 22 million. Australia is the largest country with a population of 14 million people. Next come New Zealand and Papua New Guinea, with populations of about 3 million each. None of the other islands holds even a million people. Many of the smallest islands have not been given a name.

The interior of Australia is mostly flat, dry and barren. Few people live in this desert region. Most Australians live in cities, many in the fertile regions of the south-eastern seaboard. The main cities here are Sydney and Melbourne. Each has a population of over 2 million people. There is also a fertile area around Perth in the south-west.

New Zealand is made up of two main islands. Most people live on the North Island. Wellington and Auckland are the main cities. The South Island includes the important coastal cities of Christchurch and Dunedin. However, the interior is mountainous and more thinly populated.

Inhabitants	
per sq mile	per sq km
Under 16	Under 6
16-256	6-100
256-512	100-200
Over 512	Over 200

Key

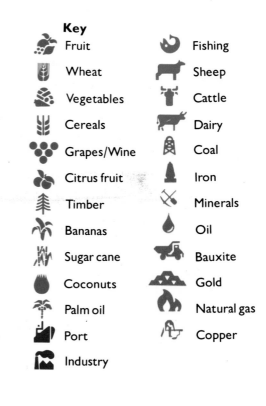 Fruit		Fishing
Wheat		Sheep
Vegetables		Cattle
Cereals		Dairy
Grapes/Wine		Coal
Citrus fruit		Iron
Timber		Minerals
Bananas		Oil
Sugar cane		Bauxite
Coconuts		Gold
Palm oil		Natural gas
Port		Copper
Industry		

KIRIBATI

Pacific Ocean

SOLOMON
ISLANDS

esby

PHOENIX ISLANDS

Coral Sea

TUVALU

MARQUESAS ISLANDS

er

VANUATU

WESTERN
SAMOA

FIJI

COOK ISLANDS

NEW
CALEDONIA

Brisbane

dney

rra

Auckland

Tasman Sea

Cook Strait

Wellington

NEW
ZEALAND

Southern Alps

Australia

Australia has six states and two territories. The states are Western Australia, Queensland, South Australia, New South Wales, Victoria, and the island of Tasmania. The two territories are the Australian Capital Territory, with the nation's capital, Canberra, and the Northern Territory whose main town is Darwin.

Australia is a fairly level land mass. A low-lying, dry, flat area called the Western Shield covers almost half of Australia. The name for this type of flat country is a plateau. Much of the Western Shield is desert. The main lake in the Western Shield is called Lake Disappointment. It is not a real lake but an area of salt marsh. Very few people live in the Western Shield except around Perth in the south-west.

East of the Western Shield, three large basins run from north to south. A basin is a large flat, lowland area surrounded by hills so that it is shaped like a basin or bowl. The Carpentaria Basin is a southern extension of the Gulf of Carpentaria. Further south is the Great Artesian Basin. The isolated town of Alice Springs is in this region. South again, the third basin is around the Murray river and its main tributaries, the Darling and the Murrumbidgee rivers.

Along the eastern coast of Australia is the Great Dividing Range. These mountains separate the wetter coastal areas from the dry interior. Most Australians live in the cities, towns and farmlands between these mountains and the Pacific coast. The five largest cities in Australia are also the main ports. Sydney has a population of almost 3 million. Melbourne, Brisbane, Adelaide and Perth are the other large cities.

Sheep-raising is very important in Australia and there are many more sheep than people. The country exports wool and lamb. Mining for silver, gold and other metals are important Australian industries.

The climate of Australia is varied. Much of the center is hot desert. In the north the climate is tropical but in the south and south-east, the climate is milder. Fruit such as apples and peaches are some of the crops grown.

Facts and Figures

Flag

Language English

Area 2,966,200 sq miles (7,682,300 sq kms)

Population 14,376,400

Australian Dollar
Currency

Canberra
Capital

▲ This map shows the states and territories in Australia. The largest state is Western Australia and the smallest territory is the tiny Australian Capital Territory.

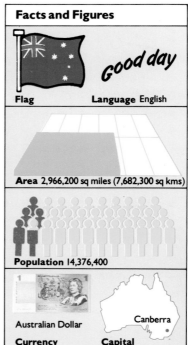
▲The Great Barrier Reef, along the coast of north-east Australia, is the largest coral reef in the world. It is 1,250 miles (2,000 kms) long. Coral is a small marine animal related to the sea anemone. There are over 200 coral species here.

▶ Sheep stations cover huge areas of land. The heavy-coated merino sheep, which is raised for its wool, is suited to areas with little rain. Sheep for meat are raised on the wetter coastal areas.

▼ Kangaroos and koalas carry their young in pouches. Koalas live in trees, feeding on leaves and shoots. Kangaroos have powerful hind legs for leaping.

Making an Australian hat
1. Take an old felt hat with a brim, string, about 20 corks, scissors and a thick needle.

2. Cut one piece of string about 4in (10cm) long for each cork. Tie one end of the string tightly around the cork. With the needle, make a hole carefully through the hat brim about ½in (1cm) from the edge. Thread a piece of the string through the hole.
3. Repeat until the corks go around the whole brim. The hat will help protect you from the sun and keep flies out of your eyes.

▶ The famous Opera House, overlooking Sydney Harbor, was opened in 1974. Sydney is the largest city in Australia and is its chief port. Its main exports are wool, wheat, flour, sheepskins and meat. There are also shipyards and oil refineries.

▲ Australia is the largest producer of bauxite in the world. This mine is in Gove Peninsula in the north. Australia also exports lead, iron ore, nickel and zinc. Oil has been discovered in Bass Strait, south Australia. This is a valuable addition to Australia's resources.

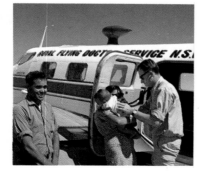

◀ The Flying Doctor service was introduced for people living on sheep and cattle stations, long distances from the nearest town and doctor. Airplanes are an important means of transport for everyone who lives in the Australian outback.

Key

Timber		Fishing	
Sugar cane		Coal	
Fruit		Iron	
Wheat		Minerals	
Cereals		Silver	
Vegetables		Gold	
Bananas		Natural gas	
Citrus fruit		Oil	
Grapes/Wine		Bauxite	
Port			
Industry			
Sheep			
Dairy			
Cattle			

Cape York Peninsula

Timor Sea

Darwin

Gulf of Carpentaria

Coral Sea

Indian Ocean

Great Sandy Desert

L Disappointment

Gibson Desert

Alice Springs

Simpson Desert

R Dawson

Cairns

Townsville

Great Barrier Reef

Rockhampton

L Eyre

Great Victoria Desert

Brisbane

R Darling

Pacific Ocean

Kalgoorlie

Broken Hill

Newcastle

Perth
Fremantle

Great Australian Bight

R Murray

Canberra

Sydney
Wollongong

Adelaide

Mount Kosciusko 7316/2230m
R Snowy

Bendigo

Melbourne

Bass Straight

Tasman Sea

Geelong

Launceston

TASMANIA

Hobart

Scale
0   200 kms
0   200 miles

▶ An aborigine plays the didgeridoo, a traditional instrument. There are about 125,000 aborigines, mostly living in the semi-desert of the northern region.

New Zealand

New Zealand is a group of islands in the south-west Pacific midway between the Equator and the South Pole. The main islands are the North and South Islands. New Zealand also includes Stewart Island and some other small islands. New Zealand is about the same size as Britain or Japan. It is 930 miles (1,500 kms) away from Australia and 6,580 miles (10,600 kms) away from South America.

New Zealand is a mountainous country and North Island has many volcanoes. The main active volcanoes are Ruapehu and Ngauruhoe. Ruapehu is 9,175 feet (2,797 meters) high. Ngauruhoe is 7,515 feet (2,290 meters high. The North Island has pools of boiling mud.

The main mountains in South Island are the Southern Alps. There are 19 mountains over 9,000 feet (3,000 meters) high. New Zealand's highest mountain is Mount Cook in the center of South Island. It is 12,349 feet (3,764 meters) high. In and around the Southern Alps are glaciers, lakes and large inlets called 'sounds'. South and east of the Southern Alps are the Canterbury Plains.

New Zealand is the world's largest exporter of dairy products and lamb. It is the second largest exporter of wool. Sheep farming is important on the Canterbury Plains. Cattle are raised in the North Island.

Facts and Figures

Flag — Language: English, Maori (Hi, Kiaora)

Area 103,747 sq miles (268,704 sq kms)

Population 3,105,800

Currency New Zealand Dollar — Capital Wellington

▼ New Zealand has 12 land districts. On the North Island are North Auckland, South Auckland, Hawke's Bay, Gisborne, Taranaki and Wellington. The South Island has Canterbury and Marlborough. Nelson, Otago, Southland and Westland.

◄ The kiwi is a small bird which cannot fly and is found only in New Zealand. It's the symbol of New Zealand and appears on coins and stamps.

► The Canterbury Plains, South Island, are a very fertile area. The land is used for sheep farming and growing wheat.

▼ Nelson district, South Island, produces many tons of apples and pears for export. There is a sunny climate, transport is good and there are modern well-equipped packing stations.

▼ The Canterbury area in the South Island is known for its production of lamb. New Zealand was the first country to begin exporting frozen lamb.

► Farming accounts for three quarters of New Zealand's exports. Wool and lamb make up 40 per cent of exports and dairy products make up 15 per cent. This dairy herd is at South Auckland, North Island.

▲ Wellington, the capital of New Zealand, is an important port. It is an exporting center for dairy produce, wool and meat.

▲ This new housing area is in a suburb of Wellington. Nearly half the population live in towns or urban areas and most houses are bungalows.

▼ There are 225,000 Maoris, who live mainly in the hot springs area of the North Island. This Maori is a sheep-shearer.

▲ Rugby football is a very popular sport in New Zealand. This player belongs to the national team, the All Blacks, who play successfully in many countries of the world.

▲ Steam, which comes from hot underground springs, is used as a cheap form of energy. The geothermal borefield at Wairakei in the North Island pipes steam to a generating station. It is then turned into electricity. Steam produces only a small amount of New Zealand's energy.

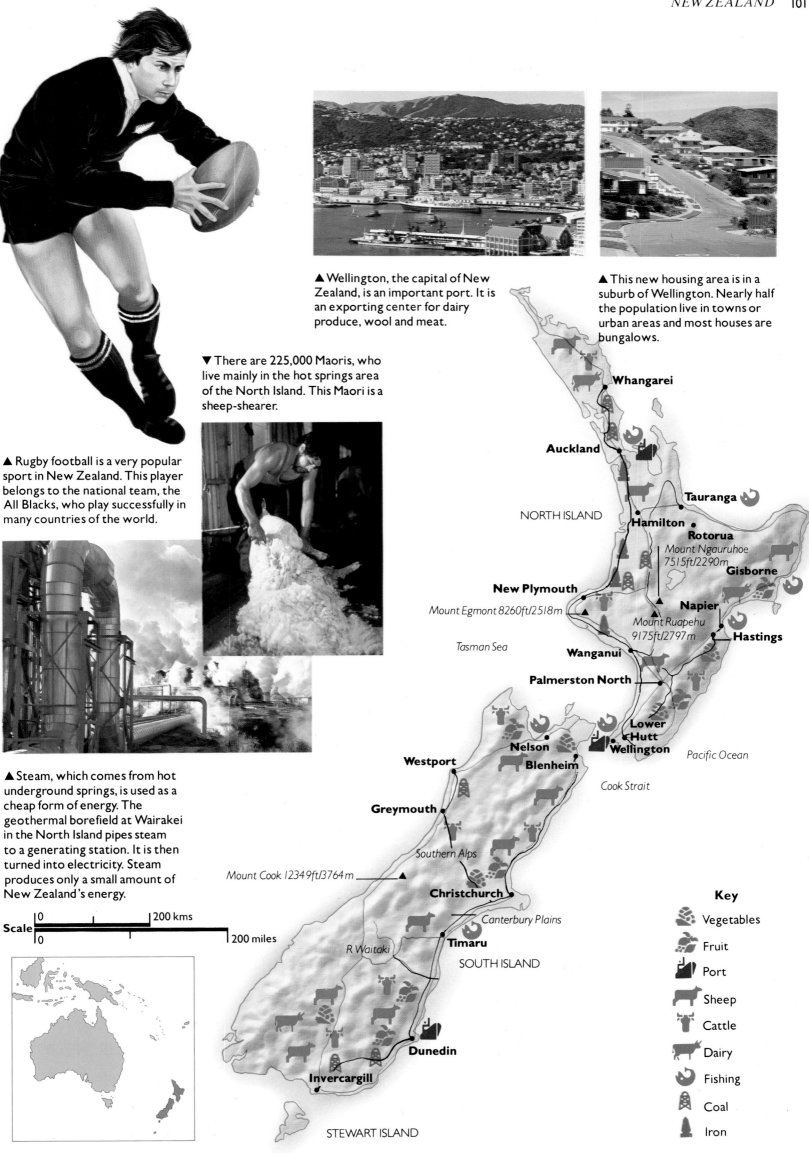

Whangarei

Auckland

Tauranga

NORTH ISLAND

Hamilton

Rotorua

Mount Ngauruhoe
7515ft/2290m

Gisborne

New Plymouth

Mount Egmont 8260ft/2518m

Napier

Mount Ruapehu
9175ft/2797m

Hastings

Tasman Sea

Wanganui

Palmerston North

Lower Hutt

Nelson

Wellington

Pacific Ocean

Westport

Blenheim

Cook Strait

Greymouth

Southern Alps

Mount Cook 12349ft/3764m

Christchurch

Canterbury Plains

Scale

| 0 | | | 200 kms |

| 0 | | | 200 miles |

R Waitaki

Timaru

SOUTH ISLAND

Dunedin

Invercargill

STEWART ISLAND

Key

Vegetables

Fruit

Port

Sheep

Cattle

Dairy

Fishing

Coal

Iron

Oceania

Oceania is the name of the many islands in the southern Pacific Ocean. There are three main groups called Polynesia, Micronesia and Melanesia. Most of the Pacific islands are either volcanic islands or coral islands. The coral islands are usually atolls. An atoll is a coral reef shaped like a ring or a horseshoe. Inside the reef is an area of shallow water called a lagoon. Coral reefs are made from the skeletons of tiny creatures like sea anemones. When the animal dies, a skeleton is left behind. Millions and millions of these skeletons gradually build up into reefs and islands.

The Polynesian islands are to the north-east of New Zealand. The main island groups are Samoa, Tonga, the Cook Islands and Marquesas. The Hawaiian Islands are in Polynesia, too, but they now belong to the United States. The Polynesians are great boatbuilding people.

The islands of Micronesia lie to the east of the Philippines and north of New Guinea. The largest groups of islands in Micronesia are called the Marshall, Caroline and Mariana islands. Tuvalu and Kiribati are also in Micronesia.

The island region of Melanesia curves around northeast Australia. Melanesia includes some of the largest Pacific islands such as New Guinea, the Solomon Islands, New Caledonia and Fiji.

The coconut palm is the most important plant in Oceania. It provides the island people with food, drink, and building materials. When the inside of the coconut is dried it is called copra. Coconut oil comes from this.

◀ A boy displays his catch at a quayside market on the island of Tonga. The Pacific islands produce copra and bananas for export. Pineapples are grown in all parts of Polynesia.

PAPUA NEW GUINEA

Port Moresby •

Coral Sea

AUSTRALIA

SOLOMON ISLANDS

Honiara •

VANUATU

NEW CALEDONIA

Nouméa

N

Scale
0 — 200 kms
0 — 200 miles

Facts and Figures

Flag FIJI HAWAII PAPUA NEW GUINEA | SOLOMON ISLANDS TONGA WESTERN SAMOA

Language
FIJI English, Fijian, Hindi
HAWAII English
PAPUA NEW GUINEA English, Hiri, Pidgin English
SOLOMON ISLANDS English, Pidgin, dialects
TONGA English, Tongan
WESTERN SAMOA Samoan, English

FIJI 7,055 sq miles (18,272 sq kms)	**PAPUA NEW GUINEA** 178,704 sq miles (462,840 sq kms)	**SOLOMON ISLANDS** 11,157 sq miles (28,896 sq kms)	**WESTERN SAMOA** 1,100 sq miles (2,849 sq kms)

Area   **HAWAII** 6,450 sq miles (16,705 sq kms)   **TONGA** 290 sq miles (750 sq kms)

| FIJI 624,000 | HAWAII 796,913 | PAPUA NEW GUINEA 3,078,500 | SOLOMON ISLANDS 214,000 | TONGA 91,000 | WESTERN SAMOA 152,672 |

Population

SOLOMON ISLANDS Solomon Islands Dollar

PAPUA NEW GUINEA Kina

WESTERN SAMOA Tala
TONGA Pa'nga
FIJI Fiji Dollar
Currency

ARSHALL ISLANDS

▼ Nobody knows who carved the ancient stone heads on Easter Island. The people are Polynesian, but the island belongs to Chile.

▲ A girl sells fabrics at a shop in Nukualofa in the Tonga Islands. The material is distinctive and colorful. Women generally make up their dresses for themselves.

▲ These women of Nukualofa are carrying food in baskets woven from coconut fronds. This is the usual way to carry things around.

Pacific Ocean

KIRIBATI

PHOENIX ISLANDS

◀ This coral atoll is in Tahiti. The island is one of the most beautiful in the southern Pacific. It produces fruit, copra and pearls which are all exported.

TUVALU

WESTERN SAMOA
●**Apia**

Nukualofa

MARQUESAS ISLANDS

FIJI

SOCIETY ISLANDS

●**Suva**

TAHITI

COOK ISLANDS

◀ Young men of Papua New Guinea have been harvesting yams. This food is an important part of the local diet.

Key

 Timber

 Coconuts

Palm oil

Sugar cane

Fruit

Bananas

Fishing

Gold

 Silver

Copper

Oil

Minerals

◀ In western New Guinea the jungle is dense and the people are primitive. This village is in the middle of tropical forest.

▼ Coconuts are the fruit of coco palms which grow throughout the Pacific islands. The white flesh is called copra. Palm oil comes from this. Desiccated coconut is shredded copra, which is used in all kinds of food.

Looking at North America

North America is shaped like a huge triangle. The largest countries in this continent are Canada, the United States and Mexico. The coasts of North America touch three oceans – the Arctic, the Pacific and the Atlantic. Its northern lands are less than 500 miles (800 kms) away from the North Pole. The southern part of North America is just over 500 miles from the Equator. The continent is so wide that it has eight time zones. This means that when it is noon at St John's in Newfoundland it is only 5am at Anchorage in Alaska.

Cape Morris Jessup in Greenland is the most northerly tip of land in the world. Although Greenland is in North America it belongs to Denmark. The Arctic Circle passes through southern Greenland, northern Canada and Alaska. The Bering Strait separates Alaska from Siberia in Asia. This narrow sea passage is only 55 miles (88 kms) wide. It joins the Arctic and the Pacific oceans.

In the south of the North American continent the Tropic of Cancer passes through Mexico and the West Indies. The isthmus of Panama joins North America to South America. The Panama Canal crosses this isthmus and links the Caribbean part of the Atlantic with the Pacific Ocean.

There are three main regions in North America. In the west a chain of high mountains stretches from Alaska to Mexico. The main range is called the Rocky Mountains. Along the eastern side of the continent is another chain which includes the Appalachian Mountains. Between them lies a huge central area which extends from north to south for nearly 3,000 miles (4,800 kms). This is the area of the Great Plains and the valley of the Mississippi, North America's longest river.

To the south of Mexico there are several small countries which make up Central America. The islands of the West Indies lie off the coasts of Central America and the south-eastern part of the United States.

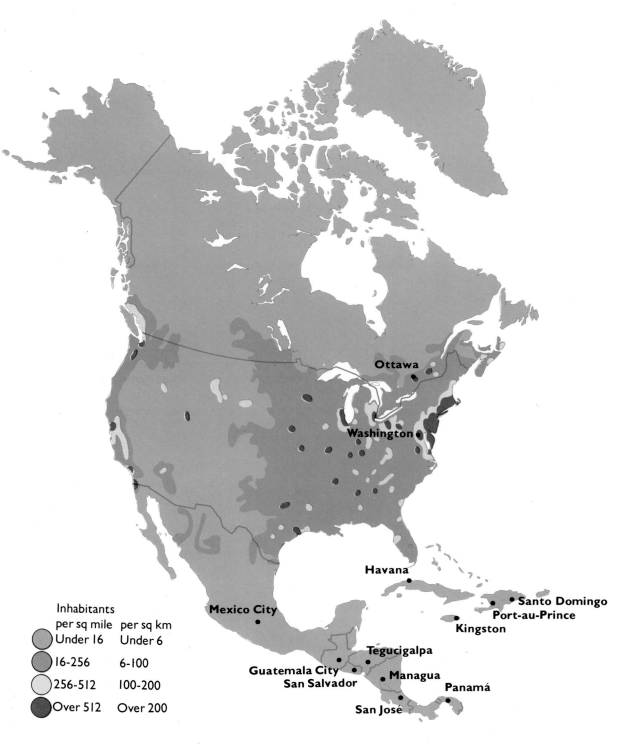

◀The total population of North America is 358 million people. Most of these are of European or African origin.

The United States has the largest population, with about 220 million people. Mexico comes next with 66 million. Canada is the third most populated country with 23 million people. In fact, Canada is slightly larger than the United States. However, much of its land mass falls inside, or near, the Arctic Circle. Most Canadians live in a few populated areas around the southern border.

The main centers of population in the United States are along the eastern seaboard. New York State alone contains 16 million people – an average of over 3,000 people per square mile (2,500 people per square kilometer).

The midwestern plains are less densely populated, and there are many desert areas in parts of the Rocky Mountains and the Great Salt Basin.

The western seaboard includes the urban sprawls of Los Angeles and San Francisco. Altogether, the United States has 16 cities with populations of more than 2 million people. Its vast urban population produces many industrial goods.

Inhabitants
per sq mile   per sq km
Under 16   Under 6
16-256   6-100
256-512   100-200
Over 512   Over 200

Ottawa
Washington
Havana
Mexico City
Santo Domingo
Port-au-Prince
Kingston
Tegucigalpa
Guatemala City
San Salvador
Managua
Panamá
San José

▼The United States is the world's leading industrial nation, and also the main producer of corn, tobacco and other agricultural goods. It is rich in coal, oil and natural gas, and it is the world's main producer of nuclear energy.

Scale

0 ——————— 1000 miles

0 ——————— 1000 kms

Arctic Ocean

Bering Strait

Brook's Range

ALASKA

Beaufort Sea

• **Anchorage** • **Dawson**

GREENLAND

Baffin Bay

VICTORIA ISLAND

BAFFIN ISLAND

• **Godthaab**

R Mackenzie

Prince Rupert•

Hudson Bay

CANADA

R St Lawrence

• **St John's**

Gulf of St Lawrence

Vancouver•

Seattle•

Portland•

Rocky Mountains

Winnipeg

Great Lakes

Quebec

Montreal•

Ottawa

Boston

Pacific Ocean

Minneapolis • **St Paul**

Milwaukee

Toronto•

Detroit

Chicago

New York City

R Missouri

Pittsburgh

Philadelphia
Baltimore
Washington DC

San Francisco

Salt Lake City

Denver•

R Colorado

UNITED STATES

Appalachian Mts

Atlantic Ocean

Los Angeles•

Cuidad Juárez• **El Paso**

Dallas•

R Mississippi

Atlanta•

Houston•

New Orleans•

MEXICO

Monterrey•

Gulf of Mexico

Miami○

BAHAMAS

WEST INDIES

Tampico• **Mérida**

Havana○

CUBA

PUERTO RICO

DOMINICAN REPUBLIC

HAITI

Guadalajara•

Veracruz

Mexico City•

JAMAICA •**Kingston**

Port-au-Prince

Caribbean Sea

BELIZE

GUATEMALA • **San Pedro Sula**

Guatemala City• **HONDURAS**

EL SALVADOR **NICARAGUA**

L Nicaragua

Managua•

San José•

COSTA RICA

PANAMÁ

Panamá

Gulf of Panama

Key

🌲 Timber

🌾 Wheat

🌾 Cereals | 🌿 Tobacco

🍎 Citrus fruit | 🏭 Port

🍇 Fruit | 🏭 Industry

🍇 Grapes/Wine | 🐄 Cattle

🌿 Cotton | 🐄 Dairy | ⛰ Gold

🌽 Corn/Maize | 🐟 Fishing | ⛏ Copper

🥦 Vegetables | 🐑 Sheep | ⚡ Energy

🍌 Bananas | 🛢 Oil | ⛏ Iron

🌾 Sugar cane | ⚒ Minerals | 🔥 Natural gas

🥜 Groundnuts | ⛏ Coal | ⚙ Steel

Canada, Alaska and Greenland

Canada is in the northern part of the North American continent and it is the second largest country in the world. It extends from the Atlantic in the east to the Pacific in the west, and from the Arctic Ocean in the north to the United States in the south. This boundary follows the St Lawrence River, the Great Lakes and the 49th Parallel which is a line of latitude. In the north-west, Canada also has a border with Alaska which is part of the United States.

Canada consists of the Arctic regions in the north, the Rocky Mountains in the west, the Laurentian Plateau in the east the the vast central prairies. The St Lawrence River is part of a seaway which connects the five great lakes of Canada and the United States with the Atlantic Ocean. The island of Newfoundland lies to the north of the gulf of St Lawrence.

Most Canadians live in the provinces of Ontario and Quebec in the south-east. Central Ontario is one of the world's important mining areas. The southern part of the province, surrounded by the lakes, is a farming area famous for its fruit. Toronto is the capital of Ontario.

The province of Quebec is French speaking. It contains Montreal which is Canada's largest city and one of the busiest ports in North America. The historic city of Quebec is the provincial capital. Canada's main capital city is Ottawa which is in Ontario on the border with Quebec.

The prairie provinces of Manitoba, Saskatchewan and Alberta all produce wheat. Alberta also has oilfields, coal mines and valuable mineral resources. British Columbia is Canada's mountainous state in the west. Its main city is Vancouver which is Canada's largest port on the Pacific. Canada is one of the world's main industrial countries. Most of its trade is with the United States. Timber, oil, natural gas and cereals are all exported.

Very few people live in the cold north of Canada apart from the Eskimos. However, there are mining camps, weather and defense stations and fur-trading posts where people buy and sell fur.

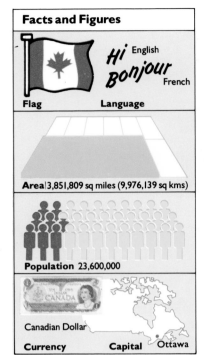

Facts and Figures

Flag	**Language** Hi (English) Bonjour (French)
Area 3,851,809 sq miles (9,976,139 sq kms)	
Population 23,600,000	
Currency Canadian Dollar	**Capital** Ottawa

▲ The city of Quebec has many fortifications. In 1759, a young man named General James Wolfe led British troops to victory in their battle against the French. He landed his troops in a cove at the bottom of the Heights of Abraham. The men scaled the cliffs to reach the city.

▲ Canada is made up of ten provinces: Newfoundland, Nova Scotia, New Brunswick, Prince Edward Island, Quebec, Ontario, Manitoba, Saskatchewan, Alberta and British Columbia. In addition, Canada includes vast Arctic regions where few people live. These are the Yukon Territory and North-west Territories.

▼ The Indians of north-western Canada have carved totem poles for hundreds of years. The totem is a ritual bond between members of a community.

▲ The Welland Ship Canal is on the St Lawrence Seaway. It links Lake Ontario with Lake Erie. The lakes are on different levels, so the canal includes a system of locks. It was opened in 1959 to connect the lakes but avoid the Niagara Falls.

► Mount Robson is the highest peak in the Canadian Rocky Mountains. The summit is 12,972 feet (3,954 meters) above sea level. It stands in a vast forest reserve of mountains, falls and glaciers, which is popular with visitors.

Cape Morris Jessup

QUEEN ELIZABETH ISLANDS

Arctic Ocean

GREENLAND

Mount McKinley 20320ft/6194m

Bering Strait

Mount Forel 11100ft/3360m

Baffin Bay

R Yukon

ALASKA

BAFFIN ISLAND

VICTORIA ISLAND

• Anchorage

Mount St Elias
18008ft/5489m

• Dawson

Godthaab

Julianehaab

Mount Logan
19850ft/6050m

R Mackenzie

Key

Timber

Wheat

Cereals

Fruit

Port

Fishing

Dairy   Oil

Cattle   Iron

Steel   Gold

Minerals   Copper

Coal   Silver

• Juneau

CANADA

Atlantic Ocean

Rocky Mountains

Hudson Bay

NEWFOUNDLAND

Pacific Ocean

• Prince Rupert

Churchill •

Edmonton

R Nelson

St John's

Vancouver

R Saskatchewan

Gulf of
St Lawrence

• Calgary

R Albany

R St Lawrence

Saskatoon

Victoria

Medicine Hat

Winnipeg

Quebec

Halifax

Ottawa

Great Lakes

Montreal

Toronto

Niagara Falls

Scale | 0 | 200 kms
       | 0 | 200 miles

◄ The Royal Canadian Mounted
Police (or 'Mounties') have a
reputation for persistence in
tracking criminals across the
wilderness of Canada's forests.

▲ Eskimos drill through the ice of
an Alaskan lake so that they can
fish in the waters below. They use
modern equipment to perform
this traditional task.

◄ Vancouver is Canada's main
Pacific seaport. Timber reaches
the city from inland forests. It is
then processed in sawmills.

▼ The spectacular cascades of the
Niagara Falls are on the border
between Canada and the United
States. One half is in Canada, the
other in the United States.

◄ Farmers sow grain on the plains
of Alberta. The region is known as
a 'prairie province'. It is famous for
its great wheat fields. Fruit and
vegetables are also grown here.
However, the other main products
of Alberta today are coal, oil and
natural gas.

United States

The United States of America is one of the world's largest countries in both size and population. The country is in the central part of the North American continent between Canada and Mexico. It extends from the Atlantic Ocean in the east to the Pacific Ocean in the west.

Within these boundaries are 48 states which each have their own government and capital city. The capital of the United States is Washington DC. DC stands for District of Columbia. Alaska, in the north-west of the continent, and Hawaii, a group of islands in the central Pacific, are also states of the union. This makes a total of 50 states. The United States flag is called the 'stars and stripes'. There are 50 stars on the flag, one for each state.

The United States has a wide variety of land forms including mountains, plateau lands, hot desert basins, plains, lowlands, coastal swamps and wooded uplands. Its climate also varies from very hot in the south to much colder weather along the Canadian border and in the Rocky Mountains.

Between the Rocky and the Appalachian Mountains lie the Great Plains and the Mississippi basin. This is some of the richest farmland in the world. Cotton, wheat, corn and tobacco are all important farm products. Beef and dairy cattle, pigs and sheep are reared in parts of the Great Plains. The United States is also a major industrial country. It is the world's largest producer of both coal and petroleum products and it has many mines and oil wells.

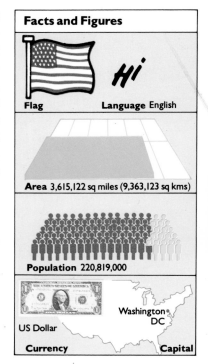

Facts and Figures

Flag

Language English

Area 3,615,122 sq miles (9,363,123 sq kms)

Population 220,819,000

US Dollar

Washington DC

Currency

Capital

▲ On 21 July, 1969, the Apollo II lifted off with three astronauts and landed on the moon. Neil Armstrong called this "a giant leap for mankind."

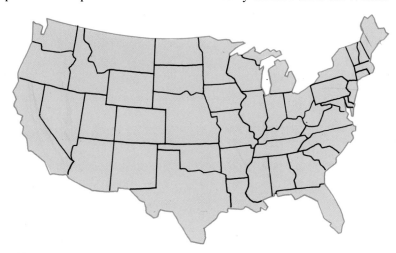

▲ The United States is made up of 50 states. Forty-nine of these are on the continent and the fiftieth, Hawaii, is an island in the Pacific Ocean. Washington DC is the capital of the country.

▼ New York City is the largest city in the United States and the third largest in the world. It is the trading center of the country.

Mount Rainier 14408ft/4392m

Seattle

CANADA

Portland

R Columbia

R Snake

R Yellowstone

Salt Lake City

R P

San Francisco

Denver

Mount Whitney 14495ft/4418m

Mount Elbert 14431ft/4399m

Rocky Mountains

R Colorado

Los Angeles

Pacific Ocean

El Paso

MEXICO

◀ American food and drink is famous all over the world. One of the advantages of the hamburger is that it can be served to customers in a very short time.

▶The Grand Canyon runs along the River Colorado and is from 4 to 18 miles (6.4 to 29 kms) wide and 217 miles (349 kms) long. Many visitors go there each year.

◀The Everglades are a marshy, tropical area in Florida. The National Park is the third largest in the world.

◀Baseball is one of the most popular sports in the United States. It comes from the English game of rounders.

▶The Walt Disney cartoon characters Mickey and Minnie Mouse are known all over the world. Disneyworld in Florida and Disneyland in California are major tourist attractions.

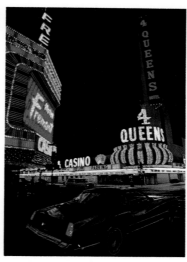

◀Las Vegas, Nevada is a popular gambling and nightclub resort. Its bright lights and famous actors and singers attract people from far and wide.

◀Many Indians still live in the western part of the United States. These are Navajo Indians of Arizona. They are the largest tribe in America.

Key

Wheat		Port		Coal	
Corn/Maize		Industry		Minerals	
Cotton		Cattle		Oil	
Fruit		Dairy		Natural gas	
Groundnuts		Fishing		Iron	
Tobacco		Sheep		Steel	
Grapes/Wine		Pigs		Uranium	

Great Lakes
R Hudson
Minneapolis
St Paul
Milwaukee
R Missouri
Detroit
Buffalo
Boston
New York City
Newark
Omaha
Chicago
Cleveland
Philadelphia
Pittsburgh
Cincinnati
Washington DC
Baltimore
Kansas City
St Louis
R Ohio
Appalachian Mountains
Memphis
Atlanta
Dallas
R Mississippi
Atlantic Ocean
Houston
New Orleans
Gulf of Mexico
Miami

Scale
0 | 200 kms
0 | 200 miles

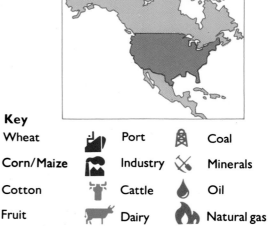

▲The River Mississippi is the principal river of the United States. Steamer and paddle boats were common in the nineteenth century.
▶These musicians are in St Louis, Missouri, which is on the Mississippi. Jazz music is very popular and many groups are formed here.

Central America

Mexico is between the United States and the Central American republics of Guatemala and Honduras. The Rio Grande forms the north-eastern border with the United States. This river also divides the mainly English speaking part of the Americas (Anglo-America) from the Spanish and Portuguese speaking part to the south (Latin America).

The eastern and western Sierra Madre, two mountain ranges, run through Mexico. Between them is a plateau. The highest peaks in Mexico are Citlaltepetl (18,700 feet/5,700 meters) and Popocatepetl (17,887 feet/5,452 meters). Both are snow-covered volcanoes which have erupted in the past.

The Tropic of Cancer crosses the center of Mexico. The country's climate is tropical in the south and more temperate in the north and in the highlands. There is dense tropical forest in the south, especially in Yucatan, which is Mexico's largest lowland area.

Corn, coffee, cotton, sugar cane, sisal and chicle are Mexico's main farming products. Sisal is the fiber from which ropes are made and chicle is used in making chewing gum. Mexico's wealth comes from minerals and from oil and natural gas wells along the Gulf coast. Mexico City, the capital, is one of the world's largest cities.

Central America is made up of the countries of Guatemala, Honduras, El Salvador, Belize, Nicaragua, Costa Rica, Panama and the Panama Canal Zone. Compared to Mexico, they are small countries. They all have tropical climates. The important products of Central America are coffee, bananas, sugar and cotton. Some minerals and oil products are also exported.

▲ The peak of Popocatepetl is covered with snow all the year round. It has not erupted for many years. However, sometimes smoke billows from the crater.

▶ The Latin American building in Mexico City is 43 floors high. Mexico's sprawling capital contains over 15 million people.

◀ Indians tend their coffee crop in the highlands of Guatemala. The Fuego volcano is in the background.

▶ A Mexican girl has a haircut. In small villages, many craftsmen work in the open air. The store's plaster walls are typical of much building in Mexico.

Facts and Figures

COSTA RICA	**MEXICO**	**HONDURAS**	**BELIZE PANAMA**	
Flag	**EL SALVADOR**	**GUATEMALA**	**NICARAGUA**	

Buenos dias
Language Spanish

Hello
BELIZE English

MEXICO 761,604 sq miles (1,972,546 sq kms)

COSTA RICA 19,652 sq miles (50,898 sq kms)	**EL SALVADOR** 8,124 sq miles (21,041 sq kms)	**GUATEMALA** 42,042 sq miles (108,889 sq kms)	**HONDURAS** 43,277 sq miles (112,088 sq kms)	**NICARAGUA** 49,759 sq miles (128,875 sq kms)	**BELIZE** 8,867 sq miles (22,965 sq kms) **PANAMA** 29,762 sq miles (77,082 sq kms)

Area

EL SALVADOR 4,663,000

GUATEMALA 6,835,900 **HONDURAS** 3,691,000 **NICARAGUA** 2,395,000

BELIZE 140,612
PANAMA 1,891,000

Population COSTA RICA 2,224,000   **MEXICO** 66,944,000

COSTA RICA Colón

HONDURAS Lempira

EL SALVADOR Colón

Currency   **GUATEMALA** Quetzal   **MEXICO** Peso

Capital

GUATEMALA Guatemala City	**MEXICO** Mexico City
EL SALVADOR San Salvador	**BELIZE** Belmopan
	HONDURAS Tegucigalpa
	NICARAGUA Managua
COSTA RICA San José	**PANAMA** Panama City

▲ The city of Tikal in Guatemala was built by the ancient Maya people of central America. Their civilization flourished over 3,000 years ago. Tikal contains temples, squares and palaces.

Corn/Maize	Industry
Wheat	Dairy
Cotton	Sheep
Sugar cane	Fishing
Coffee	Cattle
Bananas	Goats
Rice	Pigs
Port	Oil
Tourism	Iron
	Steel
	Coal
	Minerals

◄ This jungle clearing is near Tikal. Tikal is in the Peten, an immense tropical forest. Few people live here. Most Guatemalans live in the highland regions to the north.

▼ The resort of Acapulco is set among the rocky cliffs of Mexico's Pacific coastline. Skin-diving is a popular pastime here.

Scale 0 — 200 kms / 0 — 200 miles

▼ Bullfights are popular in Mexico. here, the bull has been goaded with banderillas (barbed sticks). The matador makes passes at the bull with his cape. He prepares himself for the kill.

▲ Indians fish on Lake Patzcuaro in western Mexico. The 'butterfly' shape of their nets is typical of the local fishermen. The people are Tarascan Indians. The scenery makes Patzcuaro a popular resort.

◄ The town of Antigua in Guatemala lies on an earthquake belt. It has often been hit by earthquakes and floods. Many historic buildings have been destroyed. Here, Indians sell fruit and vegetables in a market in the ruins of a Jesuit monastery.

◄ A Mexican woman weaves serapes at her loom in Oaxaca. A serape is a woolen blanket. Oaxaca is a state in southern Mexico, and most of its people are Indians. It is famous for its handicrafts which include fine pottery and leatherwork.

The Caribbean

The West Indies or Antilles are made up of many islands which form a chain over 2,500 miles (4,000kms) long stretching from Yucatan and Florida to the north coast of South America.

The islands can be divided into three groups. The first group is the Bahama Islands off the coast of Florida. Here there are over 700 islands and reefs, but only 20 are populated. Andros is the largest island but Nassau, the capital of the Bahamas, is on the small island of New Providence. Fruits and vegetables are the main products of the Bahamas.

The Greater Antilles form the second group of islands and include Cuba, Jamaica, Hispaniola and Puerto Rico. Cuba is larger than all the other West Indian Islands combined. It is famous for its tobacco, and it also produces sugar. The capital of Cuba is Havana which is a major port and the largest city in the West Indies.

The island of Hispaniola belongs to both Haiti and the Dominican Republic. Puerto Rico is associated with the United States and many of its people now live and work in American cities. Jamaica is famous for crops such as sugar cane and bananas. Kingston is its capital.

The Lesser Antilles make up the third group of West Indian islands. They extend in a curve from Puerto Rico to the coast of Venezuela. The largest island is Trinidad which is also famous for its sugar crop. Other islands in this group include Barbados, Tobago, Martinique, Guadaloupe, Dominica and Grenada. Britain, France and the Netherlands still have West Indian colonies.

The West Indies suffer from hurricanes which are strong, destructive winds. Many tourists visit the islands because of the hot summers and the mild winters.

▲ This 'shanty' town is in Dominica. Poverty is a problem throughout the West Indies. Many people live in townships known as 'shanties' built from any material available.

◀ Fishing nets are being hung out to dry in the hot sun on a beach in St Lucia. In the background, the Pitons are visible. These are cone-shaped peaks which are produced by volcanic action. Most of the island's soil is volcanic and fertile. Forests, lush vegetation and tropical fruit grow well here.

◀ A Cuban woman rolls a Havana cigar. Tobacco is one of Cuba's main exports. The fine leaves of Havana cigars are highly prized. The inner leaves are pressed, and the outer ones wrapped spirally around them.

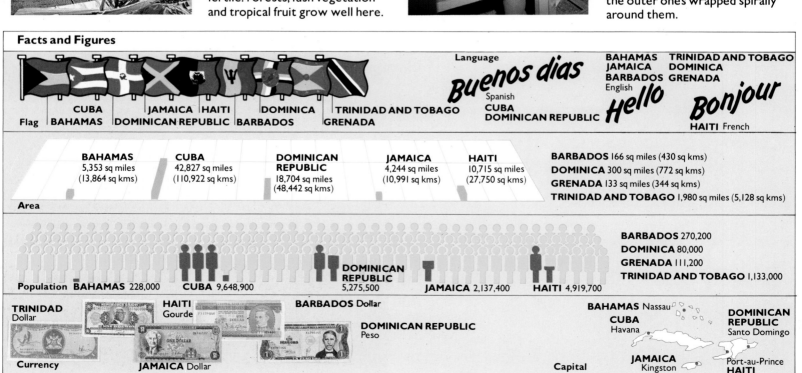

Facts and Figures

Flag	CUBA BAHAMAS JAMAICA DOMINICAN REPUBLIC HAITI BARBADOS DOMINICA TRINIDAD AND TOBAGO GRENADA	**Language** *Buenos dias* Spanish CUBA DOMINICAN REPUBLIC *Hello* BAHAMAS JAMAICA BARBADOS English TRINIDAD AND TOBAGO DOMINICA GRENADA *Bonjour* HAITI French

	BAHAMAS 5,353 sq miles (13,864 sq kms)	CUBA 42,827 sq miles (110,922 sq kms)	DOMINICAN REPUBLIC 18,704 sq miles (48,442 sq kms)	JAMAICA 4,244 sq miles (10,991 sq kms)	HAITI 10,715 sq miles (27,750 sq kms)	BARBADOS 166 sq miles (430 sq kms) DOMINICA 300 sq miles (772 sq kms) GRENADA 133 sq miles (344 sq kms) TRINIDAD AND TOBAGO 1,980 sq miles (5,128 sq kms)
Area						

					BARBADOS 270,200 DOMINICA 80,000 GRENADA 111,200 TRINIDAD AND TOBAGO 1,133,000
Population BAHAMAS 228,000	CUBA 9,648,900	DOMINICAN REPUBLIC 5,275,500	JAMAICA 2,137,400	HAITI 4,919,700	

Currency TRINIDAD Dollar HAITI Gourde JAMAICA Dollar BARBADOS Dollar DOMINICAN REPUBLIC Peso	**Capital** BAHAMAS Nassau CUBA Havana JAMAICA Kingston DOMINICAN REPUBLIC Santo Domingo Port-au-Prince HAITI

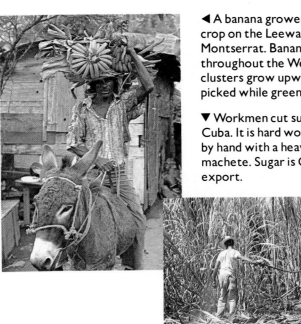

◄ A banana grower brings in his crop on the Leeward island of Montserrat. Bananas are grown throughout the West Indies. The clusters grow upwards. They are picked while green.

▼ Workmen cut sugar cane in Cuba. It is hard work, carried out by hand with a heavy knife called a machete. Sugar is Cuba's main export.

Limbo dancing
Limbo dancing is popular in the Caribbean. Get two friends to hold a long pole or stick at about the height of your shoulders. Then stand a few paces behind the pole. Bend your knees, hold your hands in front of you to balance, and lean backwards. Shuffle slowly forwards on both feet until you have passed under the pole. Repeat this with the pole a little lower each time. Be careful not to fall backwards as you might hurt yourself.

► A steel band plays in Trinidad. People developed this popular form of music by drumming on oil barrels with muffled sticks. The sound is rhythmic and melodious. It takes practice to master the art. The instruments are not as easy to play as they may look.

Atlantic Ocean

Pico Duarte 10200ft/3175m

HAITI

Port-au-Prince

Santo Domingo
DOMINICAN REPUBLIC

Caribbean Sea

PUERTO RICO
San Juan

Ponce

ANGUILLA

ST CHRISTOPHER
NEVIS
MONTSERRAT

ANTIGUA
St Johns

GUADELOUPE

DOMINICA
Roseau

MARTINIQUE
Fort-de-France

ST LUCIA

ST VINCENT

Bridgetown
BARBADOS

GRENADA
St George's

NETHERLANDS ANTILLES

Willemstad

TRINIDAD AND TOBAGO
Port-of-Spain

Coffee		Palm oil	
Citrus fruit		Corn/Maize	
Sugar cane		Tourism	
Bananas		Port	
Cacao		Industry	
Tobacco		Oil	
Rice		Coal	
		Bauxite	
		Copper	
		Minerals	

► The main sport in the West Indies is cricket. Children often play on beaches or in the streets. Here top player Viv Richards plays a typical stroke.
◄ Deserted beaches, like this one on the island of San Andres, attract many foreign visitors. Tourism is a major industry in the West Indies.

Looking at South America

South America is the fourth largest continent in the world. The isthmus of Panama joins it to Central America. South America's shape is like a triangle which becomes very narrow towards the southern tip of Chile and Argentina. Here the Strait of Magellan separates a group of islands called Tierra del Fuego from the mainland. Cape Horn is south of these islands. The Falkland Islands are part of South America. They lie over 250 miles (400 kms) off the east coast.

South America has four highland regions – the Andes, the Guiana Highlands, the Brazilian Highlands and the Patagonian uplands – and it has three lowland areas which are the Amazon basin, the Orinoco basin and the Parana-Paraguay plain. The Andes Mountains dominate the west of South America. They extend from north to south through Venezuela, Colombia, Ecuador, Peru, Bolivia, Chile and Argentina. Many of the mountains in the Andes are volcanic and are over 9,500 feet (6,000 meters) high. Even at the Equator the peaks are so high that they are covered in snow. Aconcagua (22,835

feet/6,850 meters) in Argentina is the highest mountain in the western hemisphere.

The Guiana Highlands are shared by Venezuela, Brazil and Guyana. Mount Roraima (9,220 feet/2,816 meters) is its highest point. To the north is the Orinoco basin. The eastern part, called the Llanos, is a large grassland area. The vast Amazon lowlands separate the Guiana Highlands from the Brazilian Highlands. The Parana-Paraguay lowlands lie between the Brazilian Highlands and the Andes. In the north is the Gran Chaco area which is dry scrubland. The southern part is rich grassland called the Pampas. The barren tableland of Patagonia is even further south than the Pampas.

It was mainly the Spanish and the Portuguese who colonized South America so many people who now live there are of Spanish and Portuguese descent. There are also many Indians and blacks. Spanish is spoken in twelve of the countries in South America and Portuguese is spoken in Brazil. The Indians also speak many native dialects.

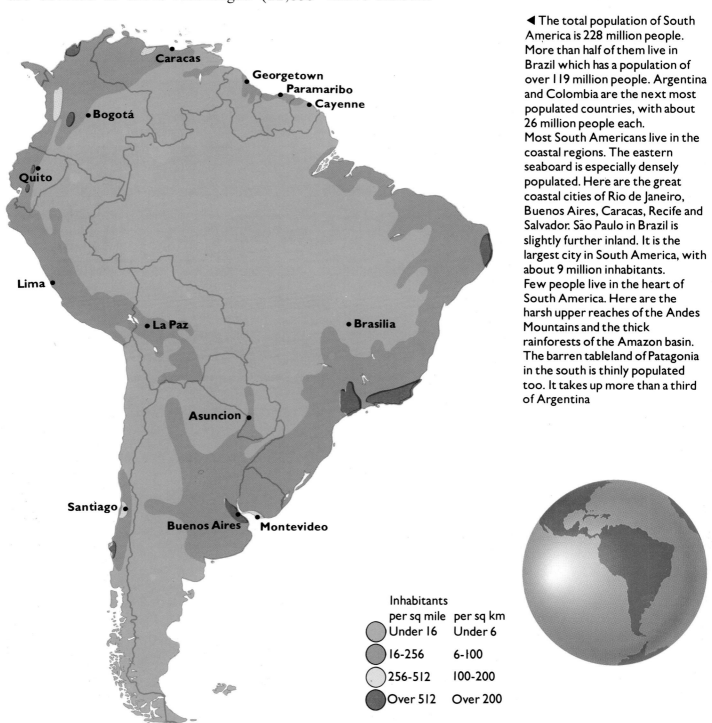

◄ The total population of South America is 228 million people. More than half of them live in Brazil which has a population of over 119 million people. Argentina and Colombia are the next most populated countries, with about 26 million people each.
Most South Americans live in the coastal regions. The eastern seaboard is especially densely populated. Here are the great coastal cities of Rio de Janeiro, Buenos Aires, Caracas, Recife and Salvador. São Paulo in Brazil is slightly further inland. It is the largest city in South America, with about 9 million inhabitants.
Few people live in the heart of South America. Here are the harsh upper reaches of the Andes Mountains and the thick rainforests of the Amazon basin. The barren tableland of Patagonia in the south is thinly populated too. It takes up more than a third of Argentina

Inhabitants

per sq mile	per sq km
Under 16	Under 6
16-256	6-100
256-512	100-200
Over 512	Over 200

Scale
0 ——————————————————— 1000 miles
0 ——————————————————— 1000 kms

Caribbean Sea

Baranquilla • — Maracaibo
Valencia • — Caracas
Barquisimeto
VENEZUELA
Medellin •
• Bogotá — GUYANA — • Georgetown
COLOMBIA — • Paramaribo
SURINAM — • Cayenne
FRENCH GUIANA
Atlantic Ocean
Quito •
ECUADOR — Andes
Guayaquil • — R Negro
R Amazon — • Manaus — • Belém
• Chiclayo
PERU — Fortaleza •
Trujillo •
Callao — BRAZIL — • Recife
• Lima
BOLIVIA — Mato Grosso Plateau
Pacific Ocean — R São Francisco
La Paz • — • Brasília
Santa Cruz
Sucre — Brazilian Highlands
PARAGUAY
R Paraguay
Antofagasta • — Rio de Janeiro
Gran Chaco — • Asuncion — São Paulo •
CHILE
R Paraná
• Porto Alegre
Andes
Mendoza • — URUGUAY
Santiago • — • Montevideo
Buenos Aires •
Concepción • — Pampas — R Colorado
• Mar del Plata
ARGENTINA — • Bahía Blanca
• Puerto Montt
Patagonia — • Comodoro Rivadavia
Punta Arenas •
Magellan's Strait
TIERRA DEL FUEGO
Cape Horn

Key

	Cereals
	Coffee
	Timber
	Rice
	Sugar cane
	Rubber
	Cotton
	Bananas
	Cacao
	Citrus fruit
	Tobacco
	Fruit
	Corn/Maize
	Vegetables
	Port
	Cattle
	Fishing
	Sheep
	Animal farming
	Dairy
	Farming

	Oil
	Iron
	Bauxite
	Minerals
	Gold
	Diamonds
	Coal
	Silver
	Copper

◄ Compared with North America, South America has little industry. Manufacturing is confined to a few major centers. This is partly because there are few deposits of coal. However, there are important oilfields, especially in Venezuela. Iron is found in the Brazilian and Guiana Highlands. The Amazon basin divides the northern regions from the south. The Andes Mountains make communications between east and west difficult. However, the mountains' rich volcanic soil is well suited to coffee-growing. There is much cattle farming on the Pampas of Argentina and Uruguay. The eastern seaports handle most of South America's world trade.

Brazil

Brazil, which covers half of South America, is the fifth largest country in the world. It has boundaries with all the countries in South America except Chile and Ecuador. Very few people live in the interior of Brazil. Most of its cities, industries and farmlands are in the coastal and hill country in the east.

The River Amazon, which is the largest river in the world, is just south of the Equator in Brazil. Its main source is the Andes in Peru less than 100 miles (160 kms) from the Pacific coast. It flows for nearly 4,000 miles (6,440 kms) to the Atlantic in the east. The Amazon has many large tributaries which drain parts of Peru, Ecuador, Colombia and Bolivia as well as half of Brazil. The Amazon's delta is over 200 miles (320 kms) wide and its muddy waters can be seen far out at sea.

The Amazon basin, or Amazonia, is a huge lowland area covered with thick equatorial forest. The Brazilian Highlands, and the Mato Grosso plateau, are to the south of Amazonia. Cattle and other livestock ranching is important here. Sugar cane, cotton, rice, tobacco, oranges, pineapples and bananas are all grown in the coastal areas of the east. Coffee grows on the mountain slopes in the south-east. Brazil produces more coffee than any other country in the world. There are also large iron ore, tin, gold and diamond mines in Brazil. The capital of Brazil is a new city called Brasilia. It is to the north-west of Rio de Janeiro which was the old capital city. São Paulo is the largest city in South America and one of the largest cities in the world.

Facts and Figures

Flag　　　　Language Portuguese

Bom dia

Area 3,286,500 sq miles (8,512,000 sq kms)

Population 119,670,000

Cruzeiro

Currency　　　Capital

Brasilia

▼ Brasilia is a new city which was opened in 1960. It was built as Brazil's new capital to encourage people to settle in the country's central region. Many of its buildings are strikingly modern.

▼ A tributary of the River Amazon winds through the dense rain forests which cover much of the river's basin. There are many remote regions known only to the local Indian peoples.

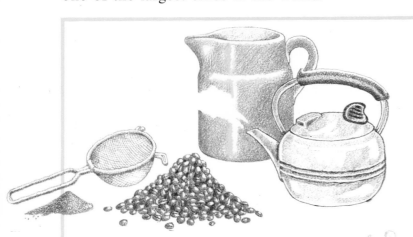

Making coffee

There are many good ways of making coffee. One of the easiest methods is to use a jug or coffee pot, ground coffee and boiling water. If you have a coffee grinder, you can grind the coffee beans freshly. However, you can use ready-ground coffee instead. Put two medium spoons of coffee for each person into the pot. Boil the water and then pour it over the coffee. Be very careful not to burn yourself. Stir the coffee once or twice and leave it for a few minutes so the grounds can settle. Put a strainer over the cup and pour the coffee through it. Take care not to spill it.

▶ Guarani Indians like these live in village communities in many parts of northern South America. Guarani of the Amazon region are know as Tupi.

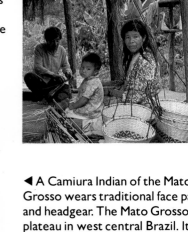

◀ A Camiura Indian of the Mato Grosso wears traditional face paint and headgear. The Mato Grosso is a plateau in west central Brazil. Its name means 'thick forest' in Portuguese. European settlers brought much cattle farming to the region in the nineteenth century. Today, modern development threatens the traditional ways of life of the native Indian peoples.

▶ Coffee workers on a plantation in Campinas tend their crop. Coffee grows well in the rich, well-drained soil of south-east Brazil.

▼ After harvesting, the beans are spread out to dry, as here in Parana. The beans are then roasted to develop their taste.

▲ Rio de Janeiro is Brazil's main seaport. Corcovado peak rises above the harbor which has an immense statue of Christ at its summit.

▶ A workman examines a pile of Brazil nuts at Manaus. The city is the main trading center on the Amazon. The nuts are the seed pods of trees which grow along the banks of the Amazon and Orinoco.

Key

◈	Diamonds	🌳	Cotton
⛰	Gold		Timber
⚒	Minerals		Rubber
⚱	Iron		Bananas
⚰	Coal		Cacao
			Coffee
			Sugar cane
			Tea
			Citrus fruit
			Port
			Pigs
			Sheep
			Cattle

VENEZUELA

COLOMBIA

R Negro

R Amazon

Manaus

R Purús

R Tapajós

R Madeira

R Xingu

PERU

R Araguaia

BOLIVIA

BRAZIL

Atlantic Ocean

● **Belém**

Fortaleza

R São Francisco

Recife

Salvador

Paraná ●

Brasília ●

Pico da Bandeira 9462ft/2890m

Belo Horizonte

Pico das Agulhas Negras 9255ft/2787m

R Paraná

Campinas

São Paulo

Rio de Janeiro

PARAGUAY

Scale | 0 ____ 200 kms
| 0 ____ 200 miles

ARGENTINA

Pôrto Alegre ●

URUGUAY

▼ Soccer is immensely popular throughout South America. Here, the Brazilian star, Pelé, performs in the national team.

Colombia, Venezuela and the Guianas

Colombia, Venezuela and the Guianas – which are now called Guyana, Surinam and French Guiana – are in the northern part of South America. They all have coastlines on the Caribbean Sea or the Atlantic Ocean and have boundaries with Brazil in the south. Colombia also has a coastline on the Pacific.

Colombia has a hot and swampy coastal plain. The Andes mountains separate it from the Llanos and the equatorial forests of Amazonia. On the coast there are important gold and platinum mines. Colombia's main ports are Barranquilla and Cartagena. Most Colombians live in the highlands. Bogota, the country's capital, is 8,700 feet (2,650 meters) above sea level. The main crop in the Colombian highlands is coffee.

In Venezuela, the Gulf of Venezuela and Lake Maracaibo lie in the north-west near the most northern part of the Andes. Petroleum, iron ore and coffee are the country's main products, There are thousands of oil wells in the Maracaibo lowlands. Caracas, the capital, is one of the most modern cities in South America.

Guyana is a tropical country between the deltas of the Orinoco and the Amazon. Georgetown is its capital and sugar and rice are the main crops. Guyana exports minerals such as bauxite from which aluminum is obtained. Surinam is also a major bauxite producer. Its capital is Paramaribo.

French Guiana belongs to France and is the only colonial country in South America. The country is famous for its shrimps which are sent to the United States and timber and minerals are also important. Cayenne is the capital of French Guiana.

Make your own maraca
1. Take an empty plastic lemon or fruit that syrup comes in. Clean it out and put in some uncooked rice or bird seeds.

2. When enough rice is inside the lemon, fit a pencil into the opening as a handle. Use sticky tape to attach it to the lemon.

3. Now cover the lemon and pencil with small pieces of newspaper. Stick these one on top of the other either with glue or with a flour and water mixture.

4. When the maraca is a good shape, leave it to dry until it does not feel at all damp. Then paint it brightly. Now it is ready for shaking in time with music.

◄ Oil rigs rise from Venezuela's Lake Maracaibo. The surrounding region is also rich in oil, Venezuela's main export.

► The glittering sprawl of Caracas is viewed here from the south. The city has impressive new government buildings, highways and shopping centers.

Facts and Figures

Language
COLOMBIA VENEZUELA Spanish — *Buenos dias*
FRENCH GUIANA French — *Bonjour*
GUYANA English — *Hello*

Flag COLOMBIA GUYANA SURINAM VENEZUELA FRENCH GUIANA

Area
COLOMBIA 439,737 sq miles (1,138,914 sq kms)
VENEZUELA 347,175 sq miles (889,180 sq kms)
FRENCH GUIANA 34,750 sq miles (90,000 sq kms)
GUYANA 83,000 sq miles (215,000 sq kms)
SURINAM 70,060 sq miles (181,455 sq kms)

Population
COLOMBIA 26,587,000
GUYANA 865,000
SURINAM 448,000
VENEZUELA 13,515,000
FRENCH GUIANA 60,000

Currency
COLOMBIA Peso
VENEZUELA Bolivar
SURINAM Surinam Guilder

Capital
VENEZUELA Caracas
GUYANA Georgetown
FRENCH GUIANA Cayenne
COLOMBIA Bogotá
SURINAM Paramaribo

Gulf of Venezuela
L. Maracaibo
Atlantic Ocean

Barranquilla
Cartagena
Caribbean Sea
PANAMA
Maracaibo
Barquisimeto
Valencia
Caracas
VENEZUELA
Maturín
R Orinoco
Cúcuta
R Cauca
R Magdalena
Pacific Ocean
Medellín
Bogotá
Nevado del Tolima 17110ft/5215m
R Guaviare
COLOMBIA
Cali
Andes Mountains
ECUADOR
PERU

Mount Roraima 9220ft/2816m
GUYANA
R Essequibo
Georgetown
Paramaribo
SURINAM
Cayenne
FRENCH GUIANA
BRAZIL

Scale
| 0 | 200 kms |
| 0 | 200 miles |

Key

Rubber	Cattle
Cacao	Fishing
Corn/Maize	Pigs
Cotton	Goats
Bananas	Animal Farming
Sugar cane	Sheep
Rice	Oil
Citrus fruit	Bauxite
Coffee	Iron
Coconuts	Gold
Timber	Diamonds
Port	Minerals

▲ Spanish influence is strong in Colombia, as in other South American countries. The people enjoy bullfights, and the *encierro* festival where bulls run loose through the streets.

◄ Most Colombians live in the highlands. Coffee is grown on hillsides like this. Colombia also produces oil, cotton and sugar.

▼ The interior of Guyana is a tropical region with dense forests and many river systems. Here, an Akawaio family paddles along the upper Mazaruni. The canoe is a dugout, carved from a single log.

◄ Colombian coffee workers lay out their harvest of beans to dry. The volcanic soil of the Andes Mountains is particularly good for growing the crop.

► Buses are colorful and crowded in Colombia. They are an important form of transport on the highland roads. There are few railroads.

Ecuador, Peru, Bolivia and Chile

Ecuador and Peru, like Colombia, have coastal plains along the Pacific. The Andes separate these plains, which in Peru are narrow, from the Amazon forests.

The Equator passes through Ecuador and bananas and other tropical fruits grow well in the humid climate. Guayaquil, at the head of the Gulf of Guayaquil is the country's chief port. A railroad from Guayaquil climbs over 9,000 feet (2,745 meters) to Quito, Ecuador's capital in the Andes. There are many volcanoes around Quito. Cotopaxi is the most active. Most of Ecuador's population live in the cooler highlands.

The Galapagos Islands belong to Ecuador. They are volcanic and they are about 650 miles (1,040 kms) away from the mainland. Unusual animals such as iguanas and giant tortoises live there.

Peru is smaller than Brazil and it has a narrow coastal belt along the Pacific. The Peruvian Andes are rich in copper, lead and zinc. All the mining areas are linked to Lima, the capital, and Callao which is its port.

The highest city in South America is La Paz which is the seat of government in Bolivia. It is 12,000 feet (3,660 meters) above sea level. The capital of Bolivia, Sucre, is in the south. The Andes cover about a third of Bolivia. In the south is high tableland called the Altiplano. This is one of the highest areas in the world where people live. Bolivia is the second largest producer of tin in the world. It also has silver, lead and tungsten mines.

Chile is a long, narrow country which stretches over 2,600 miles (4,160 kms) from the Peruvian border to the southern tip of South America, Tierra del Fuego. Its widest part is only 110 miles (176 kms). The Atacama Desert in the north of Chile is one of the driest places in the world and it is rich in mineral salts such as potash and iodine.

The center of Chile, round Santiago the capital, has a climate similar to that of California. The farmers in Chile grow olives, grapes and citrus fruits.

Southern Chile is largely covered with forest. The extreme south is uninhabited. It is a land of mountains, glaciers, fjords and islands.

▶Smoke billows from an active volcano on the border between Chile and Argentina.

▼ Volcanic mountains rise steeply from Chile's northern desert on the border with Peru.

◀ These thatched dwellings are near Pisaq in the highlands of central Peru. Three ranges of the Andes pass through the central region. Its people are mostly poor peasants. They grow just enough to feed themselves and their families. They do not sell much.

▲The ruined city of Machu Picchu is in the mountains of Peru. The Incas once hid there from the Spanish conquerors.

▼ Llamas are creatures of the Andes. The Indians use them as beasts of burden. They also use llama wool for making clothes.

Facts and Figures

Flag BOLIVIA   CHILE ECUADOR   PERU

Buenos dias

Language Spanish

BOLIVIA	CHILE	ECUADOR	PERU
424,165 sq miles (1,098,581 sq kms)	292,135 sq miles (756,626 sq kms)	108,624 sq miles (281,334 sq kms)	496,224 sq miles (1,285,215 sq kms)

Area

Population BOLIVIA 4,886,700   CHILE 10,917,500   ECUADOR 8,047,000   PERU 17,291,000

PERU Sol

CHILE Peso

BOLIVIA Peso Boliviano

ECUADOR Quito

PERU Lima

BOLIVIA Sucre

Currency   ECUADOR Sucre   Capital CHILE Santiago

COLOMBIA

Quito
Cotopaxi 19344ft /5896m
ECUADOR
Chimborazo 20561ft/6267m

Guayaquil

R Amazon

Iquitos

R Ucayali

BRAZIL

Trujillo

PERU

Andes

Lima
Machu Picchu
Cuzco
BOLIVIA

Nevado Ausangate 20945ft/6384m
R Mamoré
Nevado Illampu 20873ft/6362m

Arequipa
La Paz

Arica
Santa Cruz
Sucre

Pacific Ocean
Andes

Atacama Desert
R Pilcomayo
PARAGUAY

Chuquicamata

Antofagasta
CHILE

Cerro Ojos del Salado 22516ft/6863m

Valparaíso
Santiago

Concepción
ARGENTINA

Puerto Montt

Punta Arenas
TIERRA
DEL
FUEGO

▼ The Chuquicamata copper mine is in northern Chile. It is the biggest copper mining center in the world. Northern Chile also produces other minerals such as iron, nitrates, gold and silver.

Scale
|0 |200 kms
|0 |200 miles

▲ An Indian woman sells colorful blankets at a market in La Paz, Bolivia. Much of Bolivia is bleak, high tableland. More than half of its people are pure Indians. They often wear woolen blankets as protection against the cold. The lower eastern region of Bolivia is warmer and more fertile.

▶ An iguana moves among cactus plants in the Galapagos. These isolated islands' wildlife includes a species of iguana, which lives in the sea, and giant tortoises. There is little land worth farming on the islands. They are now a wildlife sanctuary.

▲ Lake Titicaca is high in the Andes on the border of Peru and Bolivia. It is 110 miles (177 kms) long, making it the largest lake in South America. Here some local people fish and carry goods in traditional boats called balsas. The hull and the sail are both made from reeds which are woven together.

Key

Sugar cane		Port	
Rice		Fishing	
Coffee		Sheep	
Cacao		Cattle	
Bananas		Llamas	
Cotton		Oil	
Citrus fruit		Iron	
Tobacco		Minerals	
Grapes/Wine		Copper	
Corn/Maize		Silver	
Wheat		Gold	

Argentina, Uruguay and Paraguay

Argentina is the second largest country in South America. It consists of four main regions. In the north there are sub-tropical plains and scrub-forests called the Gran Chaco. There are Pampas grasslands in the center, the Andes are in the west and there is an upland plain in the south called Patagonia.

Argentina is an important meat producer. Cattle are reared on the Pampas by South American cowboys who are known as gauchos. The Pampas also grow wheat, corn, flax and cotton.

Farming is also important outside the Pampas. Cotton is grown in northern Argentina, sugar cane in the north-west and fruit trees grow in the foothills of the Andes. Patagonia is mainly a sheep rearing area, but it has oil, coal and other mineral deposits. Buenos Aires is Argentina's large capital city. It stands on the shore of the wide Rio de la Plata and is a major port. Most of Argentina's industries are in and around Buenos Aires.

Uruguay is another country of plains, low hills and plateaus. It lies on the northern shores of the Rio de la Plata. Stock-raising is the main activity in this country. Wool, animal fats, meat and leather are its chief products. Montevideo is the capital and chief port of Uruguay. It has large meat-packing stations, flour mills and textile industries. Montevideo now has a growing tourist trade from all over the world.

Paraguay has borders with Brazil, Bolivia and Argentina. It has no sea coast but the Paraguay-Parana river provides access to the Atlantic. Paraguay has very few industries and most of its people are farmers.

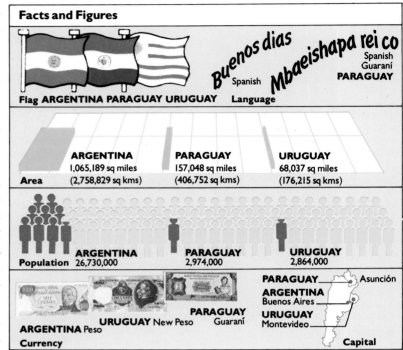

Facts and Figures

Flag ARGENTINA PARAGUAY URUGUAY

Language
Buenos dias Spanish
Mbaeishapa rei co Spanish Guaraní PARAGUAY

Area	ARGENTINA	PARAGUAY	URUGUAY
	1,065,189 sq miles (2,758,829 sq kms)	157,048 sq miles (406,752 sq kms)	68,037 sq miles (176,215 sq kms)

Population	ARGENTINA	PARAGUAY	URUGUAY
	26,730,000	2,974,000	2,864,000

Currency: ARGENTINA Peso · URUGUAY New Peso · PARAGUAY Guaraní

Capital: PARAGUAY Asunción · ARGENTINA Buenos Aires · URUGUAY Montevideo

◄ Traffic throngs down the Avenida de Corientes. This is the center for night-life and theater-going in Buenos Aires. Argentina's capital has a population of over 3,000,000 people. As one of the world's great ports it is constantly receiving influence from Europe, North America and elsewhere.

▶The Chaco of Paraguay is a dry scrubland region where cactus plants grow high. There are swamps and forests too.

▼A farm worker herds sheep in Uruguay. Over two thirds of Uruguay is given over to raising sheep and cattle.

▶ Paraguayan gauchos gallop through a ranch. Gauchos pride themselves on their courage, their sense of honor and their skillful horsemanship.

◄ A herd of of sheep is set out to graze on the uplands of Patagonia. Sheep are raised here mainly for wool. The bare plains slope gently towards the Atlantic Ocean where the land is a bit more fertile.

◄Paraguayan gauchos round up a herd of cattle and bring it to the ranch.

▼ Cattle are driven into pens by gauchos at a large ranch in Argentina, which exports beef.

▲ There are many cliffs and canyons in parts of the Argentinian Andes. These have been caused by rivers eroding rock. The steep valleys are called quebradas.

BOLIVIA

PARAGUAY

R Paraguay

Asunción

San Miguel de Tucumán

R Salado

Aconcagua 22835ft/6960m

R Parana

BRAZIL

Córdoba

Mendoza

Tupungato 22310ft/6800m

Rosario

URUGUAY

Montevideo

Buenos Aires

ARGENTINA

CHILE

Mar del Plata

Bahía Blanca

R Colorado

R Negro

Atlantic Ocean

Comodoro Rivadavia

Patagonia

TIERRA DEL FUEGO

Key

Rice

Corn/Maize

Tea

Cotton

Wheat

Citrus fruit

Grapes/Wine

Cereals

Fruit

Tourism

Industry

Port

Cattle

Dairy

Sheep

Fishing

Coal

Natural gas

Oil

Scale

0 ⊢ 200 kms
0 ⊢ 200 miles

▼ The Transandine railroad runs across the Andes from Mendoza in Argentina to Santiago in Chile. Here the range is narrow but steep, and the peaks are always covered with snow.

▲ A ferryboat carries a lorry on one of Paraguay's rivers. There are few good roads or railroads. Paraguayan products, such as meat and timber, are often carried on the river systems.

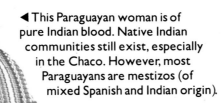

◀ This Paraguayan woman is of pure Indian blood. Native Indian communities still exist, especially in the Chaco. However, most Paraguayans are mestizos (of mixed Spanish and Indian origin).

The Arctic and the Antarctic

Antarctica lies around the South Pole and is the world's seventh continent. It is larger than both Europe and Australia and was the last continent to be discovered.

Antarctica has two deep inlets called the Ross and Weddell seas and a long, curved peninsula which is known as Graham Land. This is only 650 miles (1,040 kms) away from South America. The most southern parts of the Atlantic, Pacific and Indian Oceans surround Antarctica. These seas are always stormy and are full of ice and icebergs.

For both scientific and military reasons various countries claim parts of Antarctica. Britain, France, Norway, Australia, New Zealand, Chile and Argentina all signed the Antarctic Treaty in 1959. This gave each country an area of land along the coast.

Antarctica is a plateau which rises to 10,000 feet (3,000 meters) above sea level with mountains that reach 15,000 feet (4,500 meters). Some of these are volcanic peaks. Antarctica has minerals such as copper, nickel and coal. It may have oil as well.

Very thick ice and snow cover the whole continent except for a few coastal areas in summer which are ice-free. Antarctica has the world's harshest climate and the temperature of −126°F (−88°C) has been recorded there. Like the Arctic, Antarctica has nearly 24 hours of daylight in summer and 24 hours of darkness in winter.

Unlike at the South Pole, an ocean, not a continent surrounds the North Pole. This is the Arctic Ocean and the North Pole is near its center. The borders of this ocean are with the Arctic regions of Asia, Europe and North America. The Arctic Circle is often used as a boundary for the Arctic region. The climate at the North Pole is very cold and the temperature is nearly always below freezing point.

The Arctic Ocean flows into the Atlantic on both sides of Greenland. The Bering Strait, between Alaska and Siberia in the Soviet Union, links the Arctic with the Pacific Ocean and the Bering Sea. Compared to other oceans, the Arctic is small and because of the cold climate it is a sea of ice.

The Arctic Circle is around the North Pole. The Antarctic Circle is around the South Pole. Both are the furthest regions from the Equator so they are always cold. The Arctic is a frozen mass of water. Its shape is constantly changing as it drifts. Ice melts in some places, new ice forms in others. People can now travel under the Arctic in submarines.

◀The Arctic itself is not a land mass. However, some countries have northern regions which come within the Arctic Circle. Here, melting snow forms cold streams in Norway. No trees can grow so far north. The bare landscape is known as tundra.

▲ Blizzards occur both in the Arctic and Antarctic. The high winds and driving snow make travel difficult and dangerous.

▶ Penguins are only found in the Antarctic. They live in colonies sometimes of many thousand birds.

◀Icebreakers are ships designed for traveling though ice packs. The prow slides over the ice. The ship's weight breaks it up.

▶There are many radar stations in the Antarctic, both for scientific study and military purposes.

▶Weather stations are bases where scientists study atmospheric conditions. Results are pieced together with information from other parts of the world. Together they help to build up a total picture of the world's weather.

▲An iceberg is a block of ice that has split off from a larger mass and drifts freely in the ocean. You can see about a ninth of an iceberg on the surface. The rest is underwater. The hidden mass is dangerous to shipping.

▼The Beardmore Glacier is in Antarctica. As the glacier reaches the sea, blocks of ice break away and form icebergs.

▲The atmosphere of the Antarctic and Arctic regions can cause strange effects of light. Tiny particles of ice in the air can form glowing shapes called parhelia. These are usually two spots which look like fake suns. They appear opposite the real sun.

▲A meteorologist checks temperatures at a weather station. The information is vital for other parts of the world. For example, if a cold air current builds up in Antarctica it will soon reach neighboring regions.

▼The Antarctic is a true continent. Beneath the sheets of ice and snow lies a solid mass of rock. It is visible in many places.

Atlantic Ocean

Indian Ocean

QUEEN MAUD LAND

○ GRAHAM LAND

COATS LAND

ENDERBY LAND

Weddell Sea

Bellingshausen Sea

PRINCESS ELIZABETH LAND

• South Pole

ELLSWORTH LAND

QUEEN MARY LAND

Beardmore Glacier
▲ *Mount Markham 14270ft/435m*

Pacific Ocean

BYRD LAND   *Ross Ice Shelf*

WILKES LAND

VICTORIA LAND

Ross Sea

Scale
|0| |200 kms
|0 | |200 miles

◀Polar bears are found on the Arctic ice cap. The Antarctic has no land animals. However, the surrounding seas are rich in fish and plankton and there are many seals and penguins. The Arctic tern migrates to the Antarctic yearly.

Index

A

Abu Dhabi 74
Aconcagua, Mount 114
Addis Ababa 92
Adelaide 98
Aegean Sea 68
Afghanistan 74
Africa 86-95
Aircraft routes, major 42-3
Alaska 106, 108
Albania 68
Alberg Tunnel 60
Algarve 64
Algeria 88
Alice Springs 98
Alps:
    Austrian 60
    Bavarian 56
    Carpathian 68
    Dinaric 68
    Italian 62
    Southern 100
    Swiss 60
    Transylvanian 68
Amazon river 114, 116
America, North 104-13
American South 114-23
Amsterdam 54
Andes Mountains 114, 118, 120
Andorra 64
Angola 94
Antarctic Circle 124
Antarctica 124, 125
Antilles, Greater 112
Antilles, Lesser 112
Antwerp 54, 55
Apennine Mountains 62
Appalachian Mountains 104, 108
Arctic Circle 124
Arctic Ocean 70, 104, 124
Arctic region 124, 125
Ardennes 54, 55
Argentina 122
Asia 70-85
Aswan 89
Atacama Desert 120
Athens 68, 69
Atlantic Ocean 90, 104
Atlas Mountains 86, 88
Atmosphere 34
Australasia 96-103
Australia 96, 98-9
Austria 60

B

Bahama Islands 112
Bali 84, 85
Balkans 68-9
Bangkok 82
Bangladesh 76
Barbados 112
Barcelona 64
Basle 60, 61
Bay of Biscay 52

Belfast 50
Belgium 54
Belgrade 68
Bering Strait 104
Berlin, East 66
Berlin, West 57
Berne 60
Bilbao 64
Black Sea 68, 74
Bogotá 118
Bolivia 120
Bombay 76
Bonn 56
Bosporus 74
Botswana 94
Boundary 14
Brasilia 116
Bratislava 66
Brazil 116-17
Brazilian Highlands 114, 116
Bremen 56
Brenner Pass 60
British Isles 50-1
Brno 66
Brussels 54, 55
Bucharest 68
Budapest 66
Buenos Aires 122
Bulgaria 68
Burma 82

C

Cairo 88
Calcutta 76
Cambrian Mountains 50
Canada 104, 106
Canary Islands 86
Canberra 98
Cape Horn 114
Capital cities 14
Caracas 118
Cardiff 50
Caribbean Sea 104
Casablanca 88
Caspian Sea 74
Cayenne 118
Chad 88
Chile 120
China 78-9
Cities 12
Climate 34-5
Clouds 34
Coal 29
Coconut crop 39
Coffee bean crop 39
Cologne 56, 57
Colombia 118
Colombo 76
Communications 42-3
Continental island 16
Continental shelf 40
Continents 16-19
Contour landscape 13
Contour lines 13
Contour map 14
Cook, Mount 100
Copenhagen 58
Coral reefs 102

Core, earth's 24
Cotton crop 38
Countries 14, 22-3
Crete 68
Crops 38-9
Crust, earth's 24, 25
Cuba 112
Currents, ocean 40, 41
Cyprus 74
Czechoslovakia 66

D

Dacca 76
Danube river 66, 68
Dardanelles 74
Dar-es-Salaam 92
Darling river 98
Darwin 98
Denmark 58
Djakarta 84
Dortmund 56, 57
Drakensberg Mountains 86
Dresden 66
Dublin 50
Dubrovnik 69
Duisburg 56
Düsseldorf 56

E

Earthquakes 26, 27
East Germany 66
Economic map 15
Ecuador 120
Edinburgh 50
Egypt 88
Eire *see Ireland, Republic of*
England 50
English Channel 52
Equator 20, 33, 124
Equinoxes 33
Erosion 30
Essen 56
Ethiopia 92
Etna, Mount 62
Euphrates river 74
Europe 48-69
Everest, Mount 70

F

Falkland Islands 114
Famagusta 74
Faults 25, 27
Finland 58
Florence 62
Folds, rock 25, 27
Forests 36, 37
Fossils, how to find 29
France 52-3
French Guiana 118
Front 34
Fujiyama, Mount 80

G

Galapagos Islands 120
Ganges river 76
Garonne river 52
Georgetown 118
German Democratic Republic *see East Germany*
Germany, Federal Republic of *see West Germany*
Ghana 90
Gibraltar 64
Glacier 30, 31
Glasgow 50
Gobi Desert 70
Gothenburg 58
Grampian Mountains 50
Gran Chaco 114, 122
Grasslands 37
Graz 60
Great Britain 50
Great Dividing Range 98
Great Lakes 106
Great Rift Valley 86
Greenland 104, 106
Guayaquil 120
Guiana Highlands 114
Gulf of Aden 74
Gulf of Carpentaria 98
Gulf of Guinea 90
Guyana 118

H

Hague, The 54
Hamburg 56
Harz Mountains 56
Havana 112
Hawaiian Islands 102, 108
Helsinki 58
Hemispheres 20, 33
Himalayas 70, 76
Holland *see Netherlands*
Hong Kong 78, 79
Humidity, how to measure 35
Hungary 66, 67
Hurricanes 112
Hwang Ho river 78

I

Iberian Peninsula 64
Iceland 58, 59
Indian Ocean 70, 84
Indonesia 84
Indus river 76
Inner city 12
Innsbruck 60
International Date Line 32, 33
Iran 74
Iraq 74
Ireland, Northern 50
Ireland, Republic of 50